AN EARLY GRAVE

A totally gripping mystery with a huge twist

ROBERT McCRACKEN

THE
BOOK
FOLKS

Published by The Book Folks

London, 2020

ISBN 978-1-913516-08-6

www.thebookfolks.com

An Early Grave is the first book in the DI Tara Grogan mystery series.

PROLOGUE

It was ten years now, but Daphne would never forget.

She'd taken Meg, her springer spaniel, a different route on their morning walk. Through the meadows and down by the river. A fog was slowly rising above the trees and bushes, dawn gaining an upper hand on the darkness. Scampering over the lid of a large bin, a grey squirrel kept an eye on the wagging tail of the dog sniffing its way along the path. A keen jogger slipped by, heading towards the boat houses. They were already open, a crew preparing for an early workout. She felt snug within her sheepskin coat, old yet reliable, her collar turned up, a woollen beanie bright and cheerful on her head. The only sounds were of the few cars crossing Folly Bridge and of her own footsteps – her flat-heel boots on the cinder path. Off the lead Meg was always obedient; always came to her call.

But not today.

Suddenly, the dog was off the path and in among the trees, another squirrel darting to safety. Meg was on a mission, her head down and tail wagging. Beneath a sycamore, she began to dig. Her paws tore at the loose earth, sweeping leaves and twigs aside. In seconds the excavation was complete and the dog, front paws outstretched and sinking low on hind legs, began to bark.

Daphne marched the twenty yards across the grass towards her.

Instinctively, her hands gripped at her face when she saw what the dog had uncovered. Trying to scream, she felt only the bile rise from her stomach. Meg whimpered.

A grave. Only six inches deep. Tiny limbs – blue-grey, spattered with damp earth. A baby – naked, scarcely born or born dead.

Daphne would never forget the vision of the lifeless child, discarded and pressed into the ground.

Every November since then, she'd returned to this spot by the river. This morning, she placed a spray of white carnations beside the brass plate that marked the shallow grave where the baby boy had been discovered. No one had ever come forward to claim the child whom the police had named Baby Isis.

CHAPTER 1

Good Friday. Three years ago.

Callum Armour was already late. Very late. Not entirely his fault but Tilly would never believe him.

'Don't you dare blame poor Jian for your missing the train,' she would say. But it was Jian's project. It was his batch of samples running on the mass spectrometer in the lab, and Callum wanted to be certain the run was successful before leaving for his Easter break. Success now meant that Jian could fire ahead with the remaining work in his postdoc project. He had targets to meet, and Callum didn't want to hold him back.

Jian, twenty-eight and painfully thin, long-haired, wearing a black Megadeath T-shirt, chewing gum, peered at the monitor, inspecting each sample result generated by the computer. Callum sat next to him, tapping the fingers of his right hand on the bench, awaiting the appearance of the single peak on the display that would indicate successful detection of the drug metabolite they had been trying to isolate for weeks. This would be conclusive proof that chicken products imported from Southeast Asia were contaminated with antibiotic drugs, and Jian, his Chinese researcher, would be well on his way to completing his food safety project.

His mobile rang. He knew who it was without looking at the screen.

'Hi, love. Just about to leave.'

'You're still in Oxford?' said an exasperated Tilly.

'Train isn't till six.'

'It's ten to six now. And you're still at the lab.'

Callum glanced at his watch.

'There it is,' said Jian, excitedly. 'We found it, Callum.'

'Brilliant, Jian.'

'What?' said Tilly.

'Sorry, love. I'm on my way right now. I might still make it. How's my wee Emily today?'

'Your daughter is fine, enjoying her tea although most of it is either on her bib or the highchair.'

'Lovely. And how's my wee wife?'

'Your wife is fine, too, but will not be happy if her husband comes home late again. You haven't packed yet, and we're going to Devon tomorrow.'

'I know. I won't be late. I promise. Just tell me you love me.'

'I love you. Call me when you're on the train, and I'll meet you at Reading Station.'

'OK, bye.' He ended the call, his attention returning immediately to the monitor. A single symmetrical peak traced in red appeared on the display.

'Well done, Jian. Now we've found it, all we have to do is repeat the exercise with another two hundred samples and we could be on for a Nobel Prize.'

'I don't think so. You always make joke, Callum.'

'You never know, Jian. Keep chasing your dream, that's what I always say.'

Callum moved at speed across the small laboratory. He pulled off his white coat and reached for his jacket hanging on a hook to the left of the door. He called goodbye to Jian, who was gleefully engrossed in the data spilling onto his monitor.

'Enjoy your holiday, Callum. See you next week. I have a lot of work to do now.'

'Bye, Jian. Don't forget to go home this evening.'

'Funny man, Dr Armour. Hurry now. Catch train.'

Callum left the door to swing closed, sprinted along the corridor to his office, grabbed his rucksack from beneath his untidy desk and hurried to the stairs. He couldn't wait to see Tilly – couldn't wait to have Emily in his arms, raising her to the ceiling and watching her giggle with delight.

They would enjoy a week by the sea; the three of them playing on the sand, lunch at the Lobster Pot and a cosy fire in the evening as Tilly read aloud her latest chapter.

All good.

He was also twenty-eight, fit, healthy and, above all, a lucky man. Happiness swirled around him like a summer breeze. Callum was a man well aware he was blessed with good fortune. He had an interesting career, a wonderful wife and a beautiful daughter. All these things flooded his mind as he swept by the reception desk en route to the exit of the Chemistry building. As he pushed the door open, he heard the clerk calling out to him.

'Some mail for you, Callum,' she said, holding up a white A5-size envelope. He hurried back and took the letter.

'Thanks, Eleanor. Have a nice Easter. Have to fly. Tilly's going to kill me if I don't make the train.'

The fifty-year-old woman, with a round face and glasses perched low on her nose, smiled with understanding, well used to seeing Callum running late.

'Bye, Callum. Enjoy your break.'

He shoved the envelope into his bag as he barged through the door into the rain. He hoped the bad weather wouldn't last. Maybe in Devon the sun was splitting the trees. Callum was six feet tall, had a rapid stride, but he knew he hadn't a hope of making the six o'clock train. He would have no trouble with the six-thirty, but Tilly would not be pleased. It meant bringing Emily out after dark to meet him at the station, when she should be tucked up in bed.

* * *

Tilly waited all afternoon for his call. Finally, she had to phone to remind him that he should be on a train racing to see her instead of salivating over test results that would be waiting for him after Easter. It wasn't the first time and wouldn't be the last. She recalled the occasion when she had to go and fetch him at two in the morning. They were supposed to have dinner with friends at seven, and he'd called to tell her that he was running late. Callum didn't show. When she got to Oxford, she'd found him slumped across his desk, reams of printouts littering the floor.

'Another five minutes,' he'd murmured, oblivious to the time and her standing over him.

Tilly loved his enthusiasm. She loved his dedication, not only to his work but to her and Emily. She realised that he had a lot to put up with sometimes; she was no easy partner. A writer could never be relied upon either. While he may lose track of time and forget to come home, there were many occasions when she simply needed to get away. If she had an idea in her head, she had to run with it. On occasions that meant being alone, undisturbed, not distracted, even by Emily. At those times Callum was always there to hold things together, while she raged with her writing.

He'd called her at twenty-five to seven to say that he'd made the train. She had promised herself to shower and change, wash her brown hair, slap on some eyeliner and lipstick, to look remotely human for her husband, but her afternoon had gone awry. Emily wouldn't take her nap. Tilly had a character to flesh out. That was a disaster, because she couldn't settle on a first name for the lonely beach bum who rescues the kids from the incoming tide. It had to be something heroic. For a second, she considered using Callum but only for a second. By five to seven, it was Tilly who was running late, and oh how Callum would relish that. She'd washed Emily after her encounter with vegetable stew and rice pudding, but she had no time for her shower, a change of clothes or the slapping on of make-up. She carried Emily to the car, opened the rear door and strapped her into the car seat. A fierce wind was getting up, giving the rain that extra soak-ability. She hurried back to the cottage, gathered her anorak and handbag, and slammed the front door behind her.

Driving the small silver hatchback off the patch of gravel that was their tiny front garden and onto Bolney Road, she allowed herself a glance in the mirror. God, she looked awful. What was Callum going to say? 'Where the hell's my wife? This can't possibly be her?' Then she smiled to herself, because that's exactly the sort of thing he would say. If she turned up in evening wear, with fresh clean hair, sparkling earrings and a cleavage threatening a night of unbridled passion, he would still say, 'Where the hell's my wife?'

She loved him, couldn't wait to see him, to hold him, to run her fingers through his thick mop of black hair, to rasp the back of her hand on his unshaven face and to gaze into the dark pools of his Irish eyes. She felt blessed to have found him – to be given him. She was thankful for the day she received word that she was going to Oxford. She'd always had a plan. Oxford first, then write and write. She'd never expected Callum. Even in her wildest imagination that she battled to get into print each day, she could never have thought up Callum.

By tomorrow afternoon the three of them would be holed up in the cottage in Teignmouth that her parents had owned for years, used for weekend breaks and summer retreats. She'd lost count of the good times she'd had there as a child and more recently with Callum. She allowed herself the thought that Emily was quite possibly conceived there, in the tiny loft bedroom with its curtainless window and a view of a rolling sea.

She turned the car into Station Road where there was a level crossing to negotiate. It was never that busy. In the three years she and Callum had lived in Shiplake, she could count on the fingers of one hand the number of times she had to wait for a train to pass. There were no barriers, just the alarm and the obligatory flashing lights. Tonight, of all nights there would, of course, be a train due. She slowed well in advance of the stop sign. Emily was almost sleeping at last, and Tilly didn't want any sudden braking to jerk her out of the notion. Better that she was fast asleep when Daddy met them rather than having to deal with a screaming noise-box.

It was dusk, and the flashing red lights throbbed against the dull greens of the hedgerows. The car drew to a halt on the lane; she waited, tapping her fingers on the steering wheel, urging the train to get a move on. Still irked by her poor appearance, she returned her gaze to the mirror. It filled with light as a large car, a 4x4, pulled up behind her. She hadn't noticed any other vehicles as she emerged from Bolney Road but thought little of it. She was going to be so late for Callum.

To her right, in the distance, she caught the lights of the approaching train, and her attention left the vehicle behind. She felt a bump. Her head bounced on the headrest. Instinctively, she pulled at the handbrake as the car lurched forward. Stamping her foot on the brakes, she glanced in the mirror and squinted from the glare of the main beam of the 4x4. She felt another bump, and the hatchback lunged again, sliding towards the railway line.

Tilly screamed. Emily awoke, crying. With its wheels spinning and engine growling, the car behind roared forward sliding the hatchback across the white line on the road and beyond the flashing lights. Tilly's engine was still running. She hadn't stalled. But the 4x4 continued its shunt. Should she drive across the track? Get out? Get Emily out? Screaming at the driver to stop, she no longer had a choice. Flooring the accelerator, her wheels spun on the damp road. The 4x4 suddenly lost contact, and the hatchback shot forward. There was no time. No precious seconds for a train to slow.

The silver hatchback crumpled like a tin can. Blitzed glass and plastic sprayed over tarmac; a petrifying screech of metal grating on metal as the train shoved the captured chassis a hundred yards down the track before rolling to a halt. Lights still flashed red. The tyres of the 4x4 crackled over shattered glass and plastic but were soon humming along the road to Henley.

* * *

Callum groaned at the announcement. Train delayed due to signalling problems near Pangbourne. He called Tilly, but there was no reply. He left a message on her voicemail, saying that his train was delayed. She would be so pissed at him for being late. The passengers around him – commuters, day-trippers and students travelling home for the Easter break – muttered their complaints. Callum opened his rucksack, searching for a book to read. He noticed the letter he'd picked up on his way out of work, squeezed between the two books and a little creased. Removing it from the bag, he stared at the envelope. There was no address, no stamp or postmark, only his name typed across it: 'Dr Callum Armour'. It was a sealed envelope, so he eased his finger into the gap at the edge and ran it along to rip it open. He pulled out a card, and his eyebrows met in confusion. There was nothing written on the inside, no message or names. On the front was a picture of a large spray of flowers – white lilies. Printed in silver letters above it were the words 'With Deepest Sympathy on the Death of Your Wife'.

CHAPTER 2

As precentor and liturgist at Canterbury Cathedral, Peter Ramsey co-ordinated worship in the mighty building. When he attended Evensong, he was always left whistling or humming one of the chants performed by the choir in the service. Seeding, they call it. Tonight, he'd have some random tune rattling around in his head for the remainder of the evening unless he got to relax with some Mozart or Coldplay. He was hungry also, but he would have to make do with cheese on toast or, perhaps, that pepperoni pizza in his freezer.

The people who had attended the service, mainly regulars and a few tourists, had left the building. They walked briskly in the crisp February air through the cathedral precincts to their cars, their homes or nearby hotels. All but one. There was always one. There was always somebody who had entered the cathedral to attend the service then took the opportunity to wander around afterwards without having to pay an entrance fee. Peter watched as the figure, wearing a long dark coat, strolled down the nave. It wasn't his job to usher out visitors or to close up for the night, but he wondered if this particular visitor was waiting for someone – a member of staff perhaps. Disinclined to chase after the stranger, he remained at the steps above the nave, by the crossing, pondering a visit to Café Rouge on the high street instead of the cheese on toast.

Peter was tall but quite frail-looking, with a thin yet pleasant face. Not much meat on the bones. He didn't fit any conventional picture of a clergyman and at times looked as if he'd just returned from a weekend at Glastonbury. His silver-rimmed, penny-spectacles sat askew on his rather hooked nose; his frizzy hair was tied back during working hours into a ponytail and held in place with a blue elastic band. He was intelligent but looked delicate. His body was frequently restless. If he wasn't whistling or humming Tallis, he was tapping out *The Marriage of Figaro* with his right foot, conducting at the *Last Night of the Proms* or sweeping about the place singing *All That Jazz* from *Chicago*. And yet Peter was not entirely a happy man. At thirty-one he was, however, feeling comfortable with his current lifestyle. Nowadays, he left his sordid past well alone.

Daydreaming as he was, he'd hardly noticed the stranger mounting the steps to the north aisle of the Quire. He thought a gentle hint might be required. It was after five o'clock. Time to pack up and go home. *Antiques Roadshow* was on telly this evening, and he had still to decide what to do about food. When he reached the north aisle, he saw no one but soon realised the visitor had descended to the northwest transept into the Martyrdom.

'Excuse me,' Peter called politely from the top of the steps. 'May I be of assistance? The cathedral is actually closed for the evening. Perhaps, if you're looking for something in particular?'

The stranger stood upon the tile in the floor marked in red with the name 'Thomas'. It was believed that this was the place where Thomas Becket, Archbishop of Canterbury, had been murdered in 1170. On the wall, above a plinth of granite, hung three old and battered swords. One of them had shattered at the tip when the skull of Thomas had been sliced open.

Slowly, the stranger turned to face him.

'Good Lord,' said Peter, cheerfully. 'I never thought I'd ever see you in here.' He quickly descended the steps to greet his visitor.

'Hello, Peter. You always said you'd be an archbishop someday.'

'I'm not quite that…' Peter laughed, his hand outstretched in greeting. But, to his surprise, the visitor did not reciprocate. Feeling awkward, Peter dropped his hand to his side.

'Merely another turbulent priest?'

'Steady on. It's been such a long time.' Peter suddenly felt cold. 'Why have you come?'

'You already know the answer, Peter. To free you from your past. It's the price I must pay for your silence.'

The hand-axe appeared quickly. Peter had no time. He had no expectation of disaster. The first swipe caught his left ear and sent him sprawling over the plinth beneath the swords. The second came with greater force and truer aim – downwards, between his eyes. Peter died instantly. No need for a third blow – or a fourth. The fifth split his skull wide open. Thick dark blood flowed over the tile marked with the name of Thomas.

Pulling a small white towel from a deep pocket, the killer wiped the axe clean, stepped over the body and draped the stained cloth upon the butchered face of Peter Ramsey.

CHAPTER 3

Treadwater Estate, Netherton, Liverpool.

On days like this, Tara Grogan wondered if she was cut out for the job. She didn't even look the part. She was only five foot one and had a face that, despite her twenty-seven years, still required ID to gain entrance to some of the nightclubs she frequented with girlfriends Aisling and Kate. At work she kept her shoulder-length golden, blonde hair pulled back to a stern ponytail. She reduced it to a minimum but could never venture out without some make-up, usually resorting to mascara, a pink lipstick, and some foundation to add health to an otherwise pale complexion. Her friends still chuckled at her having to buy her clothes from the early-teenage range in Debenhams.

In flat shoes, black trousers and jacket over a white blouse, all concealed beneath the requisite white overall, she felt neither attractive nor warm. Not in here. Her skin oozed a cold sweat. A shiver had taken hold from her lower back to the base of her skull. How do you ever get used to a scene like this? Her more experienced colleagues told her it was always better to look. See the victim and you won't stop searching for the killer. The house was filling with people. She heard the team of forensics lining the hall waiting to resume their work. They'd done their initial inspection of the scene, and the duty medical officer had examined the body. Now it was their turn.

Detective Sergeant Murray stood beside her in the back bedroom. The room was sparsely furnished but for the double bed and the body lying upon it. Flimsy curtains of primrose were drawn, obscuring the dreary day.

The thin, dark blue carpet that covered the floor did nothing to lessen the creak of the boards as her boss, Superintendent Harold Tweedy, paced around the bed.

Tara needed fresh air. She'd seen enough. The image of the girl lying naked, smothered quite probably, and the sickening marks across her chest would be with her for a long time. She wouldn't need a reminder.

'Is that a word?' Tweedy asked, his voice always one of concern and empathy. Murray called him a Bible basher, a reference to his lay preaching at his local Baptist church.

DS Murray studied the letters on the girl's chest.

'Fag burns,' he said.

'Yes, but surely they form a word?' said Tweedy.

Tara cocked her head to the side. She tried to form each letter, roughly sketched and uneven. It seemed to her they had been applied to the girl's skin after death, because there was little swelling. At least she hoped the poor kid hadn't been tortured before she died. Each crooked letter was around two inches in height.

'K...U...R...W...A,' said Tara.

'*Kurwa*? Doesn't mean anything,' said Murray.

'Doesn't have to be English.'

She'd really had enough of this. The room stank of sweat and cigarette smoke. She would be sick in a minute if she didn't get some fresh air.

'Right,' said Tweedy. 'We'll get out now, and let Forensics continue their work.'

Tweedy was first out of the door, followed by Murray. Tara was thereby granted the final look at the young girl. She was no more than seventeen; lying on her back, spindly arms by her sides, legs spread apart and the sheet beneath her stained with urine. Her death-grey flesh looked bruised in places, on her neck and upper arms – the effects of lividity – the accumulation of blood under the skin after death.

The skin was smooth except for the letters branded above her tiny swellings of breasts. Her fingers were curled as though her hands had been clenched to fists but then had flexed open at the moment of death. The face was blue-grey, and to Tara was indicative of suffocation. But for that, the girl might only have been in a deep sleep. How bizarre to have three strangers staring down upon your naked body as you slept. The girl's hair was short and reddish-brown; the only warm colour in the room. Tara hurried after her colleagues as two forensics guys squeezed past on the stairs.

Outside, at the rear of the terraced house, a cordon of police incident tape had been stretched across the cul-de-sac, preventing access to the rear of the houses, the parking area and the lock-up garages. The houses were late 1950s and built in blocks of five, each block facing outwards to landscaped areas of grass, criss-crossed by pathways leading nowhere in particular. At the time, the estate was intended as the new age in social housing with pleasant areas of open space and playing fields. Treadwater had been the future of community living in Liverpool, with estates just like it going up all over the city and in many others across Britain.

She joined DS Murray and DC John Wilson at the back gate of the house. Murray, a thirty-six-year-old, had a number one cut, although baldness wasn't far off. His face and neck were fat; he had thin lips and small teeth that diminished his attempts at a broad smile. As far as Tara was concerned, he was tolerable.

A young officer of twenty-two, Wilson had round shoulders and blond hair cut in an old-fashioned short back and sides. His cheeks were puffy, giving the impression of sunken blue eyes and creating a distrusting look of someone who had already experienced too many of life's troubles. He was tall like Murray but much broader. Although most of her colleagues towered above her, Tara had sufficient confidence to know that she matched them in many other respects.

Tweedy had left them to it. The detectives were to carry out house-to-house inquiries and speak with the medical officer to establish the cause and time of death. As they dispensed with the white overalls, Murray assumed a modicum of command. He had a tendency to overlook, or deliberately ignore, that Tara was a detective inspector to his detective sergeant. She chose her moments carefully to remind him of the fact. Right now, she was prepared to let him off with it.

'John, you take the far side and work around,' said Murray. 'I'll start next door, and we can meet in the middle.'

That left the medical officer for Tara. She didn't need telling. She noticed the pair of them smirking and was about to speak out when she realised they were not looking at her but towards the entrance of the cul-de-sac.

'Here we go,' said Murray. 'Friggin' idiot.'

Tara spun round in time to see a man duck under the police tape and continue on his way along the pavement. He had a peculiar stride that seemed quick, but his length of step was short giving the impression of a man walking in an old silent movie. A small dog, the size of a Jack Russell but of no recognisable breed, waddled along twenty feet ahead. The man was wearing a double-breasted navy suit jacket with dark green jogging trousers, and a pair of brown, brogue shoes. His black hair, soaked with rain, drooped to his shoulders, and an untidy beard obscured the features of his face. A carrier bag of groceries hung from each hand. He seemed oblivious to anyone around him, and was certainly ignorant of the reason for police incident tape. Tara's colleagues sniggered.

'The local headcase,' Murray said. She looked sternly at her colleague then called out to the man.

'Excuse me, sir! There's a police investigation going on at the moment. Can you go around by the front of the houses?'

The man increased his pace. The dog appeared to do the same. Murray and Wilson giggled like a pair of schoolgirls.

'Run, Forrest, run,' Murray sniggered.

'Will you two be quiet?'

Tara went after him. By the time she'd reached the middle of the road, both man and dog had made it to the end of the cul-de-sac by the lock-ups, turned around, and were headed back the way they had come. She waited for him to draw level.

'There's a police investigation underway. Would you mind staying outside the cordon?'

He stopped and turned to face her. Bedraggled and dirty, he was thin, scrawny even, and his shoulders appeared to sag from the strain of carrying the groceries. Beneath the jacket, he wore a plain grey T-shirt that looked in dire need of washing. She drew closer, noting his dark but washed-out eyes; the whites were bloodshot. His breath stank of beer and garlic. The man seemed more interested in where his dog was headed.

'Would you mind telling me where you are going?'

'Home.'

'And where would that be?'

With a slight movement of his head, he indicated the entrance to the cul-de-sac – the opposite direction to where he had first been walking.

'Then why did you walk under the tape?'

'Midgey always comes this way.' He glanced beyond her to where Murray and Wilson were looking on, their amused grins still present.

'Well, I would appreciate it if you stayed on the other side of the tape for now.'

She watched his eyes darting from her colleagues to his dog and then back to her. When they appeared to settle on her she spoke again, hoping that at last she had his full attention.

'I'm Detective Inspector Tara Grogan.'

He was staring now, looking her up and down.

'Can you tell me anything about the people living in that house?' She pointed at the house then checked the notebook in her hand. 'Number six.'

He made no reply but maintained his staring. Unkempt beard and heavy eyes gave him a look of menace. It wouldn't be hard to suspect him of murder.

'Have you noticed anything suspicious in this area in the last few hours? Or yesterday, maybe?'

This time he shook his head slowly, but his eyes remained firmly upon Tara. She thought him rude, vacant, and certainly not forthcoming.

'Can I take a note of your name please?'

'Callum.'

She glared at his blank expression, waiting for more. She could be there all day; he had nothing to add.

'Do you have a surname?' she asked sardonically.

'Armour.'

'And your address?'

'Over there.'

'Which is?'

'Twenty-four.'

She wrote the scant details on her notepad then removed a card from her jacket pocket and handed it to the man.

'If you remember anything, those are my contact details.' He took the card without comment, and for a second they remained staring at each other. 'You can go now,' she said.

Mechanically, he turned to his right and paced away in the direction of his home. Tara watched him go, thinking him very strange and wondering why he hadn't asked what had occurred in his street that required police detectives.

'How'd you get on with our Dr Stinker then?' Wilson asked, as Tara rejoined them at the gate.

'Stinker?'

Murray laughed.

'Term of endearment round here for the likes of him.'

'Paedo,' said Wilson.

Tara shuddered at the thought.

'Is he really?'

Murray shook his head. His bulbous eyes had fire in them, feisty and spirited. He was usually well focussed on the job despite his flippant answers to sensible questions.

'No record as such,' he said. 'No reason to believe he's that way inclined, but it doesn't stop the local gobshites from sticking a label on you. We've been called out to his house at least a dozen times in the last couple of years. He's either been attacked, his house broken into, or bottles thrown at his windows. Kids. They think it's a laugh. Scares the shit out of the poor sod, though.'

'And why *Doctor*?'

'Bright spark of some sort. Went a bit loopy after his wife and child were killed. Full of conspiracy theories and all that nonsense.'

'He's harmless,' said Wilson. 'I grew up round here. So did Armour. Most people who've been here for years know him well. It's only the young ones that give him any grief.'

Tara watched the man as he opened his back door.

* * *

Stepping inside, Callum Armour stole a glance at her then shut the door firmly behind him. He set the bags of shopping on the draining board by the sink and peered through his wire-screened window towards the house where the police were milling around. In particular, he watched the girl. She was pretty, stern too, with determined blue eyes and a small mouth that he reckoned held a sharp, no-nonsense tongue. He read the small card in his hand. It had her name and the telephone number of St Anne Street station on it. He knew that name. He was certain he'd seen her before.

A few steps took him from his kitchen, through a darkened hallway and into his sitting room. The large window was screened with wire mesh like that of the kitchen. He could see out well enough, but anyone on the outside had a harder job seeing in. Despite the mesh protection, the glass had a huge crack running from the centre to the bottom right-hand corner.

The sitting room looked cramped but had little furniture. A scuffed leather two-seater sofa sat against the wall, opposite a fireplace that his late father had boarded up years ago. Instead, he had electric storage radiators in each room. It was just possible to decipher a coffee table, close to the window, covered in newspapers, magazines, empty takeaway cartons, pizza boxes, coffee mugs and a couple of photographs in cheap frames. Bundles of newspapers, textbooks and several dozen box-files occupied most of the floor space in the room. The only seat available for use was the armchair, but it was far from a conventional piece of furniture. It was constructed entirely from bundles of newspapers tied with string and used as building blocks. The dog had its favourite place and lay down on an old doormat under the coffee table.

Mumbling to himself, Callum began a search of the room, lifting one pile of magazines, transferring them to another, before upturning the lot and starting over. He knew he'd seen her face before, and his attempts to find her grew more frantic as he shuffled through magazines, newspapers and supplements, one stack toppling into another. Several minutes later, his hand finally pulled a magazine from the jumble on the floor. He stared at the cover then flicked it open and leafed through it, excitedly. On the penultimate page, he found her – the image that had struck him the second he'd fixed his eyes on Detective Inspector Tara Grogan.

CHAPTER 4

They sat around the desk of Superintendent Tweedy. A man in his mid-fifties, he had a pinched face and wore thick-framed spectacles too wide for his narrow head. His once fiery-red hair was long since greyed and the flesh was beginning to sag below a pointed chin. He looked like he needed a good feed – and as though he'd never had one. The collar of an olive-green shirt and tartan tie hung loosely around his neck, and he didn't quite fill the tweed sports jacket. He was on his feet moving back and forth to a whiteboard, where gradually he added the known facts of the girl's death on the Treadwater Estate.

Tara sat, legs crossed, with a notebook on her knee, while Murray slouched with hands in pockets and feet outstretched, and Wilson leaned over a notepad on the desk.

'Likely cause of death?' asked Tweedy.

'Suffocation,' said Tara. 'A pillow, most probably, but there was nothing found in the room. No clothing, pillows or duvet.'

Wielding the marker pen, Tweedy turned to face his team.

'Approximate time of death?'

'The medical officer estimated late evening to early hours of the morning,' Tara replied. 'We should get confirmation later today.'

He wrote again on the board.

'Thanks for that information, Tara.'

Having relayed the few details from her notes, Tara turned to a fresh page in her book, ready to write down anything of significance.

'Now, what do we know about the house?'

'No one living there permanently at the moment,' said Murray, without shifting from his position of comfort. 'House is privately owned by a Teodor Sokolowski. His home address is listed as Katowice in Poland. Seems he owns a couple of houses in Netherton and several around Merseyside. They're usually rented out to Polish workers.'

'No one in the vicinity knew of any girl living at the house,' said Wilson. 'No reports of suspicious activity and no complaints of noise from neighbours living either side.'

'No identity for the victim, as yet,' Tara added.

'OK,' said Tweedy, stepping away from his board. 'Not much to go on, so far. Alan, I suggest you check the other houses owned by this Teodor person. Try to contact him, or at least establish his present whereabouts. Tara, it might be worth visiting some of the local Polish community groups. Check if they know of anyone who is missing and has not been reported to police. John, have you made any progress on the meaning of that word?'

'Googled it, sir. It means bitch or whore in Polish.'

'The killer making a bold statement regarding his victim? Has the makings of a motive, I would suggest,' said Tweedy.

Having issued his instructions, Tweedy dismissed them to their desks.

* * *

Tara sat down at her computer to check out a list of community groups in Netherton, Bootle and Walton. Her mobile rang; the sound of Lady Gaga, *Born this Way,* broke the relative quiet in the open-plan office.

'Are you on for tonight?' It was her close friend Aisling. Straight to the point, she didn't bother with hellos.

'Absolutely,' Tara replied. 'The last two days have been pants. Stuck in the middle of a fresh murder inquiry.'

'Joys of policing?'

'Hardly that, but I'm looking forward to getting out for a few drinks.'

'Kate's booked Malmaison for dinner at eight o'clock then out for a couple of bevvies. It's going to be great! We haven't been out for ages. I'm off to buy shoes in honour of the occasion. Kate's having her hair done…'

'Have to go, Aisling. Some of us have work to do.'

'OK, I'll see you later. Bye.'

Her office phone rang, and when she picked up another female voice told her she had a visitor at the front desk.

'What's the name?'

'Mr Armour,' the desk officer replied. There was a pause. 'Sorry, a Dr Armour.' The voice fell to a whisper. 'If you ask me, ma'am, he doesn't look much like a doctor.'

Tara quickly leafed through her notebook; it took a second for the name to register. The strange guy from Treadwater.

'Did he say what he wants?'

The line went quiet, while the desk officer asked Armour his business.

'Says he'll only speak to you.'

'I'll come down.'

He looked exactly as he had done the day before. Same clothes, wet straggly hair – it was still raining outside – the same vacant expression and arms by his sides. A large carrier bag from Lidl hung from his right hand. Before she judged him too harshly, she realised that she must also look the same to him: same clothes, same hair, although she had showered since they last met. She didn't think that could be said for her visitor.

'Dr Armour, what can I do for you?' She tried to sound pleasant. She smiled and made a deliberate effort to give him his proper title. He didn't look bothered either way.

'You said to get in touch if I thought of anything.'

Several people walked by staring at the man who looked every bit the tramp. Smelt that way, too. Tara braced herself for the awkward conversation ahead.

'Do you want to come through to my office?'

He reached out the Lidl bag, but made no effort to go with her.

'This might be of help.' He stared down at her through watery eyes, his breath reeking of beer. She had no choice but to step closer to accept the bag. She took a handle in each hand and peered inside to see a battered grey box-file. Armour was already backing towards the exit.

'Are you sure you won't come through?'

He shook his head, turned and walked out.

'OK, thanks. Nice talking to you, too.'

Holding it well in front of her, she carried the bag upstairs to the office and laid it down flat on her desk. She considered donning a pair of latex gloves just to remove the box-file from the bag. There was a strong aroma of Dr Armour: stale, heavy smells of cooked food, damp clothing and dog. She shuddered. Couldn't manage it, not without gloves. She removed a pair of latex disposables from a box in the top drawer of her desk and slipped them on. To her far left, she could see Murray looking on with interest, but when she glanced over, he quickly returned to his computer screen. Removing the box-file, she returned it to the desk and dropped the bag to the floor, hoping it was well out of smelling range. It was a standard office box-file, bulging with papers, the words 'Mass Spectrometry Data' written in purple on the side. The catch on the lid was broken but was held fast by a thick rubber band. Once open, she removed the papers inside one by one, anticipating information concerning the murdered girl.

Ten minutes later, feeling very perplexed, she had a pile of dog-eared papers and grotty news cuttings littering her desk. Nothing amongst them had any relevance, as far as she could tell, to the death of the young girl on the Treadwater Estate the day before. At the bottom of the box, she was treated to a crust of toasted bread and a sprinkling of mouse droppings. Shaking the last few papers free of crumbs and mouse poo, she carried the box-file to a waste bin and tipped out the mess. She felt cheated. That filthy man had just wasted her time and probably exposed her to all kinds of diseases.

She'd learned nothing to help her with the murder case. Why had he given her all of this information? What was he trying to tell her?

CHAPTER 5

'Fancy a drive out to Treadwater?'

She'd stuffed all the papers back into the box-file, placed it back in the carrier bag, crossed the office to Murray's desk and invited him to accompany her to Armour's house. She didn't feel entirely confident going alone.

'Why, what's up?'

'I'll explain on the way.'

Twenty minutes later, Murray pulled the car into a lay-by at the front of the house, which sat back from the road and was separated from it by a pavement and a narrow strip of grass. Tara gazed at the house: number twenty-four Sycamore Drive, but not a tree in sight. It was no more appealing from the front than it had been from the rear, with a battered door and metal screens fixed to the windows.

'Wait here,' she told Murray. 'This won't take long.'

She pushed open the car door, climbed out and retrieved the Lidl bag from the boot, holding it as far away from her as possible. As she crossed the strip of grass, to her right she noticed a group of six teenagers, three boys and three girls, standing by an alley that led to the parking area behind the houses. They halted their conversation to watch the young woman approach the front door of Dr Stinker. When she glanced their way, the girls sniggered and one boy, wearing a blue Everton shirt, whistled at her. She responded with a peeved stare, but he wasn't in the least intimidated. The brief encounter merely gave rise to more laughter.

Tara stared at the front door of the house, its weathered yellow paint awash with scrapes and burn marks. The word 'paedo' had been spray-painted in dark green below the letterbox, although the smudged letters suggested there had been some attempt to wash it off. There was no doorbell or knocker, so she tapped on the wood. She waited for a few seconds before adding a more determined thump upon the door. Turning around, she saw Murray looking on from the car, his habitual bemused smirk playing on his face. Still with no reply, she knocked again.

'He doesn't answer the door,' one of the youths shouted.

'Only opens it to kids,' said the Everton shirt. The others laughed.

She tried peering through the living room window, but the screens were effective, and she saw only the grime on the glass. A car horn blared. She looked reproachfully at Murray, and he shrugged his shoulders. But it did the trick. A few seconds later, she heard movement on the other side of the door, a chain being loaded in its lock. Eventually, the door opened on the chain, and the now familiar dirty face peered out.

'Dr Armour, would you mind opening the door please?'

It slammed shut with a bang and a chain rattled. The door opened wide, and the dark shape of the man looked all the more sinister when framed by the gloominess of the hallway.

'I thought I should return this to you, Dr Armour. I'm sorry, but I don't see how any of this information is connected to the murder of the girl at number six.' She held out the bag, and he took it with both hands. His eyes didn't leave hers. 'Do you have any information relevant to our inquiry?'

He didn't reply. She was frustrated by this man, yet she felt sympathy now that she knew something of his past.

'If you think of anything that has a bearing on this current case, please get in touch. If not, I'd appreciate it if you didn't waste our time.'

She turned to go.

'More people will die,' he said in a croaky voice.

She turned back to face him.

'I beg your pardon?'

He shook the Lidl bag.

'In here.'

'I don't understand. Are you telling me that this box of papers *has* got something to do with the girl's murder?'

His nod was barely perceptible, but a tremor passed through Tara's stomach.

'Do you want to explain?'

He nodded again. She didn't fancy stepping into the house, but they couldn't struggle through this conversation on the doorstep.

'May I come in and we can discuss it?'

Armour stepped forward and peered into the road. Murray looked on intently. The teenagers watched from the entrance to the alley.

'OK,' he said, stepping back, allowing her to enter.

'Go on, Stinker! Give her one!' a youth shouted.

More laughter erupted from the group.

Armour stared blankly, waiting for her to step inside. When the door closed behind them, she felt the air cooler, although it was ripe with the stench of dog, cooked food and body odour. He led her from the darkness of the hall into the living room, brightened slightly by the evening sun squeezing through the dismal screen on the window.

Looking around, she couldn't see any obvious place for her to sit. The brown and white dog rose from its bed, came and sniffed at her shoes, wagged its stump of a tail, and waddled to a spot beneath the coffee table to lie down again. Tara waited for some guidance from her host, but he had already seated himself on a strange makeshift armchair constructed from bundles of newspapers. Gazing around her at the hoard of papers and the detritus of poor living, she spotted a tiny space on a sofa otherwise crammed with files. She forced herself to sit.

'So, tell me about the box-file?'

He had the Lidl bag on his lap, and from it he removed the battered file. After some searching among the papers, he produced a newspaper cutting and offered it to Tara. She could see it was one reporting the disappearance of a student while on a ski holiday in Austria. She looked inquiringly at Armour in a way that suggested he should explain.

'He's back.'

'I don't understand.'

'Justin Kingsley disappeared in Austria ten years ago, but he has returned to England.' He rifled the box again, growing impatient with his search. Clearly, Tara had upset the definite order of its contents. He showed her a piece reporting a copycat Thomas Becket murder in Canterbury Cathedral.

'He did it.'

'Justin Kingsley?'

Callum nodded and resumed his rummage in the box, producing next an inquest report on the death of the children's writer Tilly Reason. Tara took the paper from him and, for the second time that day, read through the story. She noted that the verdict of the inquest was accidental death.

'He did it.'

Tara felt her unease grow. Clearly, this man had no intention of giving her information about the girl murdered in the house close by. Did he know anything about the murder? She couldn't yet tell. For a second, she thought that maybe this file had come from the murder scene, or the victim had given it to him before she died, or that he killed her to get hold of it.

Tara felt a sudden urge to get out of the house. This man was a nutcase. Murray was just outside; she could make an excuse to return to the car. But it was as if Callum Armour had suddenly read her thoughts, sensed her confusion, saw the fear emerging on her face. He began talking. Openly.

'She was my wife, and Emily was my daughter. He killed them both. I know it. Then, for some reason, he killed Peter Ramsey, and I don't think he's finished.'

'It says here that the inquest recorded accidental death?'

Armour shook his head, lowering it into his hands. He wiped at his eyes and sniffed back tears.

'It was murder.'

Tara scanned through the story on the cathedral slaying.

'Kent Police are working on the basis that this was committed by a religious fanatic or someone with a grievance against the Church?'

'It was Kingsley.'

There was a sudden banging. The front door. Armour jumped in fright but made no attempt to rise from his seat. The dog went spare, barking loudly at the window. Tara stepped through the stacks of papers, made her way to the hall and opened the front door.

'You all right, ma'am?' Murray was intent upon coming inside, but she pushed him gently back.

'I'm OK. Wait in the car. I won't be long.'

'What's going on?'

'I'll explain later.' She closed the door and picked her way back to the sofa in the living room. Armour was again searching through the box-file.

'What motive could this Justin Kingsley have to kill your wife and child?'

'I've no idea.'

'And Peter Ramsey?'

'I don't know.'

'Why would he have waited so long since the time of his disappearance before killing any of these people?'

Armour stared coldly at Tara.

'I don't know.'

Further questions, she realised, would be futile. The man was living with his traumatic past and coping badly. He looked lost. His eyes moved, searching for the answers as if they should be right there in front of him printed on one of the many cuttings from newspapers and magazines littering his room. It wasn't hard to recognise a broken man nursing a broken heart.

'I'm very sorry for your loss, Callum, but I don't think I can help you. These deaths are all tragic, horrible for you, and sometimes it's hard to face up to something when you really believe differently. I'm sure the police in Kent are working very hard to catch the person who killed Peter Ramsey. Maybe, if you have some information that might be of help you can contact them directly, or I could do it for you. My job, at the moment, is to catch the person who killed the girl we found in the house behind yours.'

Tara jumped suddenly as Armour leapt from his seat and dived towards her. She struggled to her feet to avoid his lunge then blushed instantly, realising he was not coming at her.

He looked shocked by her reaction, then he began rummaging through the files on the sofa. Papers were tossed across the room as he discarded one box after another. Relieved that she wasn't under attack, she looked on helplessly as his search became more frantic.

'What are you looking for?'

Ignoring her question, he lost himself in his quest. A mobile beeped. She had a text.

'Where r u?'

It was Aisling. Tara replied that she was running late and would join them soon. Callum stood before her, brandishing a greetings card. She took it from him and gave it a cursory examination.

'With Deepest Sympathy on the Death of Your Wife,' she read from the printed card. There was nothing written inside, merely a picture of flowers below the message on the front. Slowly, she shook her head.

'I don't understand.'

He looked quite pleased with himself; the closest he'd been to smiling.

'I got this on the day Tilly and Emily died.'

'It's a sympathy card, Callum. I'm sure you received lots of them.'

'It was given to me before she died. I was on my way home. She was coming to pick me up at the station when she was killed. I had the card with me on the train.'

For the first time, she was conscious of his strange sounding accent – a blend of Scouse and Northern Ireland.

'I told the police about it at the time, but they said that I was probably mistaken. They suggested that I wasn't thinking straight, upset by the death of my wife and daughter. Eventually, one of the officers on the case tried to check up on it, but he drew a blank. Wasn't even mentioned at the inquest.'

She looked again at the picture of flowers; such paltry comfort to a man who'd had his whole life torn apart.

'You're sure about this?'

He nodded once.

There was an almighty crack and, instinctively, they both ducked. The noise came from the back of the house.

The dog barked. Tara rushed through the hall to the dreary kitchen. Callum followed her.

'It's those damned kids,' he said.

'Open the door.' She stepped back as he fumbled with a key and released a hefty bar lock. When he pulled the door open, she barged past him into a small yard. She heard laughter and running footsteps. A male voice jeered. A female giggled. Standing on tiptoe and peering over the wooden fence, she spotted one youth lingering at the end of the street – the Everton shirt.

'Why don't you grow up?' she shouted. The reply was a volley of whoops and jeers. Turning to Callum, she offered a look of sympathy. He didn't appear to notice and, with head lowered, returned to his kitchen. She watched him restore his home to a secure footing, locking the door and drawing the bolt. She smiled, a gesture of understanding, but again he dropped his gaze.

'The CCTV wasn't working,' he said on his way back to the living room. 'At Shiplake crossing,' he added. 'Justin must have known that it wasn't working and took his chance.'

'To do what?'

'He must have pushed Tilly's car onto the crossing into the path of the train, or drove it on there himself then put Tilly at the wheel. To do that he must have killed her first.'

Tiring of his theory, she felt the need to bring their meeting to a definite close.

'I'm sorry, Callum. I appreciate your frustration, really I do, but I don't understand why you're telling me this. There's nothing I can do to help you. Even if what you say is true, these deaths happened down south. I don't have the authority to start an investigation off my patch.' She noticed the despair in his eyes. Wearily, he dropped into the armchair. 'I don't see any connection between the death of your wife, a murder in Canterbury three years later and the disappearance of a student in Austria ten years ago. Did you know Peter Ramsey or Justin Kingsley?'

'We were students together: Tilly, Peter, Justin and me.'

'And that's the only link?'

'Like I said, I don't think he's finished yet. He could kill again.'

She noted his factual tone, a man with growing confidence in his theory.

'Who would he kill?'

'I think he has something against us, against the others.'

She thought back to what Murray and Wilson had said the day before – that Armour was a conspiracy theorist.

'Look, Callum, if you have something specific, some hard evidence that this Kingsley guy is intent on doing harm, I will pass it on to the relevant authorities for you. Aside from that, I don't see how I can help you any further.'

She edged her way around a stack of books to reach the hall.

'They were making movies in the house,' he said.

'Which house?' She turned to face him.

'Where you found the girl. Pornographic movies.'

'How do you know this?'

'I watched them going in with video cameras. I saw the lights, late at night, in the bedroom. Not ordinary lights, bright, like a floodlight or a spotlight.'

'Who?'

He shrugged.

Tara guessed his motive.

'Who, Callum? Men? Women? How many?'

'A few. I don't remember exactly.' Tara knew there was more, but she knew him well enough already to see that he had a calculating and stubborn streak. She would have to be patient.

'Please try. Call me if you think of anything else.'

'We were students at Latimer College, Oxford: Tilly, Peter, Justin and me.'

Tara's eyes widened. Nerves floated across her stomach. She looked Callum in the face; she saw the dazzle of conceit in his dark eyes. At last a smile, though hardly welcome, stretched across his mouth.

'I helped you. Now you have to help me.'

'Why, Callum? Why ask for my help?'

He went back to the living room, returning moments later holding a magazine. He opened it at the penultimate page and handed it to her. Immediately, she recognised the photograph of herself in police uniform. She didn't have to read the short paragraph beneath.

'You were also a student at Latimer,' he said.

Without a word, she closed the page and returned his copy of the *Oxford Alumni* magazine.

CHAPTER 6

Dr Zhou Jian breathed easy. Despite his nerves, his presentation had gone well, although his shirt now clung to his back from sweating in the heat of the auditorium. Conference delegates had received his paper '*Recent Advances in the Detection of Adulterated Food in China*' with interest. Quite a few questions were asked, and several requests made for reprints of the paper. He was pleased.

It was the culmination of two years' work, investigating cases of food contamination and the development of analytical methods for detection of the contaminants. Kudos for him and his department at Yanshan University. Not such good news for those arrested and charged with deliberate adulteration of food. The ringleaders faced the death penalty; some had already been executed. That was the kind of justice they administered in his homeland.

No one would care; the actions of a few unscrupulous businessmen had caused the deaths of more than thirty people, most of them children. It was done to make money by defrauding their customers but ultimately harming the consumer. He'd detected chemicals, such as melamine, commonly used in manufacturing plastics, being added illegally to powdered milk to increase the nitrogen concentration, and thereby used as a measure of the protein content in food. He'd uncovered instances where food processors had deliberately incorporated horsemeat and pork in beef products, and where low-grade chicken meat was passed off as organic produce. He detected drugs, such as nitrofuran antibiotics, banned for use in rearing food-producing animals because they are carcinogens, and azo dyes, also carcinogens, used to kill parasites in fish.

Jian had investigated the companies involved and had performed thousands of tests to detect contaminants in food products in order to prevent them from reaching shops and supermarkets. Consequently, he'd received a number of threats. Samples he'd collected were stolen from his lab, his wife was verbally abused by strangers in the street, acid was thrown on his car and his tyres were slashed. He was simply doing his job and never imagined that his life could be at risk. He worked for his university and his government, and he expected that same government to protect him.

Now that he'd given his presentation to the three hundred delegates in the Culture and Congress Centre on Europaplatz in Lucerne, he was going to enjoy the remainder of the conference on global food safety. This evening, he looked forward to the conference dinner. This was his first visit to Europe since he'd returned home to Qinhuangdao after his years at Oxford, as an undergraduate, a postgrad and finally two years working with his close friend Callum Armour as a postdoc. It all seemed like yesterday. He had hoped to see Callum at the conference, but a former colleague from Oxford had told him that Callum was no longer working in the field. He could understand why, after what had happened to his wife Tilly and their little daughter. It saddened him greatly. Callum had been his closest friend at Latimer College.

He fancied a walk before going to the dinner. After a shower and a change of clothes back at his hotel, he quickly checked his emails, replying to a couple and sending one to his wife Lihua, who was six months pregnant. Jian then took the lift down to the lobby of the Grand Hotel National and headed for the exit that led to the lakeside, where he hoped to enjoy the cool evening air as he strolled towards the old town. The lobby was busy with scores of conference attendees who were staying at the hotel.

'Jian,' a voice called from the lounge which opened onto the lobby. He looked across, smiled and gave a cursory wave to a bright-faced man in his thirties with untidy blond hair and wearing a checked shirt and blue jeans.

'Come and join us for a drink.'

He spoke in English with an accent unmistakably Dutch. Jian went over to the group of five people seated in comfortable leather armchairs gathered around a coffee table. He smiled his polite smile, with a slight bow of his head. He was an acquaintance of them all: Dr Koos van Leer and Pieter Schalke both from a research institute in Wageningen, Dr Clarisse Junot from Nantes, an attractive forty-year-old veterinarian, Philip Weston from York and Luca Davoli from Rome. All of them were researchers in the field of food contamination.

Van Leer dragged another chair across the carpeted floor to their table. Jian sat down and ordered a cool beer from the waiter. Soon, Jian's plan to go for a walk disappeared under intense discussions on the detection limits of triple-quad mass spectrometers in analysing mycotoxins in animal feeds, the various views on solid-phase dispersion for sample clean-up and the food safety issues associated with the export of prawns from Bangladesh to Europe. All present were intent upon sharing a few drinks before going directly into the conference dinner, hosted by the hotel.

'Dr Zhou Jian?'

For the second time that evening, Jian heard his name called across the lobby. He raised his hand in the air. The concierge paraded through the lounge carrying a silver salver scanning the room for the intended recipient of the note on the plate.

'A message for you sir,' he said. The young man, smartly dressed in a grey uniform with red trim on his lapels and on the seams of his trousers, bowed slightly and presented the salver.

'Thank you,' said Jian. He opened the small white envelope as the others continued with their conversations. No one observed Jian's reaction to the message typed on the paper within. He got to his feet immediately, smiling weakly, looking nervous yet strangely elated.

'Excuse me, please. I must leave you now.' The others looked on, but only Dr Clarisse Junot appeared to notice what Jian was saying. 'See you later at dinner,' Jian said, bowing his head then squeezing his way between chairs and the table bedecked in drinks.

'Going for that walk after all?' said Clarisse Junot.

'Yes, yes,' Jian replied. He hurried across to the reception desk and asked the young girl, seated by a computer, for directions to the Hotel des Alpes.

'It is in the old town, on the Rathausquai,' the girl explained. Rising from her seat, she lifted a tourist brochure from a pile on the counter, opened it and marked the location of the Hotel des Alps on the map inside.

'Thank you,' said Jian. He hurried outdoors and soon found his way to the lakeside. Judging by the location of the Hotel des Alps, it seemed that he would get his evening stroll after all. Now, however, he was more excited about meeting a friend he hadn't seen since his student days.

The evening air was heavy with moisture, a mist engulfing the mountain peaks of the Riga and Stanserhorn beyond the lake. Although relaxed after a nervous day, he walked in determined stride along the Nationalquai, towards the city centre. He wondered, as he had done so often recently, about returning to Europe, to England or Holland, perhaps, securing a research post, or at least another postdoc fellowship. He wanted his family to experience what he had seen, what he was seeing right now, to taste life away from an overcrowded city, stifled by poor air and with the ever-growing presence of fear. He didn't think he could stand having to deal with crooks in the food business and self-important government officials on the take for much longer. He hurried on, his stomach slowly regaining calmness like the waters of the lake.

Crossing the busy Schweizerhofquai close to the road bridge, he soon found the Rathausquai on his right. This was a quayside in the old town ushering the lake into its drain of the River Reuss. There were bars and restaurants with seating outdoors by the railings of the quay. A few people sat with glasses of wine, eating salad, or soup and bread, a prelude to their main meal of the day. Passing by the Kapellbrücke, an old wooden bridge stretching diagonally across the entrance to the Reuss, he soon found the Hotel des Alps. Outside, there was a line of tables along its frontage, each table with a parasol folded for the night. Approaching the hotel entrance, he spotted a face he remembered well from his days at Oxford. How strange, he thought, looking at the piece of paper in his hand: the message he'd received from the concierge. It was not the person whose name was written on the note but still a surprise.

* * *

Around seven the following morning, the city stretching for the day, cafés and bars were already open and serving breakfast. Traffic flowed as smoothly on the thoroughfares as the water drained from the lake. Trains departed exactly on time from the station beside the KKL, the conference centre preparing for the final day of the International Symposium on Food Quality and Hygiene in the Global Market. Dr Zhou Jian had presented his paper the day before. Today, he would not show up for the closing address; he would not join his international associates for coffee or for breakfast at the Grand Hotel National on Haldenstrasse.

A maid working on the second floor of the Hotel Schiff gazed out from the window and spied something floating in the river. She couldn't be certain; she didn't want to believe it.

'Anna, come here a moment,' she called to her younger colleague who had been cleaning the bathroom of room 215. 'Look there. What is that floating in the water?'

The girl drew a sharp breath, realising straightaway what it was.

'I'll get Nicholaus,' she called, her slim legs already drumming their way down the stairs.

Once in the lobby, she roused the concierge by the front door, and the pair of them rushed onto the quay and down the steps by the Rathaussteg to the water's edge.

'Where?' said Nicholaus, a slight young man of twenty with black greased hair and a thin nose. 'I don't see anything.'

Anna caught his arm at the elbow and forced him to look closely.

'It's a body, Nicholaus. I'm sure of it.'

Something, close to the quayside, lay entangled between the mooring rope and the hull of a small motorboat.

'Wait here,' he said, and sprinted to a café a few yards along the quay. Once there he grabbed a window pole from a waiter who was lowering the awning outside his restaurant.

'Come and help me, Josef. There's someone in the river.'

Nicholaus ran back to the steps, the waiter following but was slow on his feet.

'It is a body. I can see a hand,' said Anna.

Nicholaus pushed the pole towards the dark object in the water. After two failed attempts, he managed to get some purchase on the collar of a jacket. Nicholaus, held steady at the waist by the waiter, stretched beyond the steps, freed the body from the mooring rope and hauled it towards the quayside. Several bystanders ran to the aid of the concierge and the waiter. When they pulled the body of Zhou Jian onto the steps and turned him over, there was not a mark upon him. Anna cried in horror at the sight of the stone-grey face, and Nicholaus put his arms around her. The Chinese scientist, it seemed, had drowned tragically in Lake Lucerne.

CHAPTER 7

Night-times were the worst. Sleep, dreamless sleep, was always a blessing. He'd been alone for three years now. Time to think. Time to heal. Time to pass. He didn't do any of it well. Tilly was there when he lay down. She was there at his waking, when he ate breakfast, walked Midgey, when he read newspapers and bought drink at the mini-market. Most often, she held Emily in her arms beckoning him to join them. Sometimes, especially at night in the darkness of his bedroom, she stood alone urging him to want her, to come for her, to put everything right in their world.

There was nothing in his life that didn't trigger a worry in him. He was disturbed by his past, frightened by his present and dreaded his future. He'd grown up in this house, and now it was his prison. He was well aware of his fall into drudgery, of the filthy environment he inhabited, the foul-smelling air he breathed, and he had no inclination to do anything about it. Nothing mattered. Even now, having met the woman who could help find the killer of Emily and Tilly, he had little enthusiasm for the quest. If only he could sleep without waking – lie down on the once fresh white sheets, now grey and threadbare, close his eyes and diffuse from time to eternity. Then he would have peace.

It was daylight but early. He heard banging at the front door. It was not the usual time for those bastard kids to call. Why wouldn't they leave him alone? He'd known their older brothers and sisters. He'd gone to school with them. Did they know what their siblings got up to? Did they believe the stories about him?

He sat on the edge of his bed – the bed he'd had since he was fifteen when his mother had decided he'd outgrown his childhood bunk and should have a new divan. Pyjamas, these days, were not part of his limited wardrobe. He slept in the T-shirt and boxer shorts he'd worn the previous day and would wear for several days to come. In bare feet, he came to the top of the stairs and peered into the darkened hallway. The banging continued.

'Police, Mr Armour. Can you open the door please?' The voice was male. Callum returned to the bedroom and gazed from the window, through the metal screen. It was the same car that Inspector Grogan had come in the night before. Maybe she was outside. Did she have something already? Information on Justin Kingsley? He pulled on his jogging trousers, pushed his feet into his brown shoes and hurried downstairs. The male voice continued calling.

'Can you open the door, Mr Armour? It's the police.'

Persistent, he thought. As was his habit he left the chain in place, undid the lock and pulled the door as far as the chain allowed. Peering through the crack, he saw the detective who had accompanied Tara Grogan.

'Open the door please, Mr Armour. We'd like a word.'

'What's this about?'

'Open the door please.'

'Tell me what you want first.'

The door hit him on the head then banged against the inside wall. The chain was useless in protecting him from a stout kick at the door. Callum's hand shot to his face to stifle the blurring pain across his nose and eyes. DS Murray and DC Wilson barged in. Wilson pressed Callum to the wall and pulled his hands behind him before he had any chance to recover from the blow. Murray charged into the living room. Midgey barked noisily, as Callum heard the policeman pulling at boxes and tossing things around.

'We'd like to have a word with you at St Anne Street,' said Wilson. With a firm grip of Callum's shoulders, he ushered him outside.

If only they knew how weak he felt, they wouldn't have bothered with their show of strength. He hardly had the energy to stay on his feet never mind walk out to the car. Wilson placed him in the back seat of the unmarked Vauxhall, closed the door and waited for Murray to emerge from the house. A minute later he appeared empty-handed, slammed the door of the house and climbed into the front passenger seat of the car.

* * *

'We'd like to ask you a few questions about your neighbours, Mr Armour,' said Murray, when they'd settled into an interview room at the station.

Callum sat on a blue plastic chair with a padded seat, his hands set one upon the other and resting on a bare laminate table. His eyes, usually gritty with sleep and dirt at this time of the morning, watered from the blow to his head. He wasn't brave, hadn't felt the need to be since the heart of his life had been snatched away, but for some reason he decided to defend himself in the presence of this pair of self-important louts.

'It's Dr Armour.'

Murray winced at the reply.

'Or Dr Stinker?'

'As long as you get the doctor part right.'

'Tell us about the girl who was killed the other night in the house opposite yours.'

Callum did not reply.

'It's a reasonable question Mr… Dr Armour.'

'I'll speak to Inspector Grogan, but I'm not talking to you wise-asses.'

Murray continued as if he hadn't heard Callum's statement of intent.

'Tell me about the porno films being made at the house?'

Callum glared at Murray, realising, of course, that Tara Grogan would have shared this information.

'You must have seen who was involved? Men? Women? Perhaps you, Dr Armour?'

The pair of detectives got no further. Callum sat impassively staring at the wall ahead of him. To each question raised he offered nothing but a stale odour of sweat and a breath smelling of cheap lager.

* * *

Tara was late arriving at the station. She'd called at a community centre in Walton to meet some members of a women's group: a Mums & Tots operating primarily for the Polish community. Aniele Zagac, a friendly woman of thirty-five with excellent English, had a couple of energetic kids climbing over her as she tried to hold a conversation.

'I do not know of any Polish girls who have gone missing,' she said in reply to Tara's question. 'If you like, I will ask my friends to contact other groups and families.'

'I would appreciate that, thank you. Do you know of a man called Teodor Sokolowski?'

The woman's smile weakened as she moved her head slowly from side to side, her pale blue eyes looking uncertainly at Tara.

'He rents houses around Liverpool to workers from Poland?'

Aniele Zagac's attention, fortuitously, for her it seemed, was claimed by her children who had begun pulling at their mother's long grey cardigan and stretching it out of shape. Now she didn't have to look Tara in the face.

'I have not heard of this man,' she said, drawing both her charges close to her body, so that neither one was able to keep hold of the cardigan.

Tara handed a card to the woman.

'If you hear of anything relating to Mr Sokolowski, or of a girl who's gone missing, please let me know.'

The woman inspected the details on the card and gave a single nod.

Ten minutes' drive from the community centre and Tara pulled into St Anne Street station, a dull four-storey flat-roofed block. She was grateful for the help, but she didn't for a second believe that Aniele Zagac had told the truth about Teodor Sokolowski. Was it a case of expats closing ranks? When she reached her desk on the first floor, she found a Post-it stuck on her computer monitor informing her that she was required downstairs at interview room two. She met DC Wilson in the corridor outside the room, his back against the wall and hands busy at his mobile phone.

'Super's been looking for you, ma'am,' he said, a hint of warning in his voice.

'What about?'

'We have a suspect for the girl's murder.'

'Really?' She felt a sudden gush of excitement.

'It's that bloke Armour you were talking to the other day. Super and Murray are with him now.'

Disbelief and exasperation battled for supremacy. How did they decide that Armour was implicated in the murder?

Surely, they hadn't acted merely on what she had told Murray?

'Tara,' said Tweedy as he emerged from the interview room.

As the door closed behind him, she caught sight of Callum Armour sitting rigidly at the table staring into space.

'I'm glad you're here. This Dr Armour is proving difficult and insists on talking only to you.' Tweedy looked rather disapprovingly at Tara, like a father inquiring what his teenage daughter had been up to the night before. 'I'm happy for you to proceed, of course, but perhaps you should point out to your friend that his conversation with you will be recorded.'

'Yes sir.'

He smiled weakly as if he understood the situation, understood the relationship Tara had already established with Armour, but there was a warning in it for her. That this was not the way things were done, not in his squad. He would expect any established rapport, regardless of how tenuous it may be, to be handled most cautiously and professionally. Obviously, Murray had told Tweedy about her visit to Armour's house.

Alan Murray rose from the table as Tara entered the interview room. He shrugged to indicate he'd got nowhere. She glared icily at him. She would speak to him later about protocol and, more importantly, about having some common sense.

'Good morning, Callum. Are you going to tell me what this is all about?'

Callum rolled his eyes at Murray, who frowned and sighed.

'I'll leave you to it,' he said, opening the door and pulling it closed behind him.

'You tell me,' said Callum. 'I was dragged here out of my bed, and those two started firing questions at me about the wee girl.' It seemed that in anger his Belfast accent had gained the upper hand.

Tara knew the situation had been handled badly. Murray was too quick bringing Armour in for questioning, but she wasn't about to criticise her colleagues in front of him for trying to do their job. The washed-out, distant and unhelpful character sitting before her knew more about the murder than he had so far revealed. She stared for a moment at the swelling above his eye.

'Do you have something you want to tell me about the killing of the girl?'

He had yet to focus on her, his eyes set on an infinite point beyond the room as if staring the past full in the face, trying his best to square up to whatever evil had destroyed his life.

'Callum, you asked to speak with me. If you've changed your mind, I can always get DS Murray to come back in.'

'Why should I help you, when you and all the rest of them have done nothing to help me?'

She noticed the nerves rise in him and could hear the emotion breaking the last words in his sentence. She sat down, facing him across the table.

'How do you spend your days, Callum? Do you work?'

'Unemployed.'

'So, what do you do with your time?'

'I walk Midgey. I go to the library, the shops, the park and I go home.'

'And your evenings?'

He looked at her for the first time. Incredulity flowed from brightening eyes.

'I go out with my friends to the cinema, to the theatre, the opera and ballet. We have dinner in the best restaurants in Liverpool. We have a private box at Anfield. We drink in the liveliest clubs and get off with stunning women. What do you think?'

'I don't think that's necessary. Something you may not have realised, Callum, is that you are a suspect in this murder. For your own good, I think it's best if we cut the sarcasm, and maybe we can rule you out of the investigation as soon as we can. Tell me what you were doing two nights ago.'

'I've done nothing wrong. I want to go home. Midgey will be looking to be fed.'

'A young girl was murdered in a house close to yours. I want to know what you were doing around midnight on Tuesday.'

'I was in my bed asleep.'

'Can anyone vouch for that?'

She knew it was a stupid question for a man in his situation. He gave her a look of disgust, and once again took to contemplation of the blank wall. Tara rose from her chair. She thought that after yesterday she understood this man a little better than others around him. She had sympathy for his plight. Today, however, she found him rude and obnoxious.

'I'll pass on your request to the superintendent. If there's anything you want to tell me, Callum, you know where to find me. I won't be making this offer every time we meet.'

She left him as she'd found him, staring into his personal oblivion.

CHAPTER 8

They kept him until lunchtime but didn't happen to give him anything to eat. Didn't bother giving him a lift home either. Callum had some change in the pocket of his trousers, enough to scrape the bus fare to Netherton and to buy some milk for his breakfast. Walking to the bus stop, he wondered if it would ever do anything else but rain.

Callum thought of his native Belfast, a city he hadn't visited since he was thirteen, trying to imagine if a life spent there would have been any better. Different surely, but he doubted better. Callum didn't need any of it. He didn't need reminders of where he came from, where he'd been or what he'd done, but the great paradox of his woeful existence was that reminders were all he had: the things he collected and drew around him. Why did he need such things? He had no idea, but he hurried to get home to them.

Stepping off the bus on Glovers Lane, he wandered across to the row of shops and bought some milk, semi-skimmed, and *The Daily Telegraph*. Usually, he read the paper in Netherton Library, but today he wanted sanctuary. He made his way home. He met no one. He felt the rain trickle down his nose, dribble through his thick beard and saturate the worn collar of his T-shirt. When he reached the cul-de-sac, he could tell there was something wrong. Billy Hughes, his next door neighbour, stood under his porch, sheltering from the rain and smoking, looking up and down the road as if watching for somebody.

'See your door?' said Billy, as Callum reached the pathway leading to his house. 'Bloody kids did that.'

'Midgey! Is he all right?' He fumbled in his pocket for a key, slipped it in the lock and opened the door. The dog, tail wagging, sniffed the air as Callum bent down. 'How ya doing, Midgey? Think I wasn't coming back? I'll get you a drink and some food, and then we can go for a walk, eh?' He patted him on the head, and the dog responded by attempting to lick his hand.

'Went daft, barking and getting on,' said Billy. 'But he's OK. Been quiet all morning. Imagine them shites doing the like of that in broad daylight?'

Callum examined the scorched wood of the door. Someone had forced the letter box open, and then tried to pour petrol, or lighter fluid inside. At least the word 'paedo', which had been spray-painted on the door, was now obliterated, but how long before he or Midgey were burned to death?

'My window,' said Billy, 'I saw them from up there.' He pointed with his fag at the bedroom window above. 'I came out after them, but they ran like the clappers. Couldn't run after them, not with my knees. Our Jean got a basin of water and chucked it at the door.'

Callum nodded his acknowledgement. He didn't know whether to sound angry about the damage or grateful for Billy's intervention. He thought that maybe he couldn't care less. He had more important things to worry about. His thoughts carried him so far away that he tuned out Billy's continued explanation of the incident.

'Thanks, Billy.'

He closed the door with Billy Hughes still looking on and straining the last drag from the butt of his cigarette.

* * *

Tara spent her afternoon reviewing her notes on the murder of the girl. Murray sat with a flea in his ear on the far side of the office. She'd told him off for jumping the gun with Callum and giving her only lead in this case a bruise on his face. Tara set him the task of tracing local people who might be in the pornographic moviemaking business. She reckoned that should appeal to his facetious wit.

She had a post-mortem report on the girl. The cause of death was asphyxiation by direct interference of the main air passageways. There were no bruises, except for the effects of lividity. There were no cuts just the burn marks on her chest, inflicted after death, and red scuffs on both knees. It was apparent that sexual intercourse had taken place as there were traces of semen, and oily substances consistent with lubricant materials, found on her thighs, lower abdomen and vaginal area. A sweep of the remainder of the house revealed nothing that could be related directly to the girl. The three-bedroomed terrace was furnished with basic items: beds, a sofa in the lounge, a cooker, refrigerator and washing machine in the kitchen – all consistent with a property used and advertised as a furnished let. Fingerprints were lifted from the internal and external doors, from the kitchen worktops and the banister on the stairs.

With no positive identification of the victim, the best lead they had was to follow up on the suggestion that certain activities were taking place in the house – the making of pornographic films. The idea had still to be taken with a hefty pinch of salt considering the dubious reliability of the witness Callum Armour. A definite lead was the Polish word *kurwa* burned into the flesh of the victim. With a Polish national identified as the house owner it suggested that the girl also came from Poland, and this was a murder within that particular expat community.

Adding to her frustration over the girl's murder, were the stories she'd read in that morbid box-file presented to her by Callum Armour. Much of it was a muddle of facts and outlandish theories, but she found it hard to dismiss the account of his wife's death. Yes, it was declared an accident, but Callum was so adamant about the unsigned sympathy card and the time at which he took possession of it.

Deciding that, for the moment, she'd reached an impasse with her case, she ran a quick search on her computer, looking for stories relating to the accident which had claimed the lives of Tilly Reason and her daughter. A couple of posts from the archives of the *Oxford Mail* displayed the original report on the deaths, and she also read the police report of the incident. She skimmed through it looking for anything to give credence to Armour's beliefs that his family had been murdered at the level crossing in Shiplake.

She found plenty of articles on the dangers of ungated level crossings and noted with astonishment that out of eight thousand level crossings in Britain, two per cent did not have gates. Over three hundred accidents and near misses occurred each year. Police and motoring organisations blamed much of it on the contempt that drivers had for the warning systems in place at level crossings. It was a sad fact that many drivers and pedestrians played Russian roulette in using them. Shiplake had long been cited as a disaster waiting to happen, and Tara was relieved to note that major improvements were planned for the crossing that had claimed, among others, the lives of Callum's wife and daughter. Undoubtedly tragic, everything pointed to it being an accident, but in the three years since then Callum Armour had failed to come to terms with it. His claim about the sympathy card, however, still rankled Tara.

She wondered how she might help him, not in finding the murderer he claimed to be out there, but in more practical matters. Could she sort his problems with the local troublemakers who were causing him to live in constant fear? Could she arrange for the community policing guys to sit down with Callum and, for the first time, talk through his concerns? Perhaps she could find someone, or some organisation, to help him put his house in order – clean it up and advise him on a healthier lifestyle. Did Callum need some form of counselling? She was beginning to think more like a social worker than a detective, but she would try to help him.

She typed his name into the search engine just to see what came up. The first few hits were impressive. Callum Armour: *'Matrix ion suppression in the detection of drug metabolites, case studies,'* published in the *Journal of Mass Spectrometry*. There was a list of several other scientific publications: *The Analyst*, *Food Chemistry*, *Journal of Chromatography*, *Analytica Chimica Acta,* and *Food Additives and Contaminants*, all dating back at least three years, some as far as eight. There were a few references to the Department of Chemistry at Oxford University, a couple of links to children's writer Tilly Reason, and one to a conference on drugs and food analysis held four years ago in Brussels.

Finally, although she couldn't recall the name of the victim, she typed in 'Canterbury Cathedral murder' only to see hundreds of hits referring to the killing of Thomas Becket, Archbishop of Canterbury. Scrolling down, however, she found a BBC news report on the more recent murder of the Cathedral Precentor and Liturgist, Peter Ramsey. As she mulled over the lack of evidence for the murder of the girl in Treadwater, so it appeared detectives of Kent Police were finding it difficult to establish a motive, or to identify any suspects, in the murder of the clergyman.

Strange, she thought, that Callum Armour should think it plausible that she could and would help him, simply because she had been a student at Latimer College. Did he believe in some kind of brotherhood among the alumni, dedicated to helping each other through thick and thin? Or was he suggesting a direct link between the college and the deaths of three people? She now knew what he had studied during his time there, and perhaps he already knew that she'd studied law and had read all about her in the *Alumni* magazine.

She was beginning to regret updating her profile and submitting the photograph of her in police uniform. Maybe she should get to understand Callum Armour a little better. Why, for instance, was he pointing an accusing finger for the murder of Peter Ramsey at this student who had disappeared? What possible motive? What motive was there to kill a children's novelist? And there were years between the disappearance of Justin Kingsley, Tilly Reason's accident and the killing in Canterbury. If she were into pulling coincidences together, no matter how bizarre, why not consider Callum Armour as the link between his wife's death, the murder of Peter Ramsey and the death of a young girl on the Treadwater Estate?

CHAPTER 9

She told herself it was on her way home; she wouldn't go into the house alone, not without back-up outside. But this was not the route she would take from St Anne Street to her apartment at Wapping Dock. She drove her own car, a Ford Focus, electric-blue, but she intended leaving a note inside for her colleagues to find if, for some reason, she didn't make it out of the house.

Tara's decision to return home after Oxford had been in some ways disappointing enough for her mother Barbara, although now she had her daughter close by where she could get to see her every week. But it fair knocked the wind from the fifty-year-old schoolteacher when Tara announced that she was joining the police. Tara, her mother often said, had a chance of an exciting life, a great career as a lawyer or a barrister in London and earning good money in a city with better opportunities than Liverpool. On days like this, she was glad her mother didn't know the half of what she got up to in her job.

Turning her car into Sycamore Drive, she wondered again about Callum Armour.

'I've arranged for a community police officer to call with you,' she said, struggling once again to find a place to sit in the ramshackle room. 'They'll advise you on what's best for dealing with the harassment you've been getting from local youths.'

From his armchair of paper bundles, he glared at her through puffy eyes, reddened as if he'd been crying.

'What about harassment from the police? Who's going to advise me about that?'

She didn't reply, didn't rise to his challenge. She felt nervous enough sitting in this depressing room, and she'd forgotten to leave that note in her car.

'There is also Community Support which is a charity that helps victims of crime. Here are the contact details. You can give them a call.'

'Don't have a phone.'

'Do you have a computer?'

'Not anymore. Had a break-in a while back. They took my laptop, my TV and DVD player.'

'You should consider getting a mobile phone.'

He shook his head.

'No way. Those things pickle your brain. One day the world's going to wake up to the number of cases of brain tumours and mental disorders and finally blame it on the use of mobile phones. By then, of course, the men running the companies making a fortune will be long gone, and it'll be a heck of a fight to find those responsible.'

'Just a suggestion,' she replied. It wasn't her intention to start a debate on health and safety. She reached out some leaflets, though she suddenly realised that what Callum Armour did not require in this house was more paper. 'Some information which may be of help. You should check with social services or with the Citizens Advice Bureau about your entitlements. They might be able to help you…'

She stopped, suddenly conscious of saying too much or something that may offend him. Besides, he didn't appear terribly interested in what she had to say.

'Do you have a social worker?'

'You must think I'm a real basket case. What exactly have you heard about me? What do you think I am?'

She really didn't want to get into this. She hadn't intended to rile him. Even Midgey shifted his location from the feet of his master to the worn mat under the table. She was slow to answer, but he filled the pause.

'You know nothing about me.'

'Maybe that's down to you. You've said little on our first three meetings.'

'You want to know about the girl, don't you? That's the only reason you're here. To winkle information out of me.'

'It is my job, Callum. A young girl has been murdered, and so far you're the only person with information. You seem reluctant to share it with us.'

He shook his head and got to his feet. Tara thought that was an end to it. She'd failed to help him and failed in getting him to talk. Maybe Murray's approach was the right one. Bring him down to the station and let him stew for a day and threaten to charge him for withholding information. She rose from the uncomfortable, poorly sprung sofa.

'Not that you care,' he said, 'but there's been another killing.' He wiped his right eye with the sleeve of his sweatshirt.

'I don't understand.'

He lifted a fresh copy of *The Daily Telegraph*. It was open at the International News section and folded down to the appropriate place as he handed it to her. She read the lead-line and the few sentences printed beneath. 'Chinese scientist drowns in Swiss lake.' It was followed by a brief summary of Dr Zhou Jian's background, and that he had been attending a conference in Lucerne on food safety. His body was recovered from the River Reuss, and Swiss police were investigating.

'You knew him?'

Despite the dull hue of the living room, she saw the tears well up in his eyes. Those eyes, she thought, must have shed a potful in the last three years.

'At Oxford, we studied chemistry together, worked in similar fields for our doctorates and ended up in the same department as postdocs.'

'And you believe this is connected to the other deaths?'

Callum rubbed his forehead roughly with the palm of his right hand. He sighed deeply.

'Jian was my friend, my closest friend at Oxford. Neither of us fitted there in quite the same way as the others. I was just a kid from Belfast via Liverpool, the first person in my family ever to make it to university, never mind Oxford. I was working class and Irish, not exactly the best foundation for life amongst England's elite. Jian was different, too. We sort of identified with each other. I really trusted no one else until I hooked up with Tilly.'

Tara was still holding the newspaper. She briefly scanned the story again. Three separate incidents, four deaths, all connected to this sorry man living in squalor on a Liverpool housing estate. All linked to an Oxford college. So far, only one of the deaths was regarded as murder.

'Tell me about the guy who disappeared.' She knew this was taking her to a place she should not go. Tweedy would do his nut if he ever found out that she had visited a murder suspect on her own.

Callum lifted a box-file from a stack of five on the floor. Tara recognised its battered state, the label on the side with the words 'Mass Spectrometry Data', the box bursting with papers and letters. He sat down in his chair, the box open on his knee. Tara resumed her uncomfortable position on the sofa, still piled up with cardboard boxes and books.

'That's him,' he said, handing over the photograph she remembered seeing previously. 'Third from the left.'

The photo wasn't great, not the sharpest focus, but she examined the image of the strapping guy, broad shoulders, curly fair hair, square jaw, tight-fitting T-shirt, and seated with an arm resting casually on the back of the chair next to him. Without a smile, he stared at the camera. It seemed to Tara that he was devoid of any emotion. He reminded her of the rowing crew from her years at Latimer: athletic guys, self-assured and confident of their destiny.

Recounting in her mind the brief story of his disappearance, she found it difficult to believe that this young man could have encountered anything that would have caused him to run away. Such a relaxed pose, he looked the type who could have risen above any problem.

'He looks fine there, but not as if he's enjoying himself.'

'I suppose we'd all had a skinful by the time this was taken. It was the last night of our ski trip.'

Callum came over and knelt down beside her. For a moment they could have been a couple browsing their family holiday snaps. Tara suppressed her discomfort at his odour.

'That's Tilly,' he said, placing his forefinger on the image of a slight girl with brown hair and a beamer of a smile, her arms wide as if she were performing in a stage musical. She was standing beside a Chinese youth with dark-framed glasses, thin face and shoulder-length hair. 'Jian, obviously,' he continued, moving his finger along the picture. 'First on the left is Charlotte Babb.'

Tara noted the smiling girl with dark frizzy hair, thinking that, perhaps, she may look prettier in real life, the camera not having caught her in the best light. Her mouth seemed too wide for the narrow face, and her cheeks were rather bony. She wore a heavy sky-blue roll-neck jumper which made it difficult to gauge her true body shape. She was seated upon the knee of a very-fair-looking man sporting a lewd expression, his tongue hanging out like he was enjoying having a girl sit on his lap.

'Anthony Egerton-Hyde,' said Callum. 'You may have heard of him. Stinking rich, somewhere in line to the throne – ninety-third or something ridiculous. He's a junior minister now, Department of Health.'

She'd heard the name before but didn't think it was in either context mentioned by Callum.

She was conscious now of the improved tone in Callum's voice. For the first time since they'd met, there was enthusiasm in what he was saying and education in his speech. He didn't sound like a raving lunatic, or a headcase as Murray and Wilson had described him. The massive chip on his shoulder was greatly diminished.

'He's married to Georgina now,' he said, pointing out another girl standing next to Tilly in the photo. She seemed much taller than Tilly or Charlotte, slender, with long fair hair, not an entirely pretty face but well-tended and glamorous with it. She was dressed in tight-fitting jeans and white shirt. Even in the photo she looked expensive and yet vaguely familiar.

'What's her surname?' Tara asked.

'Maitland.'

'*The* Georgina Maitland?'

Callum nodded rather proudly.

'The one with her finger in every pie going?' Tara asked.

'That's her.'

'She's worth an absolute fortune. Fashion houses, beauty treatments, fitness, well-being, spas, good food guides, restaurants – she runs a whole empire. She was at Oxford with you?'

'She and Tilly were close friends.'

Tara found herself intrigued by the connections amongst this group of people: a highly successful entrepreneur, a government minister and a famous writer.

'That's Peter Ramsey who was murdered in Canterbury Cathedral.'

She tried to reconcile the man's face with the image she'd imagined from reading the reports on his killing. He didn't look the type to be a priest, more like a hippie on a road trip: long frizzed hair, a goatee and John Lennon glasses. Neither did he look as if he was enjoying himself. He stared, not at the camera, but at Egerton-Hyde, who was hosting Charlotte Babb upon his lap.

'Who's the guy beside him?'

'Ollie Rutherford. He was a school friend of Peter and Anthony's. Eton, I think. I didn't know him that well. There were twenty-two students on that holiday. I didn't know all of them. I was friends with Jian and, of course, Tilly and I were just getting together about then. Georgina, Charlotte and Tilly were mates as were Peter, Ollie and Anthony. Justin had been seeing Georgina, but I think it was over before we went on the holiday. Peter was quite friendly with Charlotte, although she only had eyes for Anthony. We all sort of blended because each of us was friends with someone in the group.'

'And where were you when all this was going on?'

He looked surprised by the question.

'I was taking the photograph.'

Tara glanced, quite deliberately, at her watch. He noticed and took the hint by getting to his feet. She felt it was time to leave, and yet she was truly interested in Callum's story. She took another glance at the photo before handing it over. Three of those young people, no more than twenty-one years old at that time, were now dead. The man standing over her clearly had been devastated by the loss of his wife and since then had sought answers from a box of news clippings and holiday snaps. She'd managed to get him talking, and yet there was some way to go before she felt like trusting him.

'Why did Justin Kingsley disappear?'

She was already on her feet to leave, but her tendency to question overtook her thinking.

'I don't know,' he said, looking down at the photograph. 'That night, not long after this was taken, he simply walked out of the bar, and I never saw him again.' Callum tossed the photo into the box-file.

'Did he say anything? Was there a row? Any indication that he was intending to run away?'

Callum shook his head.

'And the police in Austria never found anything?'

'One minute, we were all having a good time and the next he was gone. None of us realised he had left for good till next morning at breakfast.'

Tara managed to edge her way to the front door.

'I have to go now, Callum. I have an early start tomorrow. I hope you find some help from the contacts I gave you.'

She opened his front door.

'The wee girl's name was Audra.'

CHAPTER 10

Tara turned on the doorstep and glared icily at Callum. Was he playing a game with her? She may not look her age, or even like a policewoman, but did she look completely stupid?

'Does she have a second name?'

He shrugged, staring into her face. She fought to hold her temper.

'Is this how it's going to be, Callum? I help you along, and as reward I get a little more information about the girl? Why not tell me all of it now?'

'I think you're already closer to finding the killer of the girl than I am to finding Justin Kingsley.'

She bored into his eyes, trying to be strong, to show that she was a woman in control of the situation. She was calling the shots, not him. In a flash, she could trail him back to the station and let him sit it out with Superintendent Tweedy. The empathy she'd felt this last day or so for his plight, the willingness to help him turn things around, was fast running out. For goodness sake, she thought, right now I could be looking into the eyes of a killer.

'She's Lithuanian. Don't know her second name. I only spoke to her a couple of times when I was out with Midgey. She used to wait by the back gate of number six. No one lives there, not permanently.'

Her large blue eyes maintained an enraged glare, insistent that he should say more, tell her everything. At last, he seemed to be getting the idea.

'Usually, two or three men would show up in a car, and they would go inside with Audra.'

'What type of car?'

'I don't know. Red. More like maroon. A saloon car, not a hatchback. Maybe Toyota or Mazda, I can't be sure.'

'How long would they stay?'

Another shrug. She continued her look of displeasure. He puffed air through his lips.

'There were other girls, some older, like in their thirties or forties. They came and went. Sometimes they stayed overnight. I told you I saw bright lights in the back bedroom, and a few times I saw them carry a video camera into the house. And then for a couple of weeks there would be nothing.'

'How many girls? And don't say I don't know. Think before you answer.'

'Five maybe, but not the same girls each time. I saw Audra on about six occasions.'

'Is that it? You're sure there's nothing else you want to tell me? I can have a car here in a few minutes, and we can finish this at the station. You know, you should try trusting someone for a change. I only want to help you.'

The door slammed, ending their inflamed conversation.

What a totally ignorant man. Ungrateful with it. She owed him nothing. She turned and walked down the short path, clumps of weeds running amok in the patches of garden to her left and right.

A gathering of youths, resembling the group she had encountered the day before, stood around a car parked in front of her Focus. It was a small hatchback in white, lowered sports suspension, tinted windows, alloys and a spoiler at the rear. The driver, wearing a baseball cap, sat low in his seat, windows down, chatting to the Everton shirt who'd heckled her on her previous visit. He fiddled with a mobile phone as the driver spoke to him. Another male stood astride a kid's mountain bike, much too small for him.

Two of the three girls, arms folded, leaned against the hatchback, watching as Tara crossed a patch of grass to reach her car. The third girl held on to a buggy, a toddler, a boy no more than eighteen months old, sat restlessly within, battling to break free from his harness. The girl, Tara presumed to be the mother, didn't look much older than fifteen. She had a fresh complexion, rounded face and blonde hair falling to her waist but with roots needing attention. She wore a white vest and pink jogging trousers, but most striking of all was the bulging tummy of a girl late in pregnancy. None of them spoke as Tara reached her car, unlocked it and was about to climb inside.

She felt their eyes upon her. Considering her agitation after an hour spent in the company of an awkward, foul-smelling man, she reckoned she could handle anything these kids had to throw her way. Closing the car door again, she approached the girls.

'I take it you know about the body of a young girl being found in number six?'

'Yeah,' sang one of the girls leaning on the hatchback.

Tara saw the indignant look on the girl's face. Tight eyes. It was a look she knew well, easily recognisable on the streets of Liverpool. The look of distrust. Strangers didn't belong in a place like this. Territory was everything, and outsiders asking questions were likely to be sent on their way with a reminder not to return. The Everton shirt had that look also. Tara ignored him and concentrated on getting the girls to speak.

'Her name was Audra. She was Lithuanian. Any of you girls know anything about her?'

'We don't bother with Liths,' said the pregnant girl.

'Or Poles,' said the third girl chewing gum, an awkward-looking kid with freckles, bulging thighs in grey leggings and a pink vest.

'You a bizee?' she said, looking intently at Tara's lack of height and, what must have seemed to them, dull clothing. Tara didn't reply to the question. From the corner of her eye she saw the Everton shirt begin to stir.

'Nobody knows nothing, all right?' he said. 'Why don't you fuck off and give your mouth a rest?'

Tara ignored him and directed her question to the girls. 'Have you seen anyone coming or going from the house where the girl was found?'

'Only Poles and Liths. Nobody lives there, not for long,' said the pregnant girl.

'Shut the fuck up, Debbie. Tell the filth nothing, right?'

'What is your problem?' snapped Tara. She knew it was a mistake. You don't rile these kids. They were well used to outmanoeuvring the establishment. They could buy and sell you and then claim harassment. But it was too late. She'd had enough of his abuse. She'd had enough of this place.

In a flash, he squared up to her, except he was almost a foot taller. Her body trembled, but she didn't want him to notice. Instead, she met his stare with equally inflamed menace.

'No problem, love, as long as you fuck off. Or else you'll get my dick in your mouth.'

'Don't speak to her like that.'

It was Callum, standing on the pavement. The driver of the car, broad-shouldered and heavyset, jumped out quickly to stand beside the Everton shirt. The boy on the bike wasn't so keen and slowly eased himself behind Debbie and the child's buggy.

'Piss off, Stinker. Nothing to do with you.'

'It's all right, Callum. Go back inside. This young man was just leaving.'

'You think?'

'Either that or I have your friend's car towed away for not having tax. I'd reckon no insurance as well. If you like, I can have it searched for blow or amp. How about possession of stolen property?' She indicated the mobile phone in his hand. A pure guess.

'You don't know what you're talking about, love.' With that he backed away as Callum continued to look on.

'If you remember anything about the people using that house, you can let me know, girls.' She handed her card to Debbie then turned to her car, giving a faint grin of acknowledgment to Callum. The Everton shirt held his phone in the air and called out.

'Hey, cop!'

When she turned around, he snapped her picture.

'Something to look at when I go home.'

Callum waited until she had driven off, but the attention of the Everton shirt was swiftly refocussed upon him.

'You know what happens to touts round here, Stinker?'

Callum turned away, no stomach for a fight.

'And paedos,' said the boy on the bike, evidently feeling a tad braver. As Callum reached his door the Everton shirt stepped into the garden, aiming his mobile. Callum slammed the door, but the youth already had the picture.

CHAPTER 11

The water was hot, hotter than she usually could bear. Tonight, Tara needed it that way. She needed to wash, if it were possible, a whole day down the drain. The home of Callum Armour clung to her clothes, soiling them. The smell of old air, never replaced, never freshened, had penetrated her jacket, her blouse and trousers. Dog hairs had woven their way into the cloth and Callum's stale breath into her hair. She had to wash his house, the street, Treadwater Estate from her body.

What exactly was Callum Armour expecting from her? That she would drop everything and get justice for all the wrong in his life? Find this Kingsley and pin the deaths of four people on him? And while she was busy doing that, he could swan about the place ignoring the fact that he had information on the girl murdered on his estate? Were there any decent people left in this city – anyone with respect for the police, appreciative of their efforts to find those who perpetrated the vilest of crimes and to bring them to justice?

Wrapping the towel around her almost twice, because there wasn't much of her, as her mother often said, she padded into her bedroom pondering what she could do to unwind. She dried her hair with a hand towel but didn't feel like plugging in the dryer and straighteners. If she left it as it was, by morning it would be declared a disaster area. Despite her tiredness, she reckoned it would be a while before she could settle down to sleep.

A mug of chai tea and two rounds of toasted granary bread, a tomato sliced on top, was her treat for the evening. Legs folded beneath her on her oh-so-comfy sofa, she channel-hopped the TV unable to settle on something decent, something worthwhile, to watch. She settled on a cookery channel yet within seconds, she felt hungry again and fetched a packet of cheese-and-onion crisps from the larder. She followed the crisps with a carton of strawberry yogurt noting, by the meagre contents of her fridge, that she needed to do a shop before Kate and Aisling came the following night.

She found a channel with reruns of American sitcoms, something with laughter as she fought to erase unpleasant visions. Uppermost in her mind, the word *kurwa* burned into the white flesh of a young girl, seemingly unloved by anyone or, at least, unmissed. Most of the night she spent on the sofa, dozing, turning over, wincing from the crick in her neck, and pins and needles in her hands, until she realised this wasn't her bed and finally crawled to the comfort of pillows and duvet.

* * *

'Morning, Alan. How did you get on with the porn movies?'

She spoke loudly, deliberately so. The heads of fellow officers and clerical staff turned to look at the blushing face of DS Murray. He cleared his throat. She prolonged her satisfied grin.

'So-so,' he replied, feigning a search of his desk. She knew he would have something for her. He was good at his job, despite the odd hot-headed lapse. He handed her a sheet of A4. 'A list of known exponents in the field of adult filmmaking on Merseyside.'

There were only seven names on the paper, but it was a start. She'd already decided not to divulge the girl's name, or any of the information Callum had provided the night before. She wanted to avoid further rash questioning sessions that ended with a scolding, however subtle and veiled, from Superintendent Tweedy. Instead, she would issue a few instructions based on her latest knowledge.

'I won't hold you back,' she said to Murray. 'I'm sure you're keen to follow up on the names.'

Murray shrugged his compliance.

'While you're at it, I want you to make contact with immigrant community groups dealing with Lithuanians.'

'I thought you did that yesterday?'

'That was the Polish community. I think we should spread it out. We have no positive ID on the girl, although it seems likely that she is an immigrant. Just as likely to be Lithuanian as Polish.'

'Or Romanian, or Latvian, Estonian, Bulgarian.'

'Now you're getting it,' she said, walking off then turning round once more. 'Although I'd put money on her being Lithuanian. And don't forget to go see that letting agent about the house. We need to find out who, if anyone, is currently renting the place off Teodor Sokolowski. A list of previous occupants would be useful, too.'

The remainder of her day she spent in going through what little evidence they had so far gathered on the girl found dead on the Treadwater Estate. But it was difficult to keep thoughts of Callum Armour and his theories from interfering with her work.

Before heading home, she drove to the Liverpool One shopping mall. In WH Smiths, she went to the children's section and quickly located two of the three novels Tilly Reason had published before her death. A fourth novel had been published posthumously. She was interested in the girl who had once been a student at her old college, only four years before her. Reading something of Tilly's might help her understand what Tilly had shared with Callum and why he was so utterly destroyed by her death.

Both books had more than four hundred pages with a similar styled cover to those of the Harry Potter stories. There was a feeling from the layout of the blurb on the back cover that these books were aimed at a similar readership.

First Form Time Travellers was the title of one, *The Clock-tower*, the title of the other. The short paragraphs written on the back of *The Clock-tower* indicated that this was the second book in the series. Some of the review tags hailed Tilly Reason as a new dawn in children's writing, the books written for the enjoyment of kids of all ages, even mums and dads. Tara paid for both at the cash-desk then hurried round to Marks and Spencer food hall with a mental list of goodies to buy for her night at home with the girls.

Home for Tara was a top floor apartment on the South Quay of Wapping Dock, in the re-developed Mersey docklands. A fashionable, historic block of brown bricks, it at least provided a view across the river. The apartment had cost her, but it was her one indulgence since leaving Oxford; her one treat paid for by her life as a detective inspector.

CHAPTER 12

Callum always thought of his father when he stood on the green. Midgey scampered about working up to doing his business, while he gazed across the expanse of grass, bordered on each side by the maze of houses that was the Treadwater Estate.

'It's a lot safer for you in this part of the world, son,' his father once said, a former soldier, happy to be home in his native Liverpool. 'None of that craziness that goes on in Belfast.'

His mother didn't always agree that Liverpool was any better. She never regarded it as home and pined for the Shankill Road until the day she died. It took a few years for Callum to shake off Belfast and assume the air of a Scouser.

The smell of mown grass mingled with the odour of damp but warm evening air after a shower of rain. He wore only a grey T-shirt, heavily stained with his staple diet of beans on toast. His jogging trousers were the same pair he'd worn for weeks. He would have to wash and change soon, although the choice of clothes available in his sparse wardrobe was limited. Strange that he was even thinking such things, of being clean and looking tidy. Hadn't thought that way for years, not since Tilly. Was he now thinking like that because of a policewoman?

His father was raised in Treadwater. He used to tell him about the time as a young boy, when he paraded around the streets with dozens of kids demanding the council provide playing fields. Amazing to think that nearly fifty years on the housing estates remained separated by those fields, and that no one ever attempted to bury them under more houses. It left a more pleasing outlook. Since his return to Treadwater after Oxford, after Tilly, he had never felt safe living alone in the house, and yet only two hundred yards from there he felt perfectly at peace in the middle of the green at eleven-thirty at night.

A couple of fellow late-night walkers strolled along the paths that sliced through the lawns, their dogs prancing around, sniffing the litter and mown grass. He came out here most nights, and most nights, while he waited for Midgey to get busy, he would stare longingly towards the house in which his father had been raised. His grandmother's house, she long since dead. The place didn't look as though it had changed in the sixty years since it was built. The playing fields, too, were holding their own, and yet so much had changed. People had moved on, grown up, married and raised children; parents and grandparents had passed. He wished he could grab a piece of now, even the tiniest piece and hold on to it for ever – tuck it away like a fossil in a shoe box, keep it unchanged. Daft, of course, because even if he could look at his piece of now every day, he would continue to change. He was changing, always changing. He wondered if that was the reason Tilly chose to write about time travel; to somehow have a fixed point, a point of reference in time around which she could build her stories. Sooner or later, though, you would approach that fixed point, pass it by and disappear over the horizon. Turn back time? Oh, how he longed to do just that.

Midgey ran on ahead. He'd finished for the night and, with a faint call from Callum, skipped over the grass, across the road and soon was tracing the narrow alleys, through the parking bays and making for home. Callum didn't bother with a lead. His father had trained Midgey well. He came to the call. At nine years old, ancient in dog years, he was wise to traffic, and he didn't chase other dogs or cats. Callum followed, over the road, into the alley, through the walkways by the houses and into the next alley. Hardly a breath; such a calm evening. He heard a yelp. A dog screeching in pain. He quickened his step. Midgey.

A figure appeared to his left as he emerged from the alley into a parking bay. He turned to look. Heard another squeal. Something touched his neck. His body shook violently, pulsing. He hit the ground, his hands useless in breaking his fall. Still shaking, he felt confused by the fact that he couldn't move to get up. He saw feet. One foot swung, and he felt a deep pain in his side. But his shaking didn't stop. Laughter, a girl's giggle. Still the yelping of some poor dog. He tried to rise again, but another foot swung, and his jaw smacked shut. Another pain to his lower back, and he collapsed once again. He felt the warmth of the ground on his cheek and, in the midst of his trembling, he felt the vibration of retreating steps, heard laughter, heard a dog yelping, heard laughter, footsteps fading, heard laughter, and he didn't feel like moving. He could stay there forever. Had he captured his tiny piece of now?

CHAPTER 13

Aisling sat at one end of the sofa with Kate's right foot on her lap. Carefully, with a steady hand, she brushed the deep red liquid over the nail of Kate's big toe. Tara had been done already, hands and feet a joyful pink. She'd told her friends about Tilly Reason and Callum's theory on how his wife and daughter were killed. She did not tell them about her current investigation, the death of a Lithuanian girl called Audra. Aisling posed the first question.

'Why has he involved you in all of this?'

Tara explained the connection with Latimer College, Oxford. From there, she linked the murder of Peter Ramsey and the drowning in Switzerland of the Chinese scientist Zhou Jian.

'Sounds like a real-life Agatha Christie,' said Kate.

'Tara's far too young to be Miss Marple,' said Aisling, tapping Kate on her left foot to indicate that it now required nail varnish. Ignoring the quip, Tara continued with her story.

'Callum believes that all the murders are connected to his student days.'

'An old student with a grudge?' said Kate.

'One of his friends disappeared during their final year. Callum is convinced this guy has a score to settle with some or all of them. He's living on his nerves at the moment. Between his thinking that Kingsley is out to get him, and the local roughs throwing bricks at his house every night, and calling him a paedophile, I don't think he ever gets a wink of sleep.'

'What sort of people are you getting mixed up with?' said Aisling, sounding concerned. 'Surely you're not paid to handle all that heartache. You're not a social worker, Tara love.'

Again, Tara was not distracted from the telling of her story. She knew both girls would enjoy the next part.

'Callum showed me a photograph of all his mates at Oxford. Apart from the three people who are dead, guess who is also in the picture?'

'Wouldn't have a clue,' said Kate.

Tara and Kate watched Aisling as she thought the question through, both girls knowing that she would always rise to a challenge. Kate begged her to give in, but Aisling was determined to have a bash.

'It's either somebody famous or somebody we knew from school? Am I right?'

'Well, I'm glad you've narrowed it down,' said Kate.

'Male or female?'

'There you go; she's just cut her odds in half.'

'Both.'

'What do you mean both?' said Kate.

'There are two of them. Husband and wife nowadays, but not back then.'

'Georgina Maitland and what's his face?'

'How the hell did you know that?' cried Tara. Kate roared with laughter. Luckily, Aisling had momentarily ceased applying nail varnish as Kate threw her feet in the air.

'I read something the other day, at the hairdressers, about Georgina Maitland being an Oxford graduate. I meant to ask if you knew her, Tara.'

'Thousands of people have gone to Oxford, Aisling. I'm not mates with all of them, you know. Why say her name?'

Aisling shrugged indifference to the question.

'That Georgina Maitland is some operator though,' Aisling continued. 'Last year she was the fifth-highest-earning woman in Britain. I was reading about how she does it, you know, how she goes about making her money. I thought maybe I could get a few tips from her.' Aisling placed her feet on the sofa so that Kate could take over nail-varnishing duties. 'Here's how she does it. She finds a product, usually a fashion range, a make-up or perfume. Then she markets the hell out of it as an exclusive brand, supposedly expensive, the sort of thing only the celebs can afford. When she's got loads of exposure, like in a major fashion show, or she's paid a supermodel or actress to prance about in one of her frocks at a film premiere, she switches tack and makes the same product available on the high street.'

'That's what all the big fashion houses do. Bring out a cheaper version for the masses,' said Kate.

'No, this is exactly the same product but at high street prices.'

'But she would lose on that deal,' said Tara. 'She couldn't possibly afford to do that.'

'She could if the original, so-called designer version, was as cheap as chips to start with. All she did was stick a hefty price tag on it. The stuff is reasonable quality; it isn't complete rubbish, but it certainly ain't haute couture.'

'But the celebs would kick up a stink if they sussed it?' Kate argued.

'Why? Their reputations are at stake, too. They're not going to come out and say we've been wearing absolute tat to the Oscars. They're going to say that Georgina Maitland produces high-quality but affordable clothing. Besides, she doesn't have to do it anymore. She's made her name. Now she's into health products, beauty treatments and luxury spa centres – all at affordable prices.'

Tara was grateful for the information; it saved her half an hour on the internet.

'And what do you know of her husband?' she asked.

'Anthony Egerton-whatsit?'

'Egerton-Hyde.'

'Complete tosser. Tory junior minister. Now what have the Tories ever done for us?'

'Oh, please don't start on the politics,' said Kate. She was almost finished at Aisling's slender feet.

'So, Tara, are you going to sleep with this guy?' Aisling sounded more serious than light-hearted. Tara glared at her friend, astonished by the question.

'For goodness sake, Aisling. I'm trying to help him, that's all.'

CHAPTER 14

Superintendent Harold Tweedy was holding his regular Monday morning court with the squad of detectives he had assigned to various cases, including the murder of the young girl found on the Treadwater Estate. Tara was not pleased, but realised she had only herself to blame. She hadn't divulged the name of the murder victim, because she didn't want to further involve Callum Armour in the investigation, at least, not until she had the full measure of the man. She knew he had more to tell, but he was playing a game with her, and she was determined that eventually he would give her the whole truth. It was galling then to hear DS Alan Murray receive the plaudits from Tweedy for getting an ID on the girl.

'Thanks to Alan's hard work over the weekend,' said Tweedy, 'we now have a name for the victim, subject to a positive identification. Alan, would you care to explain?'

Murray looked fired up to deliver his findings. He had that bubbling, dedicated enthusiasm that seemed so false to Tara. It was one of the traits she'd noted in the man when they had both joined Tweedy's team a year earlier. She always felt the need to compete with him. She wasn't sure if that came from within or whether he provoked a competitive spirit between them. Murray didn't appear to behave in this manner with the other detectives in the office. She took it personally. At times, she thought it came down to her being the senior officer, despite his longer service in the police.

'OK,' he began, 'firstly, I thought I should widen the criteria for possibilities as to the victim's background. The word burned into the girl's flesh we believe to be in Polish, suggesting that the victim is of that nationality. But I thought perhaps she could hail from any of the expat communities around the city. There had been no reports of missing persons from locals, and so I contacted as many expat community groups as I could find listed.'

Tara stared coldly at the detective sergeant. Bull-bloody-shit, she fumed. She'd instructed him to do just that, and he didn't even have the decency to glance in her direction, never mind credit her with the idea.

'Anyway, cut a long story, turns out a group of hotel staff, all from Lithuania, had expressed concern to a local community liaison officer who deals specifically with Lithuanian workers, that one of their number had not reported for her shift for more than a week at the Bradbury Hotel, in the city centre. I tracked some of them down at work, and their description of their colleague matches that of the victim.'

Tara thought him long-winded. She thought it good work, of course, but Murray was milking it.

'Do you have a name, Alan?' she asked curtly.

'Audra Bagdonas – seventeen years old – Lithuanian. Been living in Liverpool for six months.'

'Address?'

'A house on Stanley Road. Shared with others, I'm told, but no names as yet.'

'Family?' Tara asked, keeping up the pressure.

'Don't know if she has family living here. If not, we'll try to get a contact through the consulate for possible family in Lithuania.'

'Thanks for that, Alan,' Tweedy said.

Tweedy always addressed his officers and staff by first name. Tara knew him to be a religious man and at times when he spoke he sounded just like a Sunday school teacher. His manner brought a certain tranquillity to the situation. They were investigating a vile murder, and yet speaking in such calm matter-of-fact tones they might have been brain surgeons or stress guidance counsellors.

'Hopefully, we have now identified the girl,' Tweedy continued. 'We need to establish a motive, and Tara's contact Dr Armour has suggested that adult films were being made at the house. We should continue to work with that lead. Alan, if you can visit the girl's home on Stanley Road? See what you can find. Tara and John, I want you to return to the scene of the killing. It's been almost a week since it happened. Ask around, now that you have a name and some background on this poor girl. See if we can rule out the possibility of a hate crime on racial grounds.'

Tara continued to seethe as they left Tweedy's office. After a Friday evening of straight talking with her friends, she felt buoyant and confident and in the right mood to stand up for herself. She made sure Tweedy was still in earshot when she spoke to Murray.

'Seems like my hunch paid off, Alan. Any joy with the porn movies?'

Murray didn't reply until he'd reached the relative safety of the detectives' open-plan operations room, beyond the narrow corridor leading from Tweedy's office. Tara reckoned that if Murray had found any information on adult filmmaking, he would be too embarrassed to share it in front of Tweedy. He was more likely to choose a time when he could embarrass her instead.

'Yes, I forgot to mention it,' he said rather sheepishly. 'Found several contacts by asking at a couple of the sex shops around Bootle. Nothing illegal, just a bit earthy. Uncensored stuff. A woman in one store told me that quite a few mucky films are made on Merseyside. Another product for the black market and, of course, the local mobs are getting some of the action. She didn't sell any of it though. I didn't believe her on that score. She also told me that many of the stars of these films are young immigrant girls. Some of them are prostitutes and others, far from home and controlled by pimps, get sucked into the porn business. In fact, the woman in the shop was Polish.'

'Do you think she's involved in any of this moviemaking?'

Murray shrugged.

'We can always pay her another visit. Make it official,' he said.

He left Tara with much more to consider than she'd bargained for, with her feeble attempt to embarrass him after his showing off in front of Tweedy. Evidence so far pointed at a sex crime, connected with adult movies, but Tweedy's suggestion of a racially motivated killing also struck a chord.

She thought immediately of the rough-cut boy who had snapped her picture outside Callum Armour's house. For that matter, she thought also of Callum who was ever slow to reveal what he knew. She found it strange that he'd known the girl's first name. Was he capable of murder when he lived in fear himself, his head bursting with theories of how his wife, daughter and student friends had perished? Why burn the letters of a Polish word, a derogatory word, into the girl's flesh? Surely the hard nut in the Everton shirt didn't have the ability to translate a word from his limited vocabulary into a foreign language. She'd be surprised if he could write his own name.

* * *

Tara and DC Wilson drove out to the Treadwater Estate. Her twenty-seven years spent without ever visiting this part of Liverpool, and now she was driving through its streets for the fourth time in less than a week. This morning, they arrived in a marked police car at the back door of the house where Audra Bagdonas had died. Three other cars sat in the parking bay. She saw signs of life in some of the houses: laundry hung on the rotary line of the house next door to the crime scene, a kitchen window open at the next house in the row and the sound of hammering from somewhere nearby that reverberated off the walls around the cul-de-sac. Tara climbed out of the car and for a moment stood gazing around her. How could somewhere so peaceful, so normal of a weekday morning, be the scene of a murder of a young girl whose life began hundreds of miles from here, in a land so different from this one?

'Take another look around the house, John. Inside and out. You've brought the key?'

'No problem, ma'am,' he replied, showing the key in the palm of his hand.

'I'll be around here if you're looking for me.'

Wilson made his way inside the house, while Tara wandered slowly down a narrow walkway at the end of the row of houses on the opposite side of the parking bay. She emerged at the front of the row and a few yards along found herself at the home of Callum Armour. She had nothing specific to ask him, unless he was ready to provide more information on the killing, but she felt compelled to check on him.

She knocked on his front door. The house was quiet; no dog barking, no sounds of chain locks or bars pulling free. A strong wind beat against her on the exposed doorstep, a chill wind for high summer. He was probably out walking that smelly dog. Forgetting almost that she was standing by his door, she gazed around the street wondering if any of the girls she'd met the previous week were about. She'd be very interested to get them on their own, away from the male of their species. What would be their take on hearing that porn films were made in the house where Audra had died? Had anyone ever approached them to take part in filming?

She was about to turn away from Callum's when a man stepped from the house next door. Billy Hughes, a hefty man, slow on his feet, greased-back hair like a well-aged Elvis, called out to her.

'Nobody in, love.'

'Do you know when he will be back?'

77

'Are you from the police?' He said it like he didn't believe for a second that the little girl before him could actually be a police detective.

'Detective Inspector Grogan. I'm investigating the murder of the young girl last week.'

'Shocking that was. Don't know what the world's coming to. An end probably. The like of that happening round here. A little foreign girl, wasn't she?'

'That's right. Did you know her at all?'

He shook his head and waddled down the garden path in his tatty slippers and navy trousers held by braces over a plain white shirt.

'There's no such thing as neighbours anymore. Used to be everybody knew each other round here. You might not know their whole life story, but you could always stop and say hello. Now? Nobody has any time for you. You never know who's coming or going. You've no idea who's living right beside you. Some of them hardly speak a word of English anyway.'

Sorry she'd asked, and still no answer to her question, she retreated down the path only to realise Billy Hughes was heading in her direction.

'And there's young Callum.' He nodded towards the barricaded house. 'Lying up in Aintree.'

'Hospital? What happened?'

'Somebody took a dislike to the lad. Used one of them taser guns on him, and then gave him a hiding.'

'How bad?'

'Bad enough. Lay in the alley all Friday night. Freezing cold when they found him. There's some bad kids round here. Callum never did anybody any harm. He's a bit messed up, but he's had a hard life. And the poor dog, too.'

'What happened to Midgey?' She said it like she had feelings for the smelly mutt, but she would never wish it harm.

'They nailed the poor brute to a fence. Vet had to put it down.'

Tara felt a shiver down her back.

'Any idea who might have done this?'

Billy Hughes shook his head.

'Round here? Could've been anybody, love.'

She thanked Callum's neighbour and hurried back along the alley to find Wilson leaning against the bonnet of the car, hands in pockets, quite content it appeared, to wait for her rather than find something useful to occupy him. Before she could reach him, a young girl, wheeling a buggy and child, emerged from the backyard of a house, three down from the murder scene. Tara's eyes met with those of the pregnant girl she'd encountered the previous week. It was obvious the girl did not wish to speak to her. She looked in a quandary over which direction to go, but it was too late.

'Hello, Debbie, isn't it?'

Resigned to her fate, the girl stopped, glared at Tara but didn't speak.

'I didn't realise you lived so close to where Audra Bagdonas was murdered.'

'I told you I didn't know her.' Debbie looked like a girl with something on her mind; a furrowed brow did not look appealing on one so young.

'You told me that Liths and Poles came and went from the house?'

'Doesn't mean I knew any of them.'

'What about men? See any men going in?'

'A couple of times, but I don't know who they were. Spoke foreign.'

'Did anyone ever ask you to go inside with them?'

Debbie shook her head, her eyes set firmly on the boy in the buggy, well turned out in a red tracksuit with blue and white trim, his gaze fixed on the police car.

Tara knew she was getting nowhere. The more questions she asked the more these kids seemed to clam up, as if they took it as a personal humiliation to be interviewed by the bizzies. She decided upon a different tack.

'So, when are you due?'

'End of the month,' Debbie replied, instinctively rubbing a hand across her bump.

'And this one is yours, too?'

'Yeah. He's eighteen months now. Isn't that right, Curtis?' She ran her hand through the child's thick black curls.'

'I'm sure daddy is proud?'

'His dad's a prick,' Debbie announced with vigour.

Tara waited for more.

'You saw him the other night. Kevin. The friggin' lizard on the bike?'

'Ah yes,' said Tara, recalling the spindly-legged youth who seemed to cower behind the girls at the merest hint of trouble. 'But he must be pleased there's another on the way?'

'He's not the dad of this one.' She patted her bump again. 'Mark's the father this time. He's the one who took your picture.'

Tara didn't know how to look or what to say. She had bags of sympathy for this young girl, and she was concerned about the kids. Debbie seemed an attentive mother, but Tara wouldn't wish that lad in the Everton shirt on her worst enemy.

'Does Mark have a second name?'

'Crawley,' Debbie replied with growing irritation.

'Why does he have a grudge against Mr Armour?'

The girl shrugged, avoiding further eye contact.

'Did Mark ever go into the house with Audra or with any of the other girls?'

'I don't know everything he does. I better go now.' She hurried away.

'Thanks, Debbie. Good luck for the end of the month.' Turning to Wilson, she said, 'I didn't think I was getting old until now.' She climbed into the car, and Wilson started the engine. 'I need to call at Aintree Hospital on the way back.'

CHAPTER 15

Wilson remained in the car, fiddling with the radio. Tara asked at reception for the ward to which Callum Armour had been admitted. A few minutes later, she stepped from the lift on the fourth floor of the tower block and entered a medical ward. After asking a nurse sitting by a desk where she might find Mr Armour, she was directed to the second bay on the right. She found Callum on a bed by a window overlooking the main hospital entrance. She almost didn't recognise him. There lay a man looking five years younger, clean-shaven, hair washed and brushed, his face, however, swollen on the right side with a purple bruise from his temple to his lower jaw. He attempted a smile when he noticed her approach, lifting his right arm and bending it at the elbow to wave. Two of the remaining three beds in the bay were occupied by men in their late sixties, Tara guessed. They both stared as she passed by.

'What happened to you?' Tara's voice was full of concern, more than she intended to show, compassion overtaking the professional nature of her visit. She quickly moved to his left, hoping his injuries would not look as severe from that side. Already, the blood was draining from her head, and she shuddered. Hospitals were not high on her list of favourite places.

'They killed my wee dog,' he said, though it was clear that talking was difficult through a swollen face.

Tara pulled a chair close to the bed and sat down. She had a sudden urge to touch him, to place her hand as comfort upon his. Just as quickly she withdrew it. Confused by her own feelings, she realised this was going to be an awkward conversation. She kept telling herself that it was purely an interview, aware also that another police officer may well have taken charge of Callum's case – that really he was no concern of hers.

'I am so sorry, Callum. Have you any idea who did this to you?'

He looked at her, this time without belligerence, stubbornness or flippancy, but didn't answer.

'Didn't you see or hear anything?'

'I didn't hear him speak, but I saw his feet. It was him.'

'You think it was Justin Kingsley?'

'Why not? He's killed my wife and child, my friends from Oxford, why not come after me?'

'Don't you think it's more likely that those kids who hang around your street did this to you? Mark Crawley, for instance?'

He fell silent once again, and she realised he was holding something back.

'We can get you moved from Treadwater, Callum. Somewhere that's safer.'

'No way. I grew up in that house. My old neighbours are all right; it's just these gangs about the place, people who didn't know me when I was a kid.'

'Maybe you should take a break, get away for a while. Is there someone I can call for you? Do you have family nearby?'

He shook his head then winced in pain.

'Parents are dead. Mum died just before Emily was born. Dad went a couple of years ago. That's why I came home. To look after him. He drank himself to death after Mum. Only fifty-six. You know the rest about Tilly.'

'Do you have friends or other relatives?'

She found this hard going, but she knew nothing about this man except for his theories of how his wife, daughter and friends had been killed. He looked to be tiring of her questions.

'I have one uncle, Mum's brother. Lives in Belfast. I haven't seen him in years. I have no close friends.'

'Tell me what happened to you, Callum. Why have you ended up living like you do? Your house boarded up, living under siege?'

'Midgey was my father's dog. Nine, he would have been. I hadn't the heart to get rid of him when Dad died. He ended up good company for me.'

'I know it's difficult at the moment, but they say whenever a pet dies you should go right out and get another one. A bit like falling off a bicycle. Getting straight back on is all part of the healing process.'

'Do you think I should have done that after Tilly and Emily died? I should have gone straight out and got myself another family?'

A nurse came into the bay, performing her observations of each patient. She seemed a pleasant girl, in the royal blue of a staff nurse, with a round face, freckled nose and short black hair. She looked at Tara and, although it was not official visiting time, she appeared to understand that Tara was no ordinary visitor.

'I'll come back later and do you, Callum,' she said smiling at them both.

'Thanks, Ruth,' Callum replied.

'What did you do after Tilly?'

'Do you mean apart from wishing every day that I had the guts to join her?'

They both let that one hang for a moment. She examined his face, blotched red in places from the shaving of his beard, removed in order to treat the gashes under his chin. She had decided he was a handsome man and tried to picture him as a student at Latimer, then as a young husband to Tilly and father to Emily. How utterly sad it was to witness the decline of a decent man, who seemed hell-bent on wasting the remainder of his life.

'I couldn't stay on at Oxford,' he said. 'I couldn't live at our house in Shiplake. For one thing, I couldn't stand the pain of having to drive over that level crossing every day. My postdoc project was nearly complete anyway, so I got myself a job teaching chemistry in a private school, of all places. At least Sussex was well away from Oxford.'

'Did it not work out?'

He laughed at the question. But at least he was engaging with her and seemingly glad of the company.

'Understatement of the year.'

'What happened?'

'Four months into the job and it was OK. Most of the teachers were friendly, and the students didn't seem to mind me. Then a fifth-former, a girl, very pretty but knew it, confident beyond her years. Precocious, I'd say in hindsight. She offered herself to me.' He closed his eyes as if he were picturing the scene all over again. 'I didn't. Honest, I didn't lay a finger on her. But for some reason, whether it was revenge for my rejecting her, I don't know, but she went to her parents, and obviously they took it to the headmaster. Luckily, for somebody, I'm not sure who, the board of governors wanted to avoid any unpleasantness. That's how they put it. I'd only been there a few months; didn't even have to resign. They let me go, for want of a better phrase.'

'And you came home to Liverpool?'

'Only option I had left. Dad was very ill by then, so I moved back to look after him.'

'When did the trouble start with the local youths?'

'It began slowly after Dad passed away. I know my appearance went to pot, and it puts some people off, makes them suspicious. Doesn't take long for rumours to start. I have wondered, though, if somehow word found its way from Sussex to Netherton about me being let go.'

'You're thinking of Justin Kingsley?'

'Why not? Easy enough for him to have set me up. Paid the girl to make the accusation. Then he spreads a few stories around Treadwater.'

'You're letting your imagination, or your paranoia, run away with you.'

'The murder of Tilly and Emily is not down to my paranoia.'

He looked away from her, watching the man across the bay struggle to climb out of bed. Tara didn't have the answers Callum needed to hear, and she resorted again to the guise of social worker.

'Maybe we can get some of your neighbours together, to make a stand against these kids? I can get the community liaison officer to advise on Neighbourhood Watch, and we have a youth diversion scheme that can perhaps deal with this particular band of kids, try to steer them into doing something positive for the area.'

He looked neither impressed nor interested in her suggestions, his response merely to reach for the newspaper lying on the trolley over his bed.

'I found this,' he said, offering her *The Guardian*. She spotted the story immediately, but didn't get to read it. 'Jian was murdered, Tara.'

She glanced at him, the first time he had called her by her first name. It seemed to herald an upward step in their precarious relationship.

'He drowned in Lake Lucerne, but that was after someone rammed a spike into his brain. That's four murders, Tara: my wife, my daughter and two friends. Three of them, alumni of Latimer College. You tell me there is no connection.'

CHAPTER 16

Superintendent Tweedy, she saw through the glass partition, stood in his office talking to Murray. She didn't think it a private conversation and tapped lightly on the door. Tweedy acknowledged her with an upward twitch of his head, and she stepped inside.

'Tara, how did you get on?'

'Not much to add, I'm afraid, sir. A neighbour, three doors down from the scene, told me that there were several girls and men who came and went from the house. She wasn't aware of the alleged activities going on inside. One other thing, Callum Armour was attacked last Friday night. He's in hospital with concussion, some cuts and bruises.'

'You think it's related to the murder of Audra Bagdonas?' Tweedy asked.

'Not sure at the moment if the attack is relevant, but I still believe Callum Armour holds more information than he has so far provided.'

'Why don't we pull him in again?' said Murray.

'He didn't say much last time,' said Tweedy. 'Unless we have the evidence to charge him with something connected to the murder I think he will remain silent.'

Tara considered it an appropriate time to explain a little of the game Callum was intent on playing.

Tweedy listened studiously as Tara related Callum's theory about his wife and daughter's killing, despite it having been declared an accident. Murray didn't look as if he believed a word, when she explained that the so-called 'Thomas-Becket-style murder' of Peter Ramsey in Canterbury Cathedral was in some way connected to the death of Tilly Reason. Tara didn't think either man would buy into the third piece of the puzzle, when she mentioned the murder of Chinese scientist Zhou Jian in Switzerland. It seemed implausible, even to her that a student who disappeared ten years ago had returned with a motive for murdering his former friends from university. She tried to convince her boss that it was worthwhile to continue trading off in order for Armour to reveal more about the murder of Audra Bagdonas.

'His head's full of crap,' said Murray.

Tweedy glared in surprise at his detective sergeant. Tara and Murray both knew well that the superintendent was not one for crude language.

'Armour has all sorts of theories about killings,' Murray continued. 'He's a paranoid conspiracy theorist, rambles about global food poisoning, airline safety and people threatening him. All rubbish. He wastes more police time.'

'Not all rubbish, Alan,' said Tara. 'He was attacked with a taser, and whoever did it also nailed his pet dog to a garden fence.'

'Dear, dear,' said Tweedy, in his usual troubled voice. 'So how do you suggest we proceed, Tara?'

She and Murray stared at each other posturing.

'I think Alan should continue with his leads: interview Audra's work colleagues and the people who shared a house with her, find the filmmakers and get a definite ID on them. I would like to spend some time on Callum Armour's claims about the murders of former students, including his wife.'

'All off our patch,' said Murray consumed by his self-confident smirk.

'If he is correct about this, then more people may be at risk. We can at least pass on our information to the appropriate authorities. Let them check it out?'

Tweedy, looking pensive, sat down at his desk, his palms together like a child in prayer. Tara saw him glance at the black leather-bound Bible that always sat on the left-hand corner of his desk. She wondered how often he found answers to difficult problems within it, or gained inspiration from it.

'OK, Tara. You may have a look into his story if it helps you to gain Armour's trust. Remember that these deaths all occurred off our patch. Please do not overstep your mark in dealing with other police forces, and if Mr Armour is not forthcoming soon with what he knows of the girl's murder then you will arrest him and charge him for withholding information. Alan, you may continue with the case as discussed.'

Murray looked far from pleased as the pair left Tweedy's office.

'You're wasting your time, you know?' he said.

'We'll see. But I want to try this, because Callum Armour knows more about the killing of Audra Bagdonas, and I can't think of a better way for him to give us that information.'

'The threat of jail usually works.'

The pair stopped by Tara's desk. She was eager to get Murray out of her hair. She wanted to prove or disprove Armour's theory as soon as possible.

'I don't think even the threat of death would be enough for him. He is a man who is living only for one thing.'

'Which is?'

'To find the person who killed his wife and child.'

'You said yourself, it was an accident.'

'If I find that to be true and there's no connection to the other deaths then we can try it your way. Until then, you get on with what the superintendent gave you to do, and let me do my job.'

Murray looked surprised by her candour and walked off. Tara didn't want him as an enemy, but it wasn't the first time she felt the need to put him in his place.

She wasted no time in gathering information on the deaths of former students of Latimer College, Oxford. Her intention was to have enough of the truth about each death to confront Callum with it and convince him that, despite his heartache at the loss of his family, there was no foundation to his theory. Or, perhaps, she would have sufficient facts to show Tweedy that there was some credence to Armour's claims. It would have been easier if she still had the tatty box-file of news clippings and photographs, but she began working from memory, typing keywords into her computer and reading the various news reports of the killings. Tilly Reason was uppermost in her mind. If there was anything that pointed to murder and not a horrific accident at the level crossing then she could move on to the others.

She remembered the chilling story Callum told her about receiving a sympathy card and reading it on the train on his way to meet Tilly. He was adamant that he wasn't mistaken about the timing of events. He'd received the card at the Chemistry Department in Oxford, only a few minutes after speaking on the phone with his wife. As Callum had told her, the report on the inquest into Tilly and Emily's death, printed in the *Oxford Mail*, made no reference to the sympathy card.

The accident, it seemed, was a case where a driver had become impatient waiting at an ungated level crossing, or was complacent in believing they could drive across before a train arrived. One passage in the police incident report, and Callum had mentioned it that first time she visited his house, stated that the CCTV at the crossing wasn't working on the evening that Tilly and Emily were killed. At the time of the inquest no witnesses had come forward. All other evidence suggested an accident. The injuries of mother and daughter were consistent with an impact of train upon car. There was nothing to suggest they had been killed beforehand and then placed inside. No one, however, could say for sure that Tilly's car had not been deliberately placed on the railway line or had not been shunted onto it by another vehicle.

But why? Tilly Reason was an up-and-coming children's author, married to an Oxford scientist. What possible motive could anyone have to do them harm? Callum had made no other suggestion about the killer's identity other than Justin Kingsley. Why? It seemed that Callum was unable or unwilling to answer that question. Kingsley disappeared seven years before Tilly Reason died. If he was the killer, and harboured a grudge against his friends, why wait so long before taking action? And why wait another three years before striking again?

* * *

Late in the afternoon, around four, she lifted the phone and dialled the number of Kent Police in Canterbury. She kept one of the news reports open on her computer as she spoke on the telephone. She explained to the desk officer who she was and asked to speak with a detective dealing with the Peter Ramsey murder investigation. A minute later, a rather upbeat male voice came on the phone.

'Hello, Detective Inspector Iain Barclay. Can I help you?'

'Hello, Inspector, I'm DI Tara Grogan of Merseyside Police.' She paused, but Barclay made no reply, merely waiting for her to continue. 'I'm investigating the murder of a young girl in Liverpool, and during my inquiries I've met a potential suspect who claims to know something in connection with the murder of Peter Ramsey in Canterbury Cathedral.'

'Oh yes?'

Barclay's interest seemed aroused although, having spoken just two phrases so far, Tara could only assume that 'Oh yes' meant that she should continue.

'His name is Dr Callum Armour–'

'Ah. Must stop you there, I'm afraid. We already know of this Dr Armour. We got a letter, several actually, but the first arrived a day or two after the Ramsey killing.'

Tara's hopes were raised, slightly. Callum was already assisting with their investigation.

'Bit of a crackpot that one,' said Barclay. 'Told us the murder of Peter Ramsey was linked to the murder of his wife, three years ago.'

'Yes, that's what he told me.'

'We checked his story. His wife was killed in an accident at a level crossing. So said the report from the inquest. He also claimed that a friend from his days at Oxford was responsible for the death of his wife and for the murder of Ramsey.'

Tara sensed that she shouldn't add a corroborative yes to this information.

'Turns out, the guy disappeared ten years ago in Austria. Sorry, I can't recall his name.'

'Justin Kingsley.'

'Mmm, that's him. I contacted his father. He's a flipping QC in London. Went through me like the proverbial dose for raking up the past regarding his son's disappearance. The lad hasn't been seen in ten years. Seems to me this Dr Armour is a bit of a time-waster – an amateur sleuth – too many murder mystery weekends.'

In Callum's defence, she ran through his theory mentioning that the murder of Zhou Jian in Lucerne, a couple of weeks ago, added weight to the argument that someone was embarked upon a series of killings linked by the victims having all been students at Latimer College. Barclay did not subscribe to her theory.

'We are working on the lines that a religious nut, someone with a grievance against the Church, is responsible for the Ramsey killing. But thanks for the information. If you find that it does begin to fit, give me a call.'

'Can I ask you to do likewise?' said Tara. 'Thank you for your time.'

'No problem.'

She got the impression from Barclay that he didn't think much of Callum's suggestions or of her for bringing them to his attention.

There was little point, she thought, in making contact with police in Oxfordshire regarding the death of Tilly Reason. She was certain they would merely quote the verdict of the inquest. That left her with the option of getting something useful from police in Switzerland.

She found a number on a website for the main police station in Kasimir-Pfyffer-Strasse in Lucerne. A female answered when she rang and, fortunately, spoke excellent English. Tara explained who she was and why she had called. Within a minute, she was put through to the senior detective handling the investigation into the murder of Zhou Jian. His name was Kurt Muetzel.

'May I help you, Inspector Grogan?' The man had quite a pleasant voice but spoke slowly, perhaps owing to English being his second language.

'I wonder if you could provide me with some details relating to the death of Dr Zhou Jian?'

'May I ask why you have an interest in this case?'

Tara explained as best she could, hopefully without sounding a complete idiot, about the connections she believed existed between the deaths of Tilly Reason, Peter Ramsey and Zhou Jian. She decided not to mention Callum's name in case the Swiss police, as that of Kent, already had experience of the man's theorising.

'These deaths, you say, occurred in Kent and Oxfordshire?'

'That's correct.'

'Then why are the police in Liverpool involved in these cases?'

Clearly, it was going to be difficult to get past Kurt Muetzel. He was understandably cautious. She embellished her role somewhat to avoid the mention of Callum Armour.

'I'm investigating the murder of a young girl in Liverpool. I uncovered this story in the course of my inquiries. I really thought nothing of it until today, when I read in the newspaper that the death of Zhou Jian is regarded as a murder. It may only be a coincidence, but it has a bearing on the credibility of a witness to the murder of the girl.'

A slight distortion of the truth, but it was an easier option than to say she was curious about Zhou Jian because she was curious about Callum Armour.

'It sounds very complicated, Inspector Grogan. I do not envy your task; we do not often investigate homicide in Lucerne. If you provide me with a verifiable email address, I will send you the information I have about the death of this unfortunate Chinese scientist.'

Tara wrote down his email address.

'Thank you, Inspector Muetzel. I really appreciate your help.'

'Assistant Chief Muetzel,' he corrected her. 'Goodbye, Inspector Grogan.'

Her face flushed at the *faux pas*, but she was pleased he had agreed to help. Immediately, she fired off an email to verify her identity.

She bought a coffee and a cherry scone from the canteen and carried them back to her desk. Twenty minutes later, an email from Assistant Chief Kurt Muetzel, with pdf attachment, sat in her inbox. When she opened it up, the first page of the seven-page document was printed in German, and for a moment she feared the rest would be the same. But it appeared that Muetzel had taken the time, at least, to do a rough translation, some in type, some handwritten, of the main points of the investigation. Tara printed out the document, knowing from habit that holding a piece of paper in her hand was more comfortable to read.

Thirty-one-year-old Dr Zhou Jian from Yanshan University in Qinhuangdao, a scientist specialising in issues of food contamination and adulteration, had been attending the Fifth International Symposium on Food Quality and Hygiene in the Global Market.

She skimmed through the information confirming what she had read in the newspapers Callum had shown her. Muetzel had enclosed a synopsis of the autopsy report. Cause of death was confirmed as drowning. The body, fully clothed, had been in the water for approximately nine hours. One abrasion to the left side of the skull with minor bruising. This suggested to Tara that Zhou Jian entered the water immediately after being struck, or perhaps hit his head as he entered it. The next few lines were of more interest. A single puncture wound was detected at the base of the skull. At autopsy, this wound showed penetration and pierce damage to the brain. The wound was consistent with the use of a thin pointed weapon such as a hat pin, needle or even a cocktail stick. There were indications of internal bleeding but no excessive loss of blood externally. Whether or not he was conscious at the time he entered the water could not be determined, but it was likely that the injury to the back of the head was sufficiently debilitating for him to fall or to succumb to a force that led to his entering the water. Cause of death was drowning, occurring most probably within a few minutes.

She'd learned little from her efforts to verify any of Callum's theory, but neither could she rule out his claims. No matter who was responsible for the deaths of Tilly Reason and her daughter, Peter Ramsey and Zhou Jian, there was not a hint of motive. Regardless of the possibility that the deaths were linked, because the adults were once students at Oxford, there was nothing to suggest that Justin Kingsley was responsible. Why had any of these people been killed? If Callum's theories were to be confirmed then she needed him to talk to her, and she needed to get another look at the contents of his box-files.

Before leaving for home, she ran a few checks on Justin Kingsley. To date, she knew only what Callum had told her and the details of his disappearance recorded in the papers at that time. Firstly, she browsed through articles relating to the missing student. As she expected there had been a flurry of activity immediately following the day Kingsley went missing. Austrian police drew a blank but, never having found a body, the official line was that he was thought to be still alive. Within a couple of months of the ski trip, Kingsley's name had largely disappeared from British press reports. Next, she examined notices of annual appeals for information on the anniversary of his disappearance, but these, too, seemed to halt by the fifth year. Finally, she ran his name through the UK police missing person database and that of Interpol. The results were not what she expected to find. Justin Kingsley was not listed as a missing person.

CHAPTER 17

Despite lying in a hospital ward for three days, Callum felt better than he had done in the last three years. The intense pains in his head were now little more than a dull background ache. The bruising on his lower ribs wasn't painful at all so long as he didn't stretch. He felt clean and rested. More than anything, he had slept untroubled except for the night-time disturbances of other patients and the titters of nursing staff going about their tasks as if it were the middle of the day. He tried not to think of all the bacteria lurking in these places: the stories of *clostridium difficile* engulfing whole wards, and methicillin-resistant *staphylococcus aureus,* known as MRSA, infections that could be resistant to beta-lactam antibiotics. He was a chemist, not a bacteriologist, but he knew what these infections could do.

He didn't wish to leave hospital feeling worse than when he came in, carrying a disease as well as a broken heart. He wouldn't give himself much chance of survival. With Midgey gone, the house would feel even more empty and desolate. So little to do with his time and yet his mind still had far too much to think about. Finding out why Tilly and Emily were murdered was always there, but now he needed to find the lowlife who had nailed his wee dog to a fence.

Also on his mind was Tara Grogan. Pleasant she may be, and pretty with it, but she was hopelessly lost. She and her colleagues were struggling through an investigation into the murder of Audra, the young Lithuanian girl; how was she ever going to track down Justin Kingsley? Bad mistake, thinking that because she had studied at Oxford, and coincidentally at his college, that she could get her head around this mystery. He knew more about murder inquiries than she did, simply from reading the papers and a few *Morse* novels. By now, he hoped, they would have finished hanging around the estate, and he would get some peace. Bizzies crawling all over Netherton only piqued the interest of mischief-makers in the street. It wasn't confined to Treadwater, or Netherton, or Liverpool either; it happened all over the country.

The doctors had done their rounds and told him he could go home. He just had to wait to be formally discharged by the staff nurse. Imagine looking forward to getting back to a place no one would ever desire to call home. He had to be mad. As he sat on the chair beside his bed waiting for the off, a nurse approached.

'Mr Armour,' she said through a tightly pursed mouth, her eyes successful in putting him down. 'A lady phoned to say she will collect you from hospital and drive you home.' The nurse turned on her heels, her message delivered.

'Did she have a name?'

She called to another nurse at the nurses' station.

'Wendy, did that policewoman who called leave her name?'

'Yes,' Wendy answered. She was a nurse who more fitted his perfect picture. 'But I can't remember. She was a detective inspector, though.'

That was all he needed. He had tried to use her, and now she had turned the table and was trying to use him. Still, it would save him the walk home.

* * *

Not for a second did Tara wish to put a foot inside that filthy house. If he was up to it, she'd decided, she would drop him home to pick up his files, and then she would drive them to a pub or a restaurant, or even a park, somewhere where they could discuss the mystery that was slowly encircling her mind. She didn't want to breathe the stench of his house, so she might as well sit opposite him in a bar while he remained moderately clean.

He looked neither pleased to see her nor grateful for the lift. Par for the course, she thought. He was leaving hospital in the same clothes in which he'd come. Thankfully, they had spent time at the laundry, although the grey T-shirt still displayed evidence across the chest of the blood spilt during the attack. She'd never seen him wear trousers other than the olive-green joggers. His shoes had seen better days and many miles. As she drove from the front car park at the Aintree Hospital, through the ticket barrier and around the one-way system, she wondered when he would ask why she had come to collect him. Or had he simply expected it? All part of the police service? Don't give him an opportunity to be awkward. Just tell him what he is doing. Give him a plan. She reckoned it was years since anyone had given him direction.

She stopped the car by the front of his house, and Callum stared at the uninviting façade of screened windows and war-battered door. She summoned the most authoritative yet pleasant voice she could manage.

'Right, Callum. I want you to pop inside and gather some of those box-files you were showing me last week. Grab a pullover; it's a bit colder today, and straight out to the car.'

He placed his hand on the door handle.

'What for?'

'We have some things to discuss, and I want to do it in more pleasant surroundings than the living room of your house.'

He turned to face her, and she glared into his eyes. She wanted to smile, to lighten the mood, to seem friendly, but she checked herself. This was a police investigation. No matter how bizarre the situation, about to discuss the deaths of people way off her patch with little clue on how to proceed, this was still her job. She must be professional. She would not sink to his level. Staring him out, she saw the smallest hint of compliance in those bloodshot eyes. He looked like someone who'd been crying forever. She didn't appreciate that the dullness in his eyes was simply down to his poor living.

Without speaking, he left the car, walked to his front door, slipped a key into the lock and pushed the door open. Briefly, he turned to face her before going in. When the door closed tight behind him, she wondered if she'd blown it. Five minutes passed; she gazed about the road, half-hoping to spy Debbie wheeling her young son along the pavement, but there was no life to be had. Treadwater was as quiet a place as it usually was. Murders, violent attacks, threats against neighbours were not so common here. She told herself once more that this estate could be lifted and set on the outskirts of any city. There was nothing special about Treadwater. Neither was there anything infamous. Another five minutes elapsed, and still no show from Callum. She debated whether she should go to the house, order him out, or call for back-up and arrest him for wasting her time. Instead, she decided this should be the moment of decision. If he didn't return, then his quest for justice for his wife and child was over as far as her helping him was concerned. She would drive away and switch her focus to Audra Bagdonas, the murdered girl, the reason why she had first met Callum Armour.

A now familiar figure appeared forty yards further down the street. Tara recognised him instantly, and he seemed to notice her car because he stopped momentarily as if deciding on whether to proceed or to turn and head in the opposite direction. Mark Crawley was alone, tall and brash. Cocky. He walked like he had a TV under each arm, a swagger born of exerting authority in his sordid world. His type would see the inside of a prison before the age of twenty. She made a mental note to check him out at the station, annoyed at herself that she hadn't already done so. While she wondered if he was responsible for the attack on Callum, she realised also that he might have killed Audra Bagdonas. With her attention centred on the approaching youth, she failed to notice Callum emerge from the house carrying two box-files under his arm. He closed his door behind him and walked to the car. Tara jumped when the passenger door opened and Callum climbed in.

'Glad you decided to join me,' she said, starting up the engine. He smiled weakly, said nothing, and she pulled away from the side of the road. She noticed the two box-files and a navy pullover sitting on his lap. She noticed, too, the menacing smirk on the face of Mark Crawley as she drove by.

* * *

It was an August day, but hardly recognisable as summer. Puffed grey clouds loomed in the sky, threatening to unleash another shower. She drove a couple of miles into open countryside, these places as unfamiliar to her as they were familiar to him. Sefton was not an area for family outings, not when you hailed from The Wirral – not for her family anyway. But today she relished the freedom and the space around her. She felt that space would help her deal with Callum. He would have to talk to her as he'd never done before. Answers, clues, hints: they must be somewhere inside that stubborn mind.

She parked outside a pub-restaurant near the parish church of Sefton. She told him to bring the box-files with him, and hoped that the pub's customers would not pick up on the fusty odours from the papers within. Callum behaved like an obedient pet, following behind her as she walked inside. She chose a table in the corner of the room. The two-hundred-year-old pub oozed warmth and rustic charm, odours of roast beef and pork wafting from plates transported by a waitress emerging from the kitchen. The building opened into a series of rooms, each with an open fireplace, exposed brickwork and surrounding walls clad in wood panelling. Two dozen or so customers were scattered about the restaurant: the lunchtime crowd. A party of middle-aged women were already eating soup, or pâté and toast. Several retired couples, and one or two business types, browsed the laminated menus set in wooden holders on each of the tables. Four men in polo shirts and trousers of whatever electrical contractor happened to be working nearby that day were busy with generous helpings of cod and chips.

No one seemed to take much notice of the couple as they took their seats. They looked an odd pairing: a determined young woman in a plain dark suit and flat shoes, doing nothing to help her lack of height, escorted by a tall, dishevelled man who didn't look as though he could afford to eat there.

A waitress, pleasant, late-thirties, but not one for a lot of chat, listed the specials of the day and took an order for drinks. Tara asked for a sparkling water. Callum, seated opposite, hesitated, looking at Tara for approval. She merely widened her eyes. He ordered a pint of lager.

'Are you hungry?'

'Been on hospital food for three days which was better than I'm used to, but yes, I am hungry.'

She handed him a menu.

'Knock yourself out.'

They both ended up ordering from one of the specials. For Callum it was sirloin steak with chips and mushrooms, for Tara, sea bass with herb potatoes. He didn't say much as they ate. She didn't mind. Having got him this far, she reckoned she could get him to open up once the table was clear of food, and they could sift through those box-files. Biding her time, she reported her work of the previous day, which she knew didn't amount to much, but would serve to demonstrate that she was serious about investigating his theory. She had told Superintendent Tweedy it would help gain Armour's trust and help her to get information on Audra Bagdonas. She had also to be honest. Callum's story would tweak the mind of any detective. There was a challenge in it that she craved. She needed to get to the truth. In a strange way, she couldn't explain, she wanted to see that her investigation could change the life of the man sitting beside her. She was aware also that she was breaking just about every rule in the book. But rules were there for the breaking. Aisling and Kate, however, would go spare if they knew what she was planning.

'Tell me why you believe Justin Kingsley is the killer? Rule number one,' she said sternly, pointing a finger at him. 'I want the truth at all times, Callum. You tell me any lies and I find out then we're finished, understand?'

He nodded obediently.

'So far, there is precious little to go on. You're going to have to think, hard. The smallest detail – you have to tell me. You try to be smart with me and I will turn you over to my superintendent, and he can charge you for wasting police time. Don't think I won't. My job is at stake here, too.'

'OK, OK, I get you.'

'And rule number two: don't get snippy with me.'

She ordered a coffee for herself. Callum declined and, like a mother bribing her child with a treat if they behaved on a shopping trip, she promised him another pint when they had finished.

He set one of the box-files on the table and opened the lid. Instantly, she caught a whiff of the foul air from inside his house, but tried her best to ignore it. Rather than begin trawling through the file, she wanted Callum to attempt answers to her questions.

'Leave that for a minute. Tell me about Kingsley. Why do you think he disappeared?'

'I can't be sure, but something went on between him and Georgina.'

'During the ski trip?'

'Yes. But I think it started a few months earlier. They had been together since the middle of our second year at Oxford. Seemed like a match, although Georgina was clearly ambitious.'

'And Kingsley?'

'Not as utterly obsessive about it, but he was pretty clear on his future.'

Callum drank some more of his beer then retrieved the group photo taken on the ski trip from the box-file. Tara watched him examine it; she watched as he relived those times in his mind. She thought it likely that he had done this many times since Tilly passed away.

'What happened the night Kingsley disappeared?'

'It was really strange. We were having a laugh at the time. Nobody thought it odd that he rose from his seat and walked out. For all we knew he was just going to the toilet.'

'Did anyone say something to offend him? Did he seem angry?'

'We were playing silly games. Or one silly game. Georgina's idea. She liked to be at the centre of things. She tried to convince us that it was a Latimer tradition for those in their final year. None of us believed her. We thought it was another way for her to show off.'

Tara cocked her head, interested to learn of a college tradition that she may have missed.

'What was the game?'

'She called it the *Five-Year Plan*.'

'Oh, I've heard of that,' said Tara in surprise. 'You're supposed to predict what you will be doing in five years' time. Your fellow students then vote whether you're a ducker or a diver. It's supposed to be based on The Slicker and The Big Man from F. Scott Fitzgerald's *This Side of Paradise*. The Slicker gets to college and becomes a success. The Big Man goes to college and turns out a failure.'

Callum's eyes widened, sparkling from the lights of the pub.

'You mean, it is a real tradition?'

'Don't know how long it's been a tradition, but we played it in my time. I was a diver, first class, but at least I got to drink more. That's the penalty for being voted a diver. A diver sinks to the bottom and is lost without trace. A ducker avoids all trouble in its path and floats on the surface. So that's what you were playing when Kingsley walked out?'

'Anthony Egerton-Hyde went first, I think. He said he intended going into politics like his father and grandfather before him. He wanted to improve his country seat, to bed and wed a damn fine filly to support his venture and to produce an heir. Everyone laughed at that, because it seemed so old-fashioned. Anthony belonged to a bygone age. Despite the laughter, we voted him a diver. He had to sink his pint. Tilly went next. Everybody loved her. She could have said she was going to be a nun and we still would have voted her a ducker. She was already well into her writing by then. Georgina and Charlotte thought her a genius and dubbed her the next JK Rowling. We all voted her a ducker. Ollie Rutherford got a thumbs-down. He rambled on about markets in the City, buying his first Maserati and a holiday home in Tuscany. No imagination, Georgina said. You can tell by now that she had assumed the role of chairperson. It descended to the point where only her vote seemed to count.'

He stared into the photo again, using it as a checklist.

'Charlotte, I think, got a thumbs-down as well. Can't remember her plans, but I'm certain it had something to do with politics. She wasn't happy to be classed a diver, but then she tended to take things far too seriously. Georgina and the others fed off that. They used to wind her up, especially about Anthony. Tilly told me once that Charlotte was besotted with him, and that Georgina encouraged her to go after him. It was as if Georgina, even when she was with Justin, knew that someday she would marry Anthony. It was cruel of her to tease Charlotte.'

'How did you fair in this game?'

He almost cracked a laugh at the question. She took it as a good sign. No harm in him enjoying himself a little as he told his story.

'Georgina always called me her Belfast Boy; it sort of stuck as a nickname. As soon as I mentioned chemistry I got an instant diver signal. "Not good enough, my Belfast Boy," Georgina said. Then Jian had a go, and they voted him a ducker, a big thumbs-up for what was more or less the same plan as mine. Of course, everybody thought it was a laugh. The Beijing Boy was a ducker, while the Belfast Boy was a diver. I saw the mischief in Georgina's eyes. Still, I got to finish my pint and order another.'

'She doesn't sound like a very nice person,' Tara said.

Callum shook his head and drank some beer.

'Everyone loved her. She and Tilly were a hell of a pair. Yes, she was overbearing, but she knew exactly where she was headed. You couldn't help liking her. It gave you a lift simply to be in her company. With most people like her you'd say they were full of shit, but with Georgina you had no reason to doubt that she would be a success. No one dared vote her a diver. Besides, her plans were so outlandish they eclipsed all the others. She stated, to the nearest million, how much money she would be earning per year after five years. Rhymed off the businesses she intended to have running, and when you read about her now, what she's worth, the empire she controls, her prediction was so accurate. I've never met anyone like Georgina.'

'You haven't mentioned Justin Kingsley playing this game.'

'Refused to play it. Charlotte and Tilly tried coaxing him, but he just sat with a grim look on his face. It was the sort of look you see in a guy who's had far too much to drink, beyond the happy point, melancholy; you know what I mean? The time when people start bearing their soul, saying things they later regret even if they are perfectly true. Justin seemed to be getting there. When he refused to play, Georgina said something like, "Perhaps my Justin has no plans." Things went a bit flat until someone realised that Peter hadn't taken his turn. He never seemed to take himself seriously.'

He stared into the picture, then looked at Tara, his expression brimming with sudden realisation.

'What's wrong? Have you remembered something?'

He closed his eyes.

'Something just made sense. About Justin. It fits now; I know it.'

'Do you want to tell me?'

'Peter started bubbling about his future, playing for laughs, talking about becoming a priest, with us poking fun about him wearing a cassock and talking gibberish from a pulpit. He took it all in good spirit, and said, "You may well laugh, people, but someday I will be Archbishop." Tilly said something like, "Ooh, I wonder which one?" And Justin grunted, "Thomas Becket."'

CHAPTER 18

'You think there's a connection between Peter's murder in Canterbury Cathedral and what Justin said before he disappeared?'

'Has to be more than coincidence.'

So far, despite his willingness to talk, Tara hadn't learned much. It was certainly not the calibre of information to shed light on a complicated business, most of which occurred some years ago and hardly around the corner in the next street. Callum still needed pressing.

'Apart from his mood that night, can you think of any reason why Justin would disappear?'

'I didn't know him that well, only through Georgina and Tilly.'

'Did he feel pressure from his studies, or from exams approaching?'

'I don't know. He was destined for the law profession; his father is a QC. Maybe it was expected of him, rather than it being a path of his choosing.'

'What reason would he have to harm his friends, first Tilly then Peter Ramsey and Zhou Jian?'

'I really can't understand Jian's death. Justin only knew him through me. I brought Jian along on the ski trip. He hadn't really socialised with the others before then. I'm not sure how well Justin knew Peter either. Again, he would have met him through his mates Ollie and Anthony at the rowing club.'

'Callum.' Tara placed her hand gently on his forearm. 'What if Justin is dead? That the night he walked out he intended to kill himself? People do such things.'

He snatched his arm away and sat upright in his chair.

'Then who killed them? If Justin didn't do it, are you suggesting that it's merely coincidence?'

He was still clutching the photograph, but he tossed it into the open box-file and began rummaging through the contents. Tara had no answers, certainly not the answers Callum wished to hear. She needed him to consider the possibility that the conspiracy only existed inside his head.

He wasn't letting go without a fight.

'Look at this,' he said angrily. 'Do you think I imagined this?'

He held out the sympathy card he'd received on the day Tilly and Emily were killed. She didn't need to examine it. There was nothing to be gained. She wanted to believe him, but her expression betrayed her.

'I picked this up before leaving the lab in Oxford. I was late for the train, and Tilly wanted me home early to pack for our Easter holidays. Jian's project was running behind; I had stayed on to help him. Tilly was driving from our house in Shiplake to meet me at Reading Station.' Tears streamed down his bruised face, his voice inflamed, while customers in the restaurant looked on. 'They were hit by a train, Tilly and wee Emily, their car crushed and shoved a hundred yards down the track. They didn't even make it to hospital. And I was sitting outside Pangbourne on a delayed train. I had this card with me, Tara. I wasn't given it the next day or the day after; it didn't come in the post. I had it with me. Whoever left that card for me knew that Tilly and Emily were going to die. The police ignored it, and it was never discussed at the inquest. Does that make it any less important? Does that mean it's all in my head? You're the detective – you tell me.'

Tara felt her face burn. She felt the eyes of the people in the restaurant upon her. Now all of them knew what she was, and what she was doing with this scruffy man. Her best option, her only sensible approach, was to continue the discussion, take the heat out of it and proceed as if nothing happened. Callum eyeballed her, but she couldn't hold his stare. His hurt, his anger gave him an irascible confidence, and she didn't feel strong enough to wear him down. She could tell him to wise up; he didn't have a shred of evidence to prove that Justin Kingsley did anything but walk out of a party and disappear.

'What else do you know about the killing of Peter and Zhou Jian?'

He drew a steadier breath, his anger standing down for the moment.

'No more than I have already told you, and that's only what I read in the papers.'

She sorted through the muddle in the box, giving no response to his answer.

'Why do you have this?' Removing several paper cuttings, she passed him the story from the *Oxford Mail* she'd read previously. It was an appeal for information regarding the Baby Isis: the discovery of a baby boy found in a shallow grave near the river in Oxford. Callum shook his head.

'After Tilly died, when I started looking into things, I collected any news stories I could find about Oxford during the time I was there. I have stuff on Shiplake, Strobl in Austria where we skied, and articles on Georgina and Egerton-Hyde. I'm just searching for answers. I don't know of any other way to do it.'

She paid the bill for lunch and suggested to Callum it was time to head back. He looked exhausted, and they both were growing irritable as she continued to ask difficult questions, and he persisted in giving only vague answers.

The rain had arrived promptly, the huge swathe of cloud that had seemed to linger in the distance found its way to the village of Sefton. They dashed from the pub to her car, and once on the road to Netherton, the wipers busy and the heater blasting to dispel the mist on the windscreen, she suggested the next course of action. She didn't dare consider the number of rules she was breaking, the advice given by her friends, and her own sensible thinking. Ten days ago, she had begun an investigation into the murder of a teenage girl. At this point she had learned little more than the girl's name. Then she'd been confronted with a bizarre case of the deaths of four people, linked through an Oxford college and the man, who right now, sat beside her. She could see only one way of progressing both cases, and that involved the co-operation of this awkward man, who carried his and most of the world's troubles on his back.

'There's only so much we can learn from those boxes of yours. If we trace all of the people in your photograph, speak with them, explain your theory, and ask if they have seen Justin, then maybe we'll form a better idea of what's been going on. We can also pay a visit to Canterbury and Oxford.'

She was conscious that he hadn't responded to her idea but, as she neared his street, she reckoned the best policy was to keep talking.

'I'll book a couple of days leave; we can fly down on Friday, and hopefully make it home by Sunday night.'

'I'm not going.'

'What do you mean? I thought you'd jump at the chance to investigate these deaths?'

'I've told you all that I know. You're the police; you investigate. It's not my job. Besides, I could be the next victim.'

Suddenly, she ran the car into a lay-by, braking hard. She couldn't drive and argue at the same time. Switching off the engine, she turned to face him.

'But I've told you, Callum, I can't go poking my nose into these cases. It's not my patch. You have to meet your old friends. Ask them about Kingsley. I'll be there to help you along. But I can't go on a professional basis, not as a police officer.'

'I'm not doing it.'

'I don't understand. You told me you wanted to find the person who killed your wife and daughter. I could lose my job doing this for you.'

'You're only doing it because you think I have more to tell you about that girl, Audra.'

'And have you?' Her large eyes looked pleadingly, but they held back her fury. She was determined not to back down.

'I'm only interested in finding justice for Tilly and Emily. Beyond that, I care little about my life or the life of anyone else.'

'But you're too young to give up on yourself. Tilly's gone, Callum. I'm sure she wouldn't want this kind of life for you. I'm sure, if she loved you, she would want you to rebuild your life and get on with things.'

'Is that an offer?'

'You're forgetting I'm a police officer, and I have girlfriends who would tear you apart for being presumptuous with me.'

It brought a smile to his face.

'I can't go,' he said.

'Why not?'

He dropped his gaze like a scolded child. Tara couldn't fathom this man. She didn't have his trust, and he certainly did not have hers. He could be the killer of Audra Bagdonas, and in some bizarre manner he was deflecting the murder investigation by dreaming up stories of conspiracy. She despised and pitied him in the same breath. But she'd had enough for one day. If he was not prepared to go with her then why should she risk her career? Gunning the engine, she glanced in her rear-view and then the wing mirror. Once the road was clear she drove away. A quarter of a mile further on, she turned into the estate and moments later pulled up by his front door.

'I'm not going there alone, Callum. If you can't be bothered to come with me then I'm afraid your investigation ends here.'

Without a word he undid his seatbelt and opened the car door.

'I don't like flying,' he said. 'Can't stand it.' Tara was dumbfounded. 'Not with all those near misses and pilots dozing off, and strange gases filling the cabins.'

Now it was her turn to smile, and she managed it with some relief. She placed her hand on his arm.

'If that's the only reason, we can go by car? Or do you have a fear of driving, too?'

Without reply he climbed out and lifted his box-files from the back seat.

'Leave those, Callum. I'd like to have another look through them. I'll be in touch.'

He closed the car door and stood watching as she drove away. He'd misjudged her. She was a very determined lady.

CHAPTER 19

'We have people who can identify Audra,' said Murray, seated at his desk and munching on a chicken tikka sandwich. 'Three girls, all Lithuanian, shared a house with her. I also found these.' There were four DVD cases sitting on the desk, all identical in black plastic without markings or labels.

'Where did you get them?' Tara drew a chair from a nearby desk and sat down, waiting as Murray finished the latest bite of his sandwich.

'Sorry, late lunch.' He held an open can of Coke in his right hand and the remainder of the sandwich in his left. 'Found them in Audra's room at the house. Buried under a pile of clothes, CDs, make-up and stuff. She wasn't exactly a tidy girl. Clothes on the floor and on the bed, shoes everywhere. I have a couple of uniforms down there now gathering up the lot. We can sift it and send anything of interest to the lab.'

'What about her housemates, did they have anything to say?'

'Funny that. They start off with perfect English, but ask them an awkward question, and suddenly they have only one language. One of them…' He set down his Coke and pulled a notebook across the desk towards him, flicking over the top page. 'Laima Gabrys, worked at the Bradbury Hotel with Audra.'

'When did she last see her?'

'Couple of days before Audra was found. I suppose that could be the day before she died, depending on the accuracy of Miss Gabrys' memory.' He glanced again at his notebook. 'Last day Audra reported for work was the day before she died, worked an early morning shift, six to two. Laima Gabrys told me they would stay over at the hotel if they had worked late the night before and were required for breakfast the following day. So it appears that Audra worked late, stayed over at the hotel, worked until two o'clock, and sometime afterwards made her way, or was taken, to the house in Treadwater.'

'Do these girls know anything about her going there?'

'That's when the questions got lost in translation, and the ability to speak in English suddenly scarpered.'

'You think Audra wasn't the only girl from that house involved in the activities going on in Treadwater?'

'Could be. But if they are involved in mucky movies you'd have thought they would have got rid of these.' He indicated the DVDs on his desk.

'Have you looked at them yet?'

He shook his head, and Tara guessed he was trying to make light of the task.

'I thought maybe we could go through them together?'

She rose from the chair with a smile. For a second, Murray looked hopeful. Despite his bravado, Tara knew he would take it seriously but fired him a warning just in case.

'Let's not make a party out of this, Alan. No need to round up the boys for laughs. If you need help, get Wilson to go through them with you.'

He nodded his acknowledgement.

'Depending on what you find, tomorrow we'll have another word with the girls.'

'You mean, I have to spend tonight watching this stuff? This is *Eastenders* night.'

'Nice try. I don't believe for a second you're the type to watch *Eastenders*.'

* * *

She carried the two box-files from her car up to the flat. Once inside, she set them on her coffee table and went for a shower. Another afternoon spent in the company of Callum Armour, and she needed to feel clean. If he did agree to travel south with her, she would insist he had a serious wash beforehand and decent clothes to wear. It would be her first order even if she had to pay for it.

Most of the scientific literature from the box-files she placed on the pile for Zhou Jian. A report she'd read briefly from the Soil Association, on issues of food contamination in Britain, and two published papers stating Callum Armour as co-author with Zhou Jian, she added to the same pile. Articles written on the subject of flight safety, health issues surrounding the use of mobile phones, the dangers of breathing fumes from diesel engines, GM crops: she dropped on the floor away from the material she considered relevant. One story that pricked at her thoughts she set with the group photograph. It was an appeal for information by Oxfordshire Police on the tenth anniversary of the discovery of Baby Isis. Even during her time at Latimer she'd heard the story. Nothing in these box-files contained much by way of happiness.

She glanced over several of Callum's bills for electricity, gas and council tax, and wondered how he managed financially. Was he entirely dependent on benefits? Had Tilly Reason left any money from her successful writing career? Among the bills were several receipts, mostly from Asda or Lidl supermarkets, nothing of any significance except, perhaps, for the name scribbled in blue ink across one of them. She assumed that it was Callum's writing. Teodor Sokolowski was a name she had already encountered in the investigation of the murder of Audra Bagdonas. He was proving to be the absentee landlord, the man who owned the house where Audra was murdered. But why did Callum have his name on a till receipt?

CHAPTER 20

He hadn't slept in his house since the night before he was attacked and wee Midgey was savagely nailed to a fence. Not that he'd missed the place much. But he did pine for Midgey. He regretted his failure to protect his only friend. The dog had been his only company in more than two years.

He'd felt clean in the hospital; the first time in over two years. Today, he'd eaten the best meal since Tilly had last cooked them a dinner of rump steak, sautéed potatoes, broccoli and vine tomatoes. He could see it on his plate, on their old dining table. The table had been the worse for wear, an antique he claimed; she didn't agree but loved it anyway. Emily lay asleep in her cot, the baby monitor switched on. They could hear her gentle sighing breaths, the odd murmur as she wrestled on the mattress threatening to wake, demanding attention and scuppering their plans for the evening. As it turned out, it was their last evening together.

His head pounded again from the trauma of the beating and the jolts of electricity that had shuddered through his body. He'd felt much better lying in hospital. Now the feeling of disorientation returned, of being unaware of what happened yet knowing it was bad, knowing that someone had stood over him intending to do him harm. His ribs ached, bruised by the kicks of his attacker. His arms and legs were stiff from the reflex of his body as it had feebly, yet instinctively, defended itself.

He went to the bathroom; three pints of beer had that effect on him. Moving afterwards to the back bedroom, thinking only of sleeping for a long time, he stepped between the stacks of books, boxes of ornaments and knick-knacks belonging to his mother, old bedding and towels and the bundles of newspapers he'd amassed in three years. He stood by the window looking into the cul-de-sac, scanning the rear of the houses with their wooden fences, garden sheds and conservatories. He stared at the back door of number six, wondering about Audra.

The pregnant girl, Debbie, emerged from the garden of the house three doors down. She looked ready to pop as she wheeled her young son across the tarmac. Suddenly, a youth, tall and wiry, appeared from an alley and ran to catch up with her. She stopped, and they spoke for a few moments. Then Debbie moved on, the youth watching as she hurried away. He was remonstrating; Callum could hear his raised voice but couldn't make out the words. The girl turned and shouted something in reply. Walking off again, in a few paces she was around the corner and out of sight. The boy, in jeans and an orange basketball vest, watched her go. His head dropped as he turned and ambled in the opposite direction. We all have problems, Callum thought. He would gladly trade all of his for whatever troubled the kid in the street.

He looked at his bed. After three nights in hospital, clean sheets, soft pillows and adjustable backrest, he didn't think he could manage to sleep in this room. When darkness came, though, it didn't much matter where he lay. His nights were always the same. Tilly and Emily floated in the air before him; now, two of his friends had joined them. If he was lucky, he would fall into sleep.

He worried what Tara would ask him to do. He'd spent the last two years doing nothing but building his grievances with the world, with the police, the social services and his neighbours. The less he did, the more he feared doing anything. Now she was asking him to go down south. That meant travel; it meant visiting places full of memories; it meant speaking to people he had not spoken to since the funeral. He wouldn't cope with it. He'd fall to pieces and make a fool of himself. Tara would have to go alone.

Downstairs, he settled into the bundles of papers he regarded as an easy chair and watched the light fade into darkness.

* * *

He heard banging on his door. Loud, insistent. Why couldn't they leave him alone? Let him sleep. He heard muffled shouts and thumping on the front door. Cold and stiff, he lay sprawled over the disintegrating chair as the bundles of paper shifted upon themselves. Still the banging. If only he was properly cold and stiff. Peace then.

But the voice he now heard was not one of menace or threat. A girl's shout, a pleading call. He rose quickly, and feeling the blood sink to his feet and his head go light, he staggered to the front door. He pulled at the bolt, undid the chain and turned the latch. Daylight rushed at him.

'I've been knocking for ages, Callum.'

'Sorry. I was sleeping.'

'Yes, well some of us have a day's work to go to.'

Tara didn't wait for an invitation, barging past him into the living room. It was hardly the right adjective for the place. He closed the door and joined her inside.

She had no time for pity this morning, no time for abhorrence at the state of the place or the state of her host. She had things for him to do, and she was adamant that he would not shirk them.

'I want all of that taken care of by close of play today,' she said, handing him a buff folder. He stared at her, taking little notice of the file. 'No excuses, Callum. You want my help in this – you do as I say.'

He rolled his eyes.

'And you needn't start that pitiful downtrodden act of yours. We all have problems, Callum. You're an intelligent man. An intelligent man wouldn't sink to this life. Now read what's inside. Two minutes, and I have to go. I'm due at the morgue by nine o'clock.'

His eyes widened, trying to show an appreciation for her calling with him before she'd even gone to work. She stood with arms folded, waiting belligerently for him to examine the contents of the file. She commentated as he began to read.

'I want you to set up appointments for this weekend, Friday to Monday, with all of those people. Make up some plausible excuse for meeting them. I can't do it. When we go to London, I go as your friend. I can't go as a police officer, understand?'

He nodded and continued reading.

'Do you have any money?'

'Yes.'

'Buy some half-decent clothes. Doesn't have to be anything formal: shirts, trousers and new shoes. Get a haircut, and make sure that beard doesn't grow back. I'm not travelling the length of England with a tramp. When you've done all of that, start clearing up around here. While you're at it, look for something in all that paperwork that might give us some clue where Kingsley got to when he bolted and why he wants to kill off alumni of Latimer College. Any questions before I go?'

'I don't have a phone. Mobiles are not good for—'

'Don't start with all that health scare nonsense. You're an Oxford graduate; figure something out. I'll call on my way home.'

She opened the front door, leaving him clasping the folder that was about to dictate his day.

'Remember what I said. You mess it up and the deal's off.'

* * *

Murray was already waiting inside the city mortuary in Pembroke Place, when Tara rushed from her car. She knew he would enjoy seeing her late and fraught, having battled traffic in the city centre at this hour of the morning. Of course, he merely offered a weak smile as if this sort of thing happened regularly. Two women stood close by, looking on as she proffered her excuses.

'This is Miss Laima Gabrys and Miss Ruta Mankus,' said Murray, doing well to remember the girls' names. 'Miss Gabrys worked with Audra at the Bradbury Hotel.'

'I thought you said there would be three?' Tara asked Murray.

'Our friend Eva did not want to see her,' said Ruta Mankus.

'That's fine. Has DS Murray told you what to expect when we go in?'

Both girls nodded once.

'Right, let's get it over with then.'

Murray led them through a set of fire doors and, thirty feet along a corridor, he turned left and held a second door open for them to enter. This was another aspect of the job that Tara didn't think she would ever become used to.

A body lay under a white cover on top of a trolley near the centre of the room. A technician, male, late thirties, sallow complexion but clean-shaven, stood close by, awaiting the signal from Murray to uncover the face for the girls to witness. Tara moved to the opposite side of the trolley. A little hint given to her by Tweedy was, in circumstances of homicide, where the person required to identify the body might also be a suspect, it made good sense to observe their reactions upon seeing the victim. Murray gave the expected nod to the technician, who then stepped forward and, with two hands, drew the sheet clear of the head and shoulders of the dead girl. Tara was surprised to see the stronger looking of the two girls, Ruta Mankus, clasp a hand to her mouth, the other hand reaching out to her companion. She whimpered; tears filled her eyes as they looked towards Tara.

'Can you please confirm if this is Audra Bagdonas?' said Murray in a formal tone. The smaller girl, Laima Gabrys, nodded slowly, her gaze never once leaving the grey-white face of the victim.

'Thank you, that's all,' said Murray to the technician. The head of Audra Bagdonas was concealed once more beneath the stiff white sheet.

Tara led the girls, followed by Murray, to one of the police interview rooms. She offered both girls a drink of water and invited them to sit to one side of a small rectangular table. Murray remained standing, while Tara sat opposite the girls.

'Before DS Murray takes some details from you both, I would like to ask a couple of questions, if you are feeling up to it?' She looked at the girls, and they both nodded. 'Tell me about Audra, what kind of girl was she?'

Ruta Mankus sniffed back some tears, but was first to answer. Her English was clear, her words carefully chosen but heavily accented.

'Audra was only a teenager. A nice, quiet girl and hard worker.'

Tara waited for the other girl to offer something but she remained impassive. Her pale complexion seemed to have lightened further.

'Did she have boyfriends?'

The girls looked at each other before Ruta answered.

'No boyfriends here in England. Boyfriend at home in Lithuania.'

'What did she do when she was not working? Did she go out with friends? Did she spend time with you?'

'Sometimes with us,' said Ruta, 'but not all the time. We did not know sometimes where she went.'

'The house in Treadwater, where she was found, did you ever go there with her?'

'No. I don't know this place.'

'Audra had DVDs in her room. Do you know anything about those?'

Tara stared at Laima Gabrys, willing her to contribute something. Ruta Mankus appeared to realise.

'Laima does not speak good English.'

Murray, standing to the side, rolled his eyes in disbelief.

'Then perhaps you could translate for her?' said Tara.

'We don't know about DVDs.'

'The house where you live, do you own it or do you pay rent?'

'Pay rent.'

'Do you know who owns the property?'

Mankus shook her head.

'Agency, we rent from an agency.'

'OK, thank you for taking the time to come here this morning. I may need to ask some more questions, but for now I will leave you with DS Murray.'

Returning to St Anne Street station, Tara made arrangements for her weekend to London with Callum. Murray returned a short while later, looking pensive.

'So, what did you make of that pair?' he asked, placing himself on the edge of her desk.

'Didn't believe a word. I think they rehearsed all of that between them. They know a lot more of what Audra was involved in before her murder. The Mankus girl was at least thirty; she should have her wits about her.'

'I can tell you that Laima Gabrys speaks reasonable English. They seemed to forget that I met them a couple of days ago. Gabrys told me then about working with Audra at the Bradbury. And that's not the only thing they got up to. If you have a few minutes, I think you should take a peek at the DVDs.'

Tara winced. Embarrassing to watch alone, never mind in the presence of a male colleague, but he seemed to be taking a professional line. She felt that she must do the same.

Murray had a laptop sitting in a small meeting room separated from their office by a glass partition. She sat down beside him; he clicked on the mouse, a disc whirred in the machine, and in a few seconds an unsteady image appeared on the screen. Murray increased the volume, although the only sounds were a few moans and the hum of background noise. In the first few minutes, none of what she saw held any significance nor was it particularly shocking in its content.

'Likelihood is, that this standard of film was intended for television, the adult channels, of course,' said Murray. Then he added, 'The woman who runs the shop in Bootle told me. No images of penetration…'

'OK, Alan. I understand. Can you move on to what is relevant?'

A lecture on the making of adult films would not make her feel any more comfortable. She felt herself flush. She wasn't a prude, but she found it difficult to understand how anyone would seek gratification from watching the likes of this. Murray clicked the mouse a couple of times, and the images switched to new scenes.

'I think this is the most relevant piece.'

Within seconds, the naked body of Audra Bagdonas was clearly visible. Apart from the scene at the mortuary, when a sheet was involved, Tara had only ever seen this girl naked. She lay on a single bed, set against a wall, her head propped on pillows, the naked frame of a man leaning over her. What he was doing was not entirely visible on camera, but it didn't take much imagination to figure it out.

'OK, so that is Audra. We now have confirmation that she was involved in making these films.'

'Keep watching,' said Murray. A minute or so passed, very slowly for Tara, and all she could do was wonder what Audra had been thinking and feeling as the man, whose head and face remained obscured, continued having vigorous sex with her. She also wondered if Audra actually had been a fully consensual participant. If not, then what she and Murray were watching was a gross act of rape. Had matters cruelly descended from Audra's rape to her murder? Had her final moments of life been filmed?

Suddenly, Audra and her partner disappeared and another girl, dressed in jeans and T-shirt, filled the screen. She sat upon a carpeted staircase, a broad smile on thin lips, brown hair lapping at her shoulders. It wasn't long before a naked male showed up, and the girl was obscured by his torso.

'Ruta Mankus, I would say,' said Murray as if Tara needed reminding of the girl she'd met just two hours earlier.

'Not surprising in the end,' she said. 'Something was going on with that girl this morning.'

'Most interesting thing is where all of it was filmed.'

'I didn't recognise anything of the house in Treadwater.'

Murray shook his head and smiled.

'That staircase is in the house where those girls live in Stanley Road. I recognised it straightaway.'

'Find out who owns the house.'

CHAPTER 21

She couldn't help feeling impressed by his efforts. For the first time, she stood in open space in his living room; most of the papers and many of the box-files were gone. There was a place to sit on the tattered sofa, and the bizarre armchair of newspapers and magazines had been dismantled.

'What did you do with all the paper?'

'Out the back for now. I'm hoping it doesn't rain before the council come to take it away.' There was a positive lift in his mood, the kind that comes with achievement. He couldn't help looking pleased with himself, and Tara was happy to give praise where it was due. 'Come and see the kitchen.' He led her through the dim hall into a tidy space, where she could now identify a cooker, a fridge and worktops free of clutter.

'Wow, you've got rid of all those foil trays, and you've washed up.'

'You haven't mentioned my hair.' He stood before her like a wife itching for praise from her husband. His hair did look better. Clean and trimmed, although it still reached his shoulders.

'You look great,' she said, then realised she sounded rather personal. 'Did you buy some clothes?'

'A couple of shirts and a pair of chinos, like you said.'

'Very good.'

'And shoes.'

She smiled at his boyish responses.

'More importantly, did you have any luck making those appointments?'

'Some of them. We're seeing Charlotte on Sunday. Ollie couldn't give me a definite yes, but told me to call him when we get to London. Anthony Egerton-Hyde, no chance.'

'Thought as much. He is a government minister, I suppose. What about Georgina Maitland?'

'Didn't get to speak with her either, but I spoke to her PA. She took a note of my name and promised to pass it on to Georgina. She'll be in her office on Friday, so I think we can turn up and assume that she'll see us.'

'Are you hopeful?'

'I think Georgina, if she knows I'm sitting in her reception, will invite us in.'

'And Justin Kingsley's parents?'

'I found Sir Edward's address in chambers, but I think our visit to him should be a surprise. I don't think he'll be too happy meeting the likes of me.'

Delighted with his work, she felt for the first time that a degree of trust had been manufactured between them. If he didn't trust her advice, he wouldn't have carried out her list of instructions. Similarly, if she hadn't begun to trust him she wouldn't be travelling alone with him to London.

'Right, I will leave you in peace to enjoy your new house. I'll pick you up on Friday morning about seven.'

He nodded as a doubtful expression crept over his face.

'It's the only way, Callum, if you want justice for Tilly.'

'You believe my story then?'

She replied with a nod of her own, despite the enormous doubts gnawing at her brain, knowing that when she returned to Liverpool she might not have a job and, if she was entirely wrong about Callum Armour, losing her job might well be the least of her worries.

Before leaving, she remembered one question she had been meaning to ask him.

'Do you happen to know who owns the house where Audra was found?'

He shook his head.

'No idea, why?'

'You have a name written on a receipt from Asda, Teodor Sokolowski. I found it in your box-file.'

'Is he the owner?'

'He is, but would you mind telling me why you have a note of his name?'

He responded with a barely perceptible shrug. In an instant that inkling of trust between them vanished.

'Before we leave for London, Callum, you have a serious think about things. I want to help you, I really do, but I know you're playing a game with me. I don't think you're playing fair.'

She left him on the doorstep, marched to her car and roared off, the noise from the engine a signal to him that Tara was less than pleased.

* * *

His hopes for dry weather were dashed an hour after DI Grogan left him. A newspaper forecast described it as summer showers, but it was rain like any other rain. Right now it was turning his bundles of paper to a sodden mess. All he had done was to shift his squalor a few yards out of doors, but still it belonged to him. Still his mess.

Of course, he didn't dump all of it. No way. Letters from Tilly, cards from Charlotte, Jian, Ollie, Tilly's parents and Georgina: he couldn't bear to throw them out. They were his only link to the past, to the time when he had Tilly and Emily. Sipping hot tea from a chipped mug, he stood amongst it all smothering his bed and littering the floor. Tara would never know he'd kept most of it. Not her business anyway.

He remained at his bedroom window, as dusk quickly slipped to night, watching the figure out the back, standing in the downpour, a hooded anorak his only protection. Callum wondered what business he had to be standing there, lingering by the alley between two houses. Was he waiting for the pregnant girl, Debbie, or for someone at number six, where Audra had died? Periodically, the stranger lifted his head and seemed to look towards him, but Callum knew there was no chance of his being seen, not in the darkness of his room and the metal screen on the window.

By the time he'd finished his tea, he realised that filling his bedroom with more paper left him without a bed. From now on he would kip on the sofa. Probably safer downstairs, anyway. Before settling down for the night, he checked once more on the figure out the back by peering through the kitchen window. The rain hadn't ceased, and the stranger was still there.

CHAPTER 22

Around the corner from Callum Armour's house, Tara pulled over, took her mobile from her bag, and sent a text to Kate, asking if she could call on her way home. Kate replied immediately with an invitation to supper. Tara was eager to speak with her, rather than Aisling, because she knew that Aisling would not take well what she had to say. Kate was more level-headed, less likely to flap under stress.

She shared a flat with Adam, a doctor currently assigned to A & E at the Royal. She was the only one of the three girls who had anything resembling a stable relationship. Aisling was unashamedly watching and waiting for Mr Handsome and drop-dead rich, test-driving a few prospects, while Tara hadn't managed more than a handful of dates since leaving Oxford. The one relationship she'd had at university, quite possibly, had put romantic notions out of her head for life. So said Aisling.

She turned her car into Canning Street in the south of the city and found a parking space thirty yards down from the cream-painted Georgian house, imaginatively transformed into four apartments. Canning Street was a pleasant area, popular with professional couples. Kate and Adam lived on the ground floor on the right-hand side of the building. As Tara climbed the front steps, she spied Kate looking out from the lounge window. The front door was open before Tara reached it.

'I pulled some lasagne from the freezer; garlic bread's in the oven. Do you want a drink?'

'Water or juice is fine. I still have to drive home.'

'So, what's all the biz, saying you needed to speak to me and without Aisling?'

Tara told Kate of her plans for the coming weekend. In doing so, she had to fill her in with quite a few details from both cases. She told her about Callum's search for answers concerning his family, and her own, professional objective to hunt down the killer of Audra Bagdonas. Unlike Aisling, who would have interrupted Tara at each and every sentence, Kate listened and allowed her to finish the story.

'I needed to tell someone, Kate. I can't discuss it at work. I could be kicked off the force for doing this.'

Neither of them had so far eaten a bite of food.

'Oh, Tara, why do you always get yourself so emotionally involved in these things?'

'I don't.'

'Yes you do. Same thing happened last year on that suicide case you talked about.'

'Callum needs my help, but he knows more about the murder of Audra than he's told me so far. I'm determined to get the truth out of him.'

'Seems to me that you can't trust him, and now you're running off to London together.'

'I know. I'm ninety-nine per cent sure he's an honest man, but I'm telling you just in case.'

'Just in case what?'

'In case you don't hear from me. I'll leave you the details of where I'm going and who I'm going to meet. I'll text you twice a day. If anything happens, and you don't hear from me, you pass the information to my superintendent.'

Kate paled at what Tara had to say.

'We have to tell Aisling; she'll go ballistic if she finds out where you've gone, and we haven't told her.'

'No, Kate. She'll insist on going with me.'

'Not such a bad idea. Maybe I should come too?'

Tara laughed nervously, for a second unsure whether her friend was serious.

'Please, Kate. I'll be fine. Telling you about it is only an insurance policy. Nothing bad is going to happen.'

'We still have to tell Aisling. We were supposed to go out on Saturday, remember?'

Tara's face was blank.

'Shopping? Aisling was going to kit you out in labels.'

'There you are. I'm already gaining from going away.'

CHAPTER 23

He looked a man transformed as he strode down the path to her car. Light blue shirt, navy chinos and brown casual shoes; he walked upright, shoulders looking broader, his dark clean hair flapping in the wind. There was no doubt that he was a very handsome guy. Smiling, but nervous with it, he placed a rather battered holdall in the boot then got into the front seat. She also felt a little nervy, like two people on their first real date, following the preliminary meeting, already aware of some of the things they liked and some of the things they found uncomfortable about their new friend. Tara was first to break an awkward silence as she drove out of the estate heading for the motorway.

'If you haven't eaten already we can have breakfast on the way.'

He seemed receptive to the idea but replied merely with a slight nod. She tried again.

'I brought your files with me. There are some things I want to discuss on the journey.'

'What sort of things?'

'Well, for starters, the questions you're going to ask the people we're meeting.'

'Some of these people were my friends once. I know what to say.'

'It's not a social visit, Callum. Someone among them may know the whereabouts of Justin Kingsley, or at least they may be able to explain why he disappeared. Your theory that Justin is a murderer is still only a theory. One of your friends may hold the answer whether or not they are actually aware of it. We have to ask the right questions. I'm the police officer, but remember, on this trip, I am merely a friend. You have to do most of the talking.'

She allowed him to ponder her instructions as she made it through the melee of rush hour traffic to the M62. Even at this point she still harboured grave doubts about this man, and she blamed that entirely on him. He was holding a lot back and not only regarding the killing of Audra Bagdonas. She had long realised that he considered Audra's murder to be his bargaining chip. But there was a lot he hadn't told her about the deaths of his wife and friends. There had to be. He continually pointed a finger at Justin Kingsley, but she couldn't yet accept that he was responsible simply because he had disappeared years before. Callum blamed a man who was not in a position to defend himself.

They ate breakfast at Knutsford service area on the M6. The conversation was a little stinted. Tara decided to leave it a while before going through her plans with Callum. A blazing row would only see them turning round at the next junction. She thought it best to give him some space for a while, difficult enough when they had to sit next to each other in the car. Soon though, she would start handing out the orders.

She treated him to coffee and muffins when they reached services on the M1. When they returned to her car it seemed as though a switch had flicked on in her head. Tara had prepared well for this investigation, and she was determined to make sure that Callum delivered on his side of the deal. She worked him hard all the way, going over questions for him to ask the people on her list, and playing out scenarios for when things got awkward. She insisted that he use her mobile to finalise appointments and to use the internet to check addresses and get directions. He protested at first, but at each of his protestations she had only to remind him why he was doing it in the first place. The number one objective of their quest, she told him, was to get justice for Tilly and Emily. So far, she had not resorted to threats of returning home before they'd even started. By the time they reached the M25, Callum had fallen into line, recognising that she was the boss, and that he had a long way to go before she would consider him a worthy assistant.

By one-thirty, having parked at Heathrow and taken the tube, they reached Chancery Lane where they entered a plain grey-stone building, the chambers of Emmett and Company. Callum explained to the receptionist that they wished to speak with Sir Edward Kingsley QC.

'I'm afraid that is quite impossible without an appointment,' said a pleasantly attractive woman in her forties.

'This is a personal matter regarding Sir Edward's son,' said Callum. The ash-blonde paused briefly, took a note of their names, asked Callum to wait then made a call.

* * *

Five minutes later, Daniel Jacobsen, a middle-aged man in a dark suit, white shirt and bold striped tie, emerged from a door behind the reception desk to greet them. Stocky rather than tall, he had a thick neck, shaved head and prominent nose. He told them in a polite but quite stern manner that a meeting with Sir Edward Kingsley was out of the question. Looking them up and down, he didn't seem impressed. Callum, despite his new clothing and clean face still looked washed out, while Tara wore a slim-fitting dress in navy with a cream bodice, a navy jacket, navy tights and three-inch heels. She'd brushed her hair with a centre parting, but still barely looked beyond the age of consent never mind whatever age one might consider a female detective inspector to be. Jacobsen seemed surprised, shocked even, when Tara addressed him.

'Mr Jacobsen, we have travelled quite some distance to speak with Sir Edward regarding the disappearance of his son Justin.'

'Miss Grogan, you have both told me your names, but that is all I know about you. Sir Edward is due in court this afternoon. At present, he is extremely busy, and I will not disturb him without good reason.'

'I'm a friend of his son Justin. I need to speak with Mr Kingsley,' Callum said.

The eyebrow of the clerk was definitely elevated by Callum referring to his boss as Mr Kingsley. Tara admired Callum for at least trying, but they were getting nowhere with Jacobsen. So much for keeping her professional role out of things.

'I'm Detective Inspector Tara Grogan, Merseyside Police.' She offered Jacobsen her warrant card. Taking it from her, he examined it closely, and a weak smile broke on his lips. Tara continued. 'We need to speak with Sir Edward in relation to his son's disappearance.'

'You're a long way from Liverpool, inspector.'

'There are lives at stake here, Mr Jacobsen.'

He seemed bemused by Tara's persistence, entertained, perhaps, by this slight pretty girl with an authoritative manner.

'Very well. I'll see what I can do. Please take a seat.'

They waited another five minutes until a young female clerk, with long fair hair, dark-framed glasses and clicky heels escorted them to the first floor of the chambers.

The narrow hallways were congested in places with clerks and barristers coming and going, many headed to afternoon sessions at court. Tara and Callum didn't make it as far as any office that might have belonged to Sir Edward Kingsley. Instead, the tall silver-haired QC stood in a cluttered outer office with Daniel Jacobsen at his side. Kingsley had a long, wrinkled face and looked around sixty-five, although his true age was only fifty-eight. His eyes were a weak shade of blue, but they glared at the two people standing before him.

'What is this about?' he asked without pleasantness, dispensing with introductions and handshakes.

Having revealed her identity as a police officer, Tara now took the lead. 'This is Callum Armour, Sir Edward. He was a friend of your son Justin when they were at Oxford.' Kingsley remained impassive. 'We were wondering if you have seen your son recently or perhaps know of his whereabouts?'

He glared at the senior clerk, Jacobsen.

'No. I have not. And I am wondering, inspector, what relevance that has for the Merseyside Police?'

Tara could see the end of her career screaming down from above. It was totally naïve to have thought this would be easy. Then Callum jumped in.

'My wife and daughter were killed three years ago, Mr Kingsley. Two friends from Oxford have been murdered recently. All of them were friends of Justin.'

'And?'

Tara took over, already convinced that they would get nothing from this man.

'We believe these deaths may be connected with your son's disappearance.'

Kingsley cut her off.

'Are you suggesting that my son is responsible for these deaths?'

Tara let that one hang for a moment. 'We are exploring that possibility. It would help us if we could speak to Justin.'

'Yes, I'm sure it would. But I repeat, inspector, that I have not seen my son. Now if you'll excuse me, I have more pressing matters to address.'

'I'll show you out,' said Jacobsen, a heavy frown on his face. Clearly, he would get his due chastisement later from his boss for having wasted his time.

'What could be more pressing than to find your son if he has been missing for the last ten years?' said Tara as they strolled towards Chancery Lane station. 'Did you notice that twice he said he hadn't seen his son? He didn't say he had no contact with him, that he hadn't spoken to him, or that he didn't know where he was.'

Reluctant to share with Callum, she realised Sir Edward Kingsley's response could well fit with the fact that his son was no longer listed as a missing person. Parents and son might well be in regular contact, but was Justin deliberately hiding from the rest of the world? If that were true, what were his motives for doing so?

The tightness in her stomach, she was sure, would be with her for the remainder of the weekend until she returned to work. There was no doubt in her mind that Sir Edward Kingsley was the kind of man who followed up on things. She was certain he would contact someone back home, the chief constable, for instance, and Tweedy would get to hear of it. Callum seemed all fired up to be finally involved in the hunt, but she had messed up badly right at the start. He had done well; she should have kept her mouth shut.

CHAPTER 24

Neither of them knew London particularly well. Tara had made several visits during her time at Oxford, and a couple of shopping trips with the girls since her return to Liverpool. Callum and Tilly had begun to pay more frequent visits, particularly after Tilly had been published, when she came up for meetings with agents and editors.

Tara thought they would be better off leaving the car outside the city and travelling in by train or tube, so she had parked at Heathrow, lifted a map from a tourist information stand and negotiated their way around the city using the Underground. They travelled from Chancery Lane to Tottenham Court Road and, from there, walked to Bedford Square, to a building housing the private offices of Georgina Maitland. At least this time they had something resembling an appointment, she thought. She worried now that Callum was over-optimistic that a woman who headed a business empire would spare the time to meet with an old chum from Oxford.

Already nervous about meeting Georgina Maitland, the experience at the chambers with Kingsley had her insides hopping and her head pounding. She managed to tidy her make-up, straighten out the creases in her dress and brush her hair, before Callum quite boldly strode to the front door of the terrace and pressed the buzzer. He seemed relaxed and curiously elated by the prospect of meeting his friend.

'Don't forget, Callum. This time, you really are on your own with Georgina. She can't be told that I'm a detective, understand?'

'I get you.'

When the buzzer sounded, allowing them to enter, he placed a hand on her back and guided her inside. Tara had imagined the place to be a frantic nerve centre of the Maitland business empire. Instead, she found the reception area in which they stood to be quiet and bright, with two girls seated either side of a sturdy old desk, one speaking on the telephone, the other working at a computer. Callum explained to the girl at the computer, a pleasant and plump redhead, who they were. She immediately lifted a telephone.

'Georgina, your friend Callum Armour is here,' she said in a slightly rounded but easily recognisable Glaswegian accent.

'Georgina is ready for you,' she said putting down the phone. 'If you'd like to follow me.'

The girl led them up a flight of stairs, clinically white from the walls to the balustrade, the starkness broken only by pieces of brightly coloured abstracts on the walls. She opened a panelled door, entered and held it open for Tara and Callum.

'Callum! My Belfast Boy!'

Tara was a bystander to the reunion as Georgina shuffled precariously in very high heels from the window, around her desk, to throw her arms over Callum.

'Hello, Georgina, it's good to see you.'

'I've missed you so much, darling.' They kissed on both cheeks and hugged tightly. 'Bring some tea please, Katrina.' The redheaded girl acknowledged the instruction with a smile and closed the door on her way out.

'Georgina, this is Tara Grogan, a good friend of mine.' Tara flushed instantly.

'Wonderful to meet you, Tara.'

'And you,' Tara replied. 'Callum has told me great things about you.'

Georgina's appearance could not have been further removed from what Tara had expected. Standing in her private office, and only for that fact, Tara would not have

135

picked Georgina out of a police line-up, or even judged her a runner-up in a Georgina Maitland lookalike contest. Tall and slender as she already knew, but painfully thin, unhealthily so. Long legs perched on blue shoes with enormous heels, she stood in a white smock tunic and white cropped leggings.

Georgina took hold of Callum's arm and sat him down on a studded brown-leather sofa. Tara was left to sit opposite in a club armchair. The office had a very traditional, antique feel about it, oak panelling and regal-looking wallpaper. Not the type of place she associated with this woman at all.

'It's so good to see you,' she said. 'I think about you every day, you know? And Tilly, of course.' Her expression rocked from sheer delight to chronic sadness and back again in a single breath. 'Poor Tilly, I miss her so much.' She smiled at Tara. 'But look, you have someone new... and beautiful.'

'No,' said Callum, jumping in hastily. 'It's not like that. We're just good friends.'

'Well, you need to get a move on. I'm sure Tara isn't going to wait on you forever. You need to let go, darling. Tilly would never have wished you to be on your own. And what do you do, Tara?'

The question came suddenly. She had to think of something.

'I work in promotions. In Liverpool. Concerts, shows, exhibitions, that kind of thing.' She reckoned Aisling wouldn't mind her borrowing her identity for a bit.

'Tara was at Latimer,' said Callum. Not what she would have wanted him to say next, but it was too late.

'Really? Same time as us?'

'No, I graduated six years ago.'

'My word. It's been ten years since we finished. Imagine that, Callum?'

There was a knock on the door, and Katrina entered carrying a large tray with silver teapot, china mugs, and rather spectacular-looking cupcakes with beautifully ornate decorations. She placed it on the coffee table between the sofa and Tara's chair.

'Thanks, honey,' said Georgina. The girl smiled and left without a word.

'So tell me, Callum, I was so excited when I heard you wanted to meet up. I haven't seen you since…'

'Tilly's funeral.'

'Yes. Worst day of my life.' She pulled a tissue from a wooden carved dispenser on the table and dabbed at her eyes. 'Sorry. I'm completely useless.'

She squeezed Callum's arm. He leaned towards her, kissing her gently on the cheek.

'I miss her so much, you know,' she said once more but directly at Tara. 'And to what do I owe this rare pleasure, my Belfast Boy?' Again, before anyone could reply, she rolled into another spiel. 'We gave him that name. Tilly, Charlotte and me – our Belfast Boy. You were like a new puppy that first day we met at Latimer. All alone, no one to talk to. Lucky we found you.'

Callum smiled. Embarrassed but admiring nonetheless. Tara could sense he was going over things in his head, hopefully preparing to ask the questions she had told him to.

'Did you hear that Peter Ramsey was killed?'

'Yes, poor Peter. Terrible thing to happen. It said in the papers the killing resembled the murder of Thomas Becket. Who would do such a thing?'

'There are a lot of very disturbed people out there,' said Tara, suddenly realising it sounded like something the police would say.

'Tony was devastated. Did you make it to the funeral?'

'Bit far for me,' Callum replied.

'We were both out of the country. I sent flowers.'

'Then Zhou Jian was killed in Switzerland.'

Georgina frowned, looking puzzled by the name, but Callum sensed her confusion. 'He was a friend of mine really.'

'Oh yes. I remember him. Didn't we call him our Beijing Boy to go with our Belfast variety?'

Callum smiled warmly.

'He was murdered, too, Georgina.'

'Really? How shocking. You don't think there's a connection by any chance? With Peter, I mean?'

'Four people are dead.'

'Four?'

'Tilly and Emily.'

'Oh, darling, I'm so sorry. Yes, of course, Tilly and little Emily. But that was a terrible accident.'

Tara watched Georgina closely; she wasn't so much overbearing as completely overpowering. But Callum sat in awe. How had he survived three years of her?

'I don't think so,' he said.

'But the inquest? It was declared an accident.'

'I think their deaths have something to do with Justin.'

'Justin?' Georgina laughed and placed her hand on Callum's thigh. Tara thought it quite nervous laughter. 'But he's been gone for at least ten years, darling.'

'That's why I've come to see you, to ask if you've seen or heard from him recently?'

'Please, Tara, help yourself to some tea. Callum, you should do mother.'

Callum duly obeyed and poured the tea into three delicate Aynsley mugs.

'Try a cupcake. It's part of my new range; they're very fruity.'

Callum helped himself, and Tara felt obliged to join in, choosing a cake with a pale green topping and a sprinkling of what appeared to be cranberry pieces.

'That's key lime and cranberry,' said Georgina, who refrained from eating her own fayre.

Tara hoped Georgina hadn't forgotten the answer to the question she seemed to be avoiding. But the bubbly woman happily took up the thread once again.

'I think about Justin often, but I've not seen or heard from him since the night he walked out.' She reached for another tissue. 'Sorry. I'm such a blub.' She did the eye-dabbing thing again. 'But why do you think Justin has something to do with these deaths?'

'I'm not sure,' Callum replied. 'Perhaps, a grudge of some kind.'

'The only person he could have a grudge against is me. How could you think he would ever harm Tilly? Anyone who ever met her would never wish to hurt her. If you believe that someone killed her, that it wasn't an accident, then it must have been a total stranger, a madman.'

She threw her arms over Callum, sobbing into his shoulder. When finally she released him, she attempted a change in subject. 'Tell me, what are you doing with yourself these days? You don't look at all healthy.'

'Not much. I went back home to Liverpool two years ago. My father was ill, and I needed to look after him. He passed away.'

'And since then? Are you still working on that Nobel prize?'

He smiled at her joke and shook his head.

'I've told you before; you can always come and work for me. I'll soon find plenty for those idle hands.'

Tara reckoned Callum had bottled out of asking any more probing questions. She decided to weigh in.

'We were wondering if you know of any reason why Justin left the way he did?'

Georgina glared icily at Tara, looking stunned by the pertinence of her question.

'We were all having a great time,' said Callum. 'Then he upped and left.'

Georgina bowed her head and fiddled with her crumpled tissue.

'Justin and I had broken up before then, Callum. I hadn't told anyone except for Tilly. I wasn't going to go on that blasted ski trip, but she insisted things would be fine. I'd thought Justin and I could still be friends.' She sighed heavily. 'Sometimes, you can't paper over the cracks.'

'Do you think that's why he left, because of your break-up?' Callum asked.

'To get back at me? Who knows? He didn't bother to leave a note or tell anyone where he was going.'

'Do you believe he is still alive?' Tara asked.

'What a marvellous girl you've found in Tara, Callum. Only a dear friend would take such interest in your past.' She proffered the teapot, but neither Tara nor Callum accepted. 'That's more than enough of all that tragedy. It's been really wonderful to see my Belfast Boy after such a long time. Please, Callum, think about my offer. It would be a fresh start for you, new beginnings and all that.'

Georgina got to her feet, and to Tara it signalled that their time was up. No matter how informal their meeting, it was still for Georgina a meeting.

'I would really have loved for us to get together this weekend – you, Tony, Charlotte, Ollie and me – but I'm afraid we're off to the country. Tony's family seat and all that aristocratic nonsense.'

Callum nodded and smiled, while Tara recalled something she'd read about Georgina. She also had some wealthy blood in her veins.

'I count myself lucky to be included in any of my husband's schedule these days. I thought I was the busy one. But can't look a gift horse and all that. Have to cherish our brief moments together. So, what are your plans, Callum? Are you staying in town for the weekend?' She glanced impishly at Tara.

'Actually, we were hoping to speak with Anthony. Thought you might be able to help on that score.'

'Oh dear. Hard to pin down these government ministers.' She looked deep in thought for a moment then caught hold of Callum, slipping her arms around his neck. Once again, Tara was the bystander. 'Look, we're supposed to be having dinner together this evening. It's a charity thing, celebs and all that tosh. Sorry I can't manage a ticket, but I'll try and steal Tony away before the thing starts, and maybe you can have a quick chat.'

'That would be great, Georgina, thanks.'

'Can't promise he'll shed any more light on the topic of Justin, but I'm sure he'd be delighted to see you again. Give me your number, and I'll call you.'

Since Callum did not possess a mobile phone, Tara wrote down her number on a sheet of Georgina Maitland personal stationery.

'Before you go, I have something for you, Tara.' Georgina went to her desk and retrieved a hard-bound book with her picture on the dust cover. 'My latest.' She quickly scribbled something on the first page and gave it to Tara. 'I hope you like it and perhaps find it useful.'

'That's very kind, thank you,' said Tara, opening the cover of *Live Your Life* to view Georgina's inscription. 'Best of Luck, Tara,' it read. Underneath she'd signed it 'Georgina.'

CHAPTER 25

Georgina was true to her word, and within an hour she had her PA Katrina call Tara with the address of a restaurant in Covent Garden and an exact time of ten to eight.

'We have a few hours to kill,' said Callum – a peculiarly different Callum. 'Do you think we can manage to get hold of Ollie Rutherford?'

They were retracing their steps to Tottenham Court Road station. Tara's feet were beginning to throb. High heels were more of a rarity for her these days. Thank goodness, she thought, for flat heels in her normal day job. If she still had a job by next week.

'I'll leave that decision to you,' she said curtly.

'What's wrong? Did you not like Georgina?'

'Well, I can see how she's got to the top in business, especially the lifestyle business. She was upbeat about everything, even when she was supposedly crying her eyes out. Hard to find that degree of optimism in my game.'

'She is great though.'

'She has the knack of controlling a conversation, except when I asked a question. She didn't like that. Did you see the look she gave me? And she managed to avoid answering.'

'We didn't learn much, but at least you got to meet her.'

It was going to be difficult getting Callum to say anything negative about Georgina, Tara thought.

'Actually, I think we've learned quite a lot,' she said to deliberately contradict him.

'You do? Like what?'

'I think we can be certain that Justin Kingsley is still alive?'

'Why do you say that?'

'Georgina's reluctance to answer the question. If she really believed Justin was dead, surely she had nothing to lose by saying so? If she believes that he is still alive but has nothing to back it up, considering they were close once, you'd think she would have jumped to defend her theory. Instead, she sidestepped the question completely. I think she knows that Justin is very much alive, but she doesn't want us to find him. And one more thing, as far as the UK police and Interpol are concerned, Justin Kingsley is not listed as a missing person. I don't know why, but I think he is merely lying low.'

'So therefore I'm right; he is the killer?'

'I didn't say that.'

She allowed Callum the use of her phone to contact Ollie Rutherford. By the time they'd reached the tube station, he'd arranged to meet up for drinks at a pub off Charing Cross Road. Apparently, Ollie was bound for an evening at the theatre with his girlfriend. Callum and Tara were welcome to join him in his pre-theatre drinks session.

When Callum returned her phone, she noticed there had been a flurry of activity: three missed calls and four texts. On the tube ride to Leicester Square, she scrolled through the text messages. The first was from Aisling, having heard from Kate that she, Tara, had gone off with that strange bloke from Treadwater. 'RU OK?' – was the main thrust of the message. The second one also came from Aisling. 'WAYN? WAYD? Where are you now? What are you doing?' The third text was Kate to say that she'd told Aisling, and Aisling wasn't pleased. The fourth message reminded her exactly what she was doing and why she was doing it. It came from DS Murray. The owner of the house rented to the Lithuanian girls on Stanley Road, including Audra Bagdonas, was none other than Teodor Sokolowski.

She replied to all of her messages, telling Aisling that she was fine and strolling around London. The missed calls she ignored; they, too, were from Aisling.

* * *

Ollie Rutherford was tall and very sure of himself. He looked Tara up and down with something akin to lurid mischief in his grey eyes.

'Delighted to meet you, Tara,' he shouted above the din of the pub, crammed with Friday evening revellers.

'Glad to see old Callum's got back on the bike, so to speak.'

On first impressions, Tara didn't like him. He was cocky, arrogant in the way he looked at people, her in particular, and the kind of man she most despised. He reminded her of someone she'd known at Oxford, and that hadn't ended well.

Callum and Ollie went off to battle their way to the bar, while Tara sat with Ollie's girlfriend, Stephanie. She was a brunette with close-cropped hair, slim, and wearing a short black dress revealing bleach-white skin and who seemed content to browse her phone and ignore her company. Tara hoped that Callum still realised the purpose of the meeting and had managed to put his rehearsed list of questions to Rutherford.

'Callum tells me you're looking into the deaths of our old mates,' said Rutherford, setting a glass of white wine and a bottle of Budweiser on their small round table.

By his remark, she wasn't sure if Callum had let slip about her being a police officer.

'Don't you think it's odd that three young people all graduates of Latimer College have died in tragic circumstances?' Tara asked.

'Absolutely.' He took a long drink from the bottle of beer.

Callum returned with a sparkling water for Tara and his pint of Guinness. Rutherford maintained a smile, aiming it directly at Tara. He was good-looking, she had to admit, with fair hair combed back on his head, although there were signs of a receding tidemark. She already knew him to have been a rower, and it appeared he had continued with some form of physical pursuit. She imagined a well-developed six-pack beneath his white shirt and red tie with a yellow pinstripe.

'Of course, I didn't know the Asian chap, what's his name? But Ramsey, silly sod, was at school with Hyde and me. Absolutely tragic.'

Stephanie seemed to exist only in parallel to her partner, such was the draw of Facebook, Twitter, or whatever forum she was currently engrossed in.

'Have you ever set eyes on Justin Kingsley since the night he disappeared?' Callum asked.

'Dead, surely?'

'We don't know for certain.'

'What did Georgina say? Her fault he scarpered in the first place. Strange chap, anyway, don't you think?'

'We were a strange bunch,' Callum replied. 'We weren't all mates together; more like we were just connected one with another.'

'You mean, like that actor chap – Kevin Bacon – six degrees of separation?'

Tara took to sipping her water. She was already wishing it was a pint of vodka. This guy irritated the heck out of her.

'I suppose so,' said Callum.

'Can you think of any reason why Justin would want to kill someone?' Tara asked.

'Same as the rest of us,' said Rutherford, putting the bottle to his lips. 'Rebellion,' he added after a swig. 'We all have something we'd like to put right, don't we?'

'We do not all commit murder,' she replied.

'True. But Kingsley had a lot going on in his head by the time he took his leave. Maybe now he feels he can change things that are wrong in his life by bumping people off.'

'I don't see a motive in what you say. What did he have going on when he disappeared?'

'His split with Georgina. I only heard about that afterwards.'

'Anything else?'

'His beef with his old man. Since he was a kid Justin was destined for the legal profession. It's what his father did, his mother and grandfather. Wouldn't be surprised if old granny had a slot in the Bailey, too.'

'You think that Justin felt pressured into becoming a lawyer? Did he have something else in mind?'

'Rowing, certainly. That's where I first met him, on the river. Interested in sailing, too. Not much of an academic when you think about it.'

'Why murder Tilly?' Tara asked.

Ollie Rutherford's face paled; his mouth fell open.

'Tilly?' He looked in horror at Callum. 'You think she was murdered? It was an accident surely? Is that why you're doing this, Callum?'

Callum told him about the card he'd received on the day Tilly died. Ollie looked sick.

'And you think Kingsley is the murderer?'

'He's a suspect,' said Tara.

'You sound like a copper,' said Rutherford. Tara didn't respond. 'If Justin murdered someone as sweet as Tilly, he would have no qualms about killing any one of us. Thanks, Callum, hell of a reunion.'

* * *

They took their leave of Ollie Rutherford, and his less talkative friend, and made their way to Covent Garden. It didn't take long to track down the brasserie in King Street where they were to meet with the Tory junior minister for the Department of Health, Anthony Egerton-Hyde. When they stepped inside the restaurant the maître d' asked if they had a reservation. It was clear to see that if they didn't, they had little chance of getting a table. Callum explained to the fraught-looking man, Italian by the sound of him, that they were intending to meet with Anthony Egerton-Hyde. He disappeared into the dining room, and a few moments later returned and briefly addressed them.

'He is coming,' he said, his attention already switching to another couple waiting beside them.

Tara noticed a tall man, in a dark suit and cream shirt without a tie, his sandy hair thinning on top, weaving his way through the tables towards them. She spotted Georgina at the back of the restaurant chatting with five others, three women and two men seated around a circular table. Her appearance had changed since their meeting earlier in the day, the white top replaced with a black and silver affair and long sparkling earrings. Suddenly,

Georgina appeared to gaze sternly at Tara. It wasn't entirely hostile, but Tara got the feeling that if they were to meet again alone Georgina might not be the jovial host she portrayed when they'd first met. The two women stared at each other until Tara heard the man speaking.

'Callum, so good to see you. Must be two years since we last met.'

'Three,' Callum replied, shaking the politician's hand keenly. 'This is Tara, a friend of mine.'

'Delighted to meet you, Tara. Sorry it has to be brief, but I hope Georgie explained? It's really a business dinner with a few friends, all for a charity we support.'

'It's OK, we understand,' said Callum. 'Thanks for sparing the time.'

'Georgie tells me you have a theory about the deaths of our old chums?'

Like any government minister, he had been briefed prior to his meeting. Georgina, Tara surmised, had probably told him to play down the conspiracy theories.

She let Callum tell his story, while she watched Egerton-Hyde's reactions. They stepped outside, it being much quieter in the street than inside the restaurant. Tara could see why Georgina would find this man attractive. He was tall, well-spoken and supremely confident. She'd read somewhere in the last few days that he was tipped for high office. Already, he was one of the youngest men in the present government. A junior minister at thirty-one. Georgina and Anthony were a highly-rated pair. She watched him, while Callum explained his concern about the re-emergence of Justin Kingsley. At first, Anthony showed little emotion in his fine features but he did appear to take what Callum was saying seriously. His response, however, was much the same as they'd heard from Georgina and Ollie Rutherford.

'But why would Justin want to harm any of them, Callum? They were his friends, except for the Chinese chap – none of us knew him that well.'

'I can't explain it either,' said Callum. 'But Latimer College and Justin's disappearance are the only things that connect all of the killings.'

'Ollie Rutherford suggested that Justin may be aggrieved from his break-up with Georgina,' said Tara, past caring whether any of these people felt she was poking her nose in where it didn't belong.

'Really? If that's the case then maybe he's out to get me? After all, I married Georgina. But that's ridiculous; we didn't get together until after we left Oxford. That was ages after Justin disappeared.'

'The deaths are connected in some way, Anthony. I can feel it. Justin is the only person shrouded in mystery.'

'Bit unfair, though. The chap's not around to defend himself. He may well be dead.'

'If we can prove that he is dead then we'll have to look elsewhere for our murderer.'

Anthony looked quite shaken by this remark. His fixed smile ebbed away. They'd given him something other than the affairs of government to think about. Tara wondered how much of the subject had he discussed with his wife.

'I'm sorry that I have to cut this short. Unfortunately, Georgina and I are heading to the country for a few days, or we could have met up again. What are you going to do now, Callum? Have you a plan of action to find Justin?'

'Nothing much beyond meeting up with you guys,' Callum replied. 'We're going down to Canterbury tomorrow to see where Peter was killed. Hopefully, we can speak with some of his colleagues. And I want to visit Charlotte on Sunday.'

'Charlotte? Do you think she'll be able to help?'

Tara sensed some alarm in Egerton-Hyde's voice.

'She's the only surviving person we have yet to see,' Callum replied.

'What do you mean, the only surviving person?'

'If Justin is responsible for all of this, I think it has something to do with the people who were together on the ski trip to Austria in our final year. Apart from Georgina, Ollie, you and me, with Peter, Jian and Tilly gone, that leaves only Charlotte. If Justin is the killer, one of us, or perhaps all of us, have wronged him in some way.'

'Or else he's completely lost his mind,' said Anthony.

They paused on that thought for a moment. Then Anthony turned his attention towards Tara.

'Georgie tells me that Callum has found himself a girl at last. She didn't say she was a raving beauty.'

Tara realised she was supposed to blush, maybe curtsey, too, at the charm of Egerton-Hyde, but her thoughts were with Georgina and the reason behind her cold stare a few minutes earlier. She was faintly aware of shaking the hand of Egerton-Hyde before he retraced his steps into the restaurant. She wondered what Aisling would make of the likes of him. Of course, she would revel in the company of a staggeringly upper-class man, but would she be taken in by such brazen charm? She smiled at the thought that Aisling probably would. She, however, was not convinced of the man's sincerity. He and Georgina seemed an odd pairing.

CHAPTER 26

Neither one felt like saying much after Egerton-Hyde had departed. They found a pizzeria further along King Street and had a quick bite to eat. Tara was bemused by her companion. It was getting late. They were seated in a restaurant in the centre of London, her car parked at Heathrow, and he had yet to ask where they would spend the night. It seemed to be a case of 'she's paying, she can decide where we go.' Of course, she knew exactly what they were going to do. If he was quietly wondering about where he would sleep, she wouldn't put him at ease by telling him.

It was close to ten when they began making their way back to Heathrow. After collecting her car, she drove a short distance then pulled into the car park of a Holiday Inn. A day earlier, while at work in St Anne Street station, she had booked two rooms on-line. She was amazed that even as she checked them both in at the hotel reception, he never once said thank you or well done. It was like he expected it. He would probably have argued that it was her idea to come to London anyway. She bid him goodnight, leaving him with instructions to meet her at nine for breakfast.

* * *

He was excited at seeing his friends, particularly Georgina, after such a long time. He hadn't set eyes on any of them since the funeral. In the year that followed Tilly and Emily's passing, Georgina and Charlotte had kept in contact by telephone and by writing letters. Once he'd returned to Liverpool, the contact amounted to Christmas cards and a brief note close to the anniversary of the tragedy. His fault entirely. He'd shut himself off from the rest of the world in his home on Treadwater Estate. People soon give up on you once you stop returning calls and don't respond to letters, and repeatedly turned down invitations.

He lay on his back in the dark, the double bed feeling great after a long day of driving, walking, jumping on and off the tube; the whole time having to think about Justin Kingsley and whether his old friends really believed what he'd told them. They hadn't gained much, although Tara now seemed convinced that he was right about Justin. He got the impression also that she harboured suspicions about Ollie, Georgina, Charlotte and Anthony. Keeping her options open, he supposed, was part of a detective's training.

He'd enjoyed spending the day with her. She'd taken charge of all the travel arrangements and dictated the questions he had to ask his friends. He liked her taking control. She was so like Tilly bossing him around, although Tara was much more serious with it. Apart from her hair colour she bore some resemblance to Tilly – her height, or lack of it, her childishly young face, large eyes and peeved expressions. Despite those similarities, he had yet to see her laugh. Tilly, especially, had an infectious laugh. But isn't that what they say? You choose your next lover because they remind you of the one you've just lost.

* * *

She lay on the double bed, her head resting on three pillows, the first novel by Tilly Reason open in her right hand. Tilly's widower was one floor below and several rooms away. *The First Form Time Travellers,* written for children, made for light reading. She hoped it might distract her from thinking about all those people she'd met today and the others she had discussed. Foolishly, she wondered if she might discover a clue to the identity of the killer concealed in the narrative, a secret code or hidden meaning tucked away in the plot. Just as quickly she realised that life was never that simple. The solution to this mystery would not be handed to her on a plate.

She felt exhausted but, oddly, not at all drowsy. The television on the wall above the dresser showed the BBC News Channel, but she had long since muted the sound in the hope of dozing off. It was much too late to phone Kate, especially if she had to rise for an early shift at the Royal. She sent her a text stating that she was in her room, alone, and things had gone well during the day. She repeated the same to Aisling who called within seconds of receiving it.

'Are you sure you're OK?'

'I'm fine, Aisling, really. I've discovered that Callum is at least bearable as long as you tell him exactly what to do.'

'Isn't that true of all men?'

Ending the call, she tossed her phone on the bed, setting the novel to the side and picking up the heavy volume Georgina had given her: *Live Your Life*, the title in huge gold letters. The collage of photos of Georgina, highlighted the lifestyle choices to be discussed within. The tag line below the title read, 'A template for the modern woman'. Tara leafed through it briefly then settled on the contents page. Each chapter was devoted to lifestyle choices: fashion, health and fitness, work-life balance, marriage, family commitments, friendships and everything a thirty-something woman needs to feel fulfilled, including sex tips. Continuing to browse, she noticed the chapters were liberally sprinkled with biographical information about the author. Georgina was the daughter of a wealthy businessman and a 1970s fashion model and raised in Hampshire with her younger brother and two older sisters.

Further on, she found a graduation photograph, taken on the lawn outside Latimer Chapel. Tara had one similar to it. There were references to her marriage to the up-and-coming Anthony Egerton-Hyde, Tory MP and heir to the Egerton-Hyde seat in Norfolk. Georgina explained how she juggled a frantic business career with love and devotion to her husband, although, Tara noted, the sex tips did not appear in this section. With greater interest, she read Georgina's views on raising a family. The author expressed the desire to have children at some point in the next few years. This formed part of a discussion on when it is best for a professional woman to have children, regurgitating, Tara thought, the well-worn debate on women who leave such matters too late.

An hour passed with reading. She'd even ventured into the section on sex tips and had to admit there might be some things worth learning. She could have a laugh over this with Kate and Aisling when she got home. Switching off the bedside lamp, but keeping the television on, she lay down hoping to sleep.

As her eyes began to rest, her mind suddenly returned to thoughts of why she had embarked on this investigation, this quest on behalf of Callum Armour. She needed to find out more about the relationships between the students captured in the photo from the ski trip ten years ago. Somehow, those people held the key to Kingsley's disappearance. Maybe one of them knew why he had returned, apparently, intent on murder. As sleep finally arrived, her last thought gave her an uneasy feeling. She would have preferred that Callum had not told Egerton-Hyde of their plans to visit Canterbury and of their intention to meet with Charlotte Babb.

CHAPTER 27

Breakfast was a strained affair. Callum showed up late, dressed again in his new clothes but unshaven.

'What's wrong?' he asked when he noticed her frowning at him.

'What happened to your effort to remain tidy?'

'Not meeting anyone today, are we? And you're not exactly dressed as you were yesterday.'

She wore a leopard-print stretch top and slim-fit jeans. This guy was all charm. There was only so much she could take. He'd lost his wife and child, understandably devastating, but was he going to live the rest of his life being rude because every day he wanted to play the victim?

'No one specific,' she replied. 'But if you do not return to your room and make yourself a bit more presentable, I am out of here right now. Alone!'

He looked at her, but she stared him out.

'Can I have breakfast first?'

Demonstratively, she looked at her watch. 'You've got five minutes to do as I ask. You decide if you have time for breakfast. We're already late as it is.'

* * *

An hour later they were on the M25, anticlockwise, headed for Kent. Her frustration with Callum continued to simmer. That combined with his apparent sulk resulted in a lack of meaningful discussion of the case. Case? First time she had thought of it as such. She was in for so much trouble when she returned home, she hardly dared think about it. But she was fast running out of sensible things to consider. She switched on the CD player and let rip with the Foo Fighters, hoping it would annoy the hell out of him. What had Tilly Reason ever seen in him?

She had followed the signs for the cathedral, but found herself on a road that seemed to encircle the old city. Eventually, she chose one of several signs indicating a car park and drove into a long strip of pay-and-display spaces beneath the city walls. On foot, they turned right into Burgate and five minutes later stood admiring the magnificent Christ Church Gate.

Tara paid for them to pass through the gate into the cathedral precincts. It was impossible not to look upwards, even as she wasted little time in entering the glorious building. She had come here, firstly, to get a view of the murder scene, although she doubted it would tell her much and, secondly and more importantly, to find someone who had known Peter Ramsey well. Conducting a police-style interview was, of course, out of the question. She was certain that Kent Police, and in particular Detective Inspector Iain Barclay, had performed a thorough investigation. Any friends or colleagues of Ramsey were likely to have already endured a police interview. They would certainly wonder why a Liverpool cop was interested in the case. She already knew the circumstances of the murder, but what she hoped to gain was information on Peter Ramsey: the kind of man he was and what motive anyone could have for taking his life.

Entering the nave by the south-west door, she lifted a guide leaflet and soon identified the location of the Martyrdom. Callum wandered off into the nave. She would have preferred him to stay close by in case they came across someone who knew Peter Ramsey but she let him go. Maybe he could do just that on his own. It might save her the trouble of pretending to be his friend.

Comparison stories on the murders of Peter Ramsey and Thomas Becket had been rife. It had been open season for press speculation; it sold newspapers. From where she stood in the Martyrdom, it was difficult to imagine any murder ever having taken place. A man and woman, in their early twenties, gazed upon the spot where it was believed Thomas Becket, Archbishop of Canterbury, had perished in 1170. They inspected a small bouquet of flowers, carnations and chrysanthemums, lying close to the floor tile marked 'Thomas'. Tara read the notes on her leaflet on the murder of Becket, wondering about the comparison made to Peter Ramsey. She paused on the supposed words of Henry II, 'Who shall rid me of this meddlesome priest?' Four of his knights had duly obliged. Had Ramsey been regarded by someone as a meddlesome priest? When the couple moved on, Tara examined the small card attached to the flowers. It read simply, 'In remembrance of Peter Ramsey.'

Emerging from the Martyrdom, she spied Callum standing on the crossing above the nave, close to the Quire entrance, in conversation with a man dressed in a black cassock. As she approached them Callum turned and smiled, holding his hand out to her.

'This is my friend Tara,' he said.

The man smiled warmly. He looked about forty, sturdily built, the leather belt around his waist a little strained. He had light brown hair, curling and drooping over his ears, and he wore gold-rimmed glasses.

'Very nice to meet you, Tara,' he said, in a sedate voice and offering his hand. 'I'm Stephen Hadleigh, Canon Pastor.'

'Hello,' Tara replied, feeling her hand caressed in his gentle grip.

'May I ask if you are from the press? We have had so many reporters here, inquiring about Peter. I don't think we can say much more about the tragic event.' The man looked nervously from Tara to Callum and back to her.

She decided that he deserved the absolute truth. Besides, she wouldn't feel right telling fibs inside a church. Callum seemed to wait for her lead.

'No, Stephen, we're not from the press. I am a police detective, but I'm not assigned to the murder investigation in any way.'

Removing her warrant card from her handbag, she gave it to him. He studied it for a few seconds before handing it back.

'Why are the Merseyside Police interested in Peter?'

'They're not. I'm here only as Callum's friend. He knew Peter well from their time at Oxford.'

'I just wanted to see where he died,' said Callum. 'And to speak to someone who knew him during his time here.'

'Oh, I see.' Hadleigh did not appear entirely convinced. He looked Callum up and down, perhaps wondering, Tara thought, that Callum didn't seem like an Oxford graduate. She could only imagine what he would have thought if he'd seen him a few days earlier. Navy trousers, heavily creased, and a casual striped shirt, he didn't look particularly dapper.

'My wife died three years ago. She also knew Peter at Oxford.'

'Ah, might that have been the author Tilly Reason?'

'Yes, it was Tilly. Our daughter Emily died at the same time.'

'I'm so sorry for your loss. Peter was very upset by the news. He was living with us at the time, my wife Alice and our two children.'

'Stephen, this may sound very peculiar,' said Tara, 'but we believe there may be a connection between Tilly's death and Peter's.'

'Goodness me. But if I remember correctly, Callum, your wife died in a car accident?'

'I think she was murdered.'

'But why? What possible connection?' Hadleigh was looking at Tara.

'We don't know,' she said. 'There's been a third murder, another of Callum's friends from Oxford. His name was Zhou Jian. Do you recall Peter mentioning the name?'

Hadleigh shook his head, deep in thought or deep in shock.

'I realise the local police are investigating Peter's murder,' Tara continued, 'but can you think of any reason why someone would want to kill him?'

'No, absolutely not. Peter was such an easy-going chap. He didn't take life too seriously. Strange, you might think, for someone in our profession but it was part of his charm, the reason why he related so well to the people who come here.'

'Did he ever mention the name Justin Kingsley?' Callum asked.

Tara inwardly applauded his question.

His gaze to the floor, Hadleigh again shook his head. Then he looked at his watch.

'I'm not entirely the best person to answer your questions, but if you have a few moments I could call Alice, get her to come over. She and Peter used to natter away over coffee every morning after service. If you give me fifteen minutes, we could meet up at the coffee shop just outside Christ Church Gate.'

* * *

Twenty-five minutes later, Stephen and Alice Hadleigh entered Starbucks and joined Tara and Callum at a table by the window, looking out to the war memorial in the ancient square. Stephen had cast off his clerical attire and wore a check shirt with short sleeves and beige trousers. Alice Hadleigh, a slightly plump lady in a green flowery dress, had thick curly hair and a round face. She smiled instantly and offered her hand to Tara as her husband introduced them. Once they were settled with mugs of coffee, Alice, in a cheery voice, took up the reins of the conversation.

'You were asking about Peter? He spoke of you several times, Callum.'

'We were wondering,' Callum replied, 'if he ever mentioned Justin Kingsley?'

Alice nodded several times as if she fully appreciated the implications of the question.

'Yes, he did, many times. Peter cherished his days at Oxford. Happiest days of his life, he often said. Particularly, Callum, after your wife died, he never stopped talking about college. Peter wasn't one for looking on the dark side of things, but he often wondered what had become of this Justin Kingsley. He thought it strange that he'd lost two friends from his college days at such young ages. He appeared very fond of Tilly. He used to read her books to our children.'

'Did he believe that Justin was dead?' Tara asked.

'Yes, I think so.'

'Did he ever mention anyone he thought might do him harm?'

'Not to me.'

'Anything that may have troubled him?'

'Nothing except for the obvious.'

Stephen Hadleigh sat back from the discussion with a deep-set frown on his smooth face.

'The obvious?' asked Tara.

Alice looked at Callum with some degree of surprise.

'Stephen doesn't like to speak of such things, but Peter was gay.'

Tara glanced at Callum for some corroboration, but he looked as surprised as she did.

'He didn't have a partner, or anything like that. Certainly not since he came to Canterbury but he did tell me that it was highly unlikely that he would ever marry.'

'That doesn't make him gay, Alice,' said her husband, sitting with arms folded, clearly finding the conversation very uncomfortable.

'I know that, darling, but Peter did tend to confide in me. He told me once over coffee that physical love, particularly with women, held no attraction for him. And there were the letters.'

'Letters?' Tara repeated.

'Yes. Peter lived with us for most of the time he was here. He only moved to his own flat about six months before he died. He left behind a few boxes and things that he didn't have room for in his new place. We still had them when he was killed.'

'We thought we should go through the stuff and send anything important to his parents in Gloucester,' said Hadleigh.

Alice waited for her husband to finish speaking, but clearly she wanted to be the one to explain.

'I found a bundle of letters tucked away in a cardboard box. Most were simply correspondence he'd gathered over the years. He had a pen-pal in New Zealand since he was nine years old. Isn't that amazing? Anyway, there were a few letters from his pen-pal, a few from his sister at home and at least a dozen from a friend at Oxford. They were quite intimate in places. And then, in the most recent of the letters, there seemed to have been some disagreement or break-up. It wasn't entirely clear.' Alice ceased talking and took a sip of her coffee.

'Do you know who that person is?' Tara asked.

Alice Hadleigh shifted position on the leather sofa, her bright face suddenly fraught with the realisation of what she was about to say.

'Stephen told me that you are not working officially on this case, Tara. And that you, Callum, believe there is a connection between Peter's death and that of your wife?'

'That's right,' Callum replied, 'and also with the murder of Zhou Jian in Switzerland. He was a good friend of mine.'

'Oh, my Lord. What is going on?'

'Mrs Hadleigh,' said Tara, 'do you know who wrote those letters to Peter?'

'Stephen felt we should pass them on to the police, you know. In case they were of use in their investigation. They were from a long time ago, ten years or more, I'm sure.'

'Can you tell me the name, Mrs Hadleigh?'

Alice Hadleigh stared into her coffee. It seemed she had tuned herself out of the conversation.

'Alice dear, please answer the question for these good people,' said her husband, his hand set on her lap, his expression now strained.

'All the letters were merely signed, Eggy,' she said. 'I'm sure you can guess, Callum?'

'Anthony Egerton-Hyde.'

CHAPTER 28

'I thought you were an intelligent man, Callum. Still, at every turn I get surprises.'

'I didn't think it was relevant.'

They were seated in her car, still parked below Canterbury's city walls. Tara was damned if she was driving anywhere until she had it out with him.

'I'm the cop. I'm the one who decides what is relevant. I asked you to tell me everything connected to your friends at Oxford.'

'I didn't know that Peter had a thing going with Anthony. As far as I was concerned, they were mates. They went to the same school. You know what they say about those public schools?'

'You didn't know Peter Ramsey was gay?'

'No. I don't think anyone did.'

'Well it seems that Egerton-Hyde was well aware of it. Can't you see what this means?'

'Those letters were from a long time ago. Alice said there was nothing recent passing between Peter and Anthony.'

'At least two of the letters, Alice said, were written after they graduated from Oxford. It's a motive, Callum. A possible reason why Peter was murdered.'

'You're suggesting that Anthony Egerton-Hyde is the killer, not Justin?'

'It is possible. You've directed all your attention at Kingsley. He disappeared ten years ago. No one seems to know why. But you've branded him a murderer. Anthony Egerton-Hyde is a public figure. He's married to a famous woman. If he's never admitted to being in a gay relationship, do you think he would want it to come out now?'

'But he always joked about finding a beautiful filly to produce his heir and to run his family seat. He was always fondling the girls. And what about Tilly? And Jian? Why kill them?'

Tara had to admit she had no ideas on that score.

'Callum, there doesn't appear to be any reason whatsoever why Kingsley or Egerton-Hyde would have killed Jian. It's cheap to say it, but maybe it's not connected to the other deaths. Jian was under threat at home in China. He'd crossed a lot of people in what he published about food safety. You told me that yourself.

You've heard of these Chinese mafia gangs. It isn't difficult in this day and age for his murder to be arranged, even in a country like Switzerland.'

'And what about Tilly and Emily?'

'Were you ever threatened or felt you were in any danger because of your job? Jian and you worked on the same projects.'

Callum shook his head.

'Our kind of research had a much lower profile in the UK than in China. We discovered traces of toxins and chemicals that shouldn't be in our food, but at most it amounted to product recalls, a few court cases and fines. It was bigger news in China. Company directors were jailed or even executed for causing widespread health issues in food. I suppose Jian definitely rattled a few cages there.'

'Is it possible that someone who had been affected by your work set out to get back at Jian and you?'

'You mean someone killed Tilly and Emily to get at me? Someone who didn't like the research I was doing?'

'I'm just asking you to consider the possibility. Did you ever receive threats?'

He shook his head once again.

'No, except for the sympathy card. And your theory doesn't explain who killed Peter. He had nothing to do with Jian's work or mine.'

She placed her left hand on top of his right; he was warm to the touch. She felt his frustration, saw the despair in his eyes as they watered. She wanted to hold him, to help him break free of his deep cycle of anger, confusion, loneliness and more anger. He pulled his hand away.

'No. You're wrong. I don't know what happened to Jian or Peter. But I do know that my Tilly was murdered. I don't have a motive. I don't have any proof that it was Justin, but it always seemed to me a logical place to start.' He wiped his eyes with the back of his hand.

* * *

Morning promise of a sunny day became the reality of a wet afternoon. An incessant drizzle sprayed the car as they drove around the M25 towards their hotel at Heathrow. Little was said. Callum fell in and out of a sleep, his head rolling as the car slowed in traffic, jerking awake when Tara braked hard. She tried to think of the next move, but she arrived repeatedly at the same conclusion that her explanation to Callum was correct. It would be a matter for the Kent Police to establish a link between Peter Ramsey and Anthony Egerton-Hyde. She wondered if Georgina Maitland had any involvement in trying to protect her husband's reputation. It might explain her cold expression at the restaurant.

She might be completely wrong about Egerton-Hyde, or Callum could be right about Justin Kingsley, but where did they go from here? He had arranged a meeting for Sunday with Charlotte Babb, the one remaining living person from Callum's photograph she had yet to meet. According to Callum, she had continued living in Oxford after she graduated from Latimer College. Hers might be an interesting take on the fate of this group of friends.

Suddenly Callum sprang to life in the car, awake and studying the road signs along the motorway.

'Do you mind if we go somewhere? It's not far from here. Come off at the next junction.'

It seemed she had little choice than to meet his request. The sign ahead on the M25 indicated Junction 10 for Guildford.

'Where are we going?'

'If you pull into the next garage. I want to buy something.'

She found his dryness hard to take. Not once had he asked how she felt. Was she tired from driving? Did she enjoy being a cop? How was her time at Oxford? Did she have a boyfriend? And did he appreciate her for running off to London to help some down-and-out with daft notions of killings and conspiracy theories? He knew nothing about her and showed no interest in her whatsoever.

Keeping her patience, she pulled into a service station. She checked the fuel gauge and noticed she could do with topping up with petrol. While she was filling the car at the pump, he got out and strode across the forecourt. She watched him as he browsed a rack of flowers by the window of the shop. By the time she was heading over to pay he was already inside.

'What number was the pump?' he called out as she entered.

'Six,' she replied, rocked suddenly by the realisation that he was actually about to pay for something.

'Thank you,' she said as they walked back to the car together. Although he'd paid for the fuel, she had bought a pack of crisps, a bottle of water and a *Hello* magazine.

'No problem,' he said, clutching two bunches of flowers, one of red roses, the other pink carnations. 'All they had,' he said, showing her what he'd bought.

'Where are we going?'

'It's not far. I want to show you where they are buried.'

He directed her off the A3 to Guildford and into open countryside. Within a mile or so, she saw a churchyard directly ahead, located by a fork in the road.

'This is it,' he said, still clasping his flowers.

There was a short lay-by with one car parked, but there was ample space for her to pull in behind. Thankfully, the rain had ceased. They both got out, and Callum walked ahead up a short lane bordering the churchyard. He opened a wooden gate, and they entered. Tara read the sign with gold lettering on a blue background: 'Church of St Nicholas'. She had guessed at the year of its foundation, but was astounded to discover she was out by more than three hundred years. This tiny church, with a high roof and stone tower, was as old as England itself if you regarded the Norman Conquest as the start of it all.

She followed Callum as he passed by the main door, set within the tower, and skirted around the side of the building. Once at the rear, he began zig-zagging his way through the gravestones. The beech trees growing close to the building and casting shade over the graveyard soon gave way to a brighter open space. He stopped on a rise above the road where it was possible to see for some distance over the surrounding fields. Tara, twenty yards off, came to a halt when she saw him drop to his knees. She watched, allowing him time alone, his head bowed over a grave. When she thought it appropriate, she came towards him, hearing his sobs, his shoulders rising and falling in a grievous rhythm.

The headstone seemed as old as the others scattered around, but it held a recent inscription. 'Tilly Reason aged twenty-eight years and daughter Emily Armour aged eighteen months.' Instinctively, she placed her hands on his shoulders, his pain running through her like a discharge of electricity. She squeezed him gently and, still on his knees, he turned his body into hers. She fought back tears as he clutched at her waist. The flowers lay on the ground, dropped, not placed.

See the victim, and you won't stop searching for the killer. Words spoken to her when she'd viewed her first murder scene. Today it was merely a gravestone, but the names upon it and the grief of the man kneeling before it gave rise to the same intention. Having seen where Tilly and Emily lay, she realised that she couldn't stop looking for their killer.

CHAPTER 29

When Callum got to his feet, Tara took his arm and walked him slowly back through the gravestones, around the church and down to her car.

He spoke in a weak voice. 'I'm sorry if I embarrassed you, me crying like that.'

'It's all right, Callum. No need to apologise.'

They rested their bodies against the car, looking back towards the church. Despite the dampness of the day, the air remained warm and still. She wished for a breeze to blow to help refresh their mood.

'She was baptised in this church – confirmed and married, and Emily was also christened here. Hatches, matches and despatches, my dad used to say. I suppose, while I'm here, I should pay a visit to my in-laws, if you don't mind?'

'Not at all.'

'It's not far.' He nodded up the road. 'We can walk from here.'

A hundred yards further along the road, past a village shop, formerly the post office, they came to a sweet-looking old house. It sat back from the road and was separated from it by a mixed hedge of laurel and golden privet. Several healthy rose bushes of pinks and yellows framed the ground-floor windows, and in the centre of the lawn a multi-armed bird feeder was the focus of attention for a solitary house sparrow. A glazed-metal plaque, black with white lettering and fixed to the right-hand gatepost, identified the house as St Nicholas' Vicarage. The Reverend Timothy Reason answered the chime of the bell.

Opening the door, he stepped back in what Tara regarded as a mixture of pleasant surprise and immediate unease.

'Callum! What on earth? Come in, come in.'

The vicar showed no outward signs of his profession. He stood in one of those American college-style sweatshirts, grey with 'Track and Field' across the chest in white, although the print was badly faded. He wore jeans holed in several places about the knees and a pair of leather slippers. He had brown hair fighting in all directions and turning silver at the sides. His eyes seemed friendly, peering down his nose through a pair of flimsy-looking reading frames.

'Hello, Tim, sorry for turning up without warning, but we were passing.' Tim stared intently at Tara, which prompted Callum to quickly introduce her. 'This is Tara Grogan.'

'How do you do, Tara?' He shook hands with her then stepped backwards. 'Come in, come in,' he repeated.

He led them down a darkened hallway into a lounge at the back of the house with a huge picture window providing a view of a well-maintained lawn with several trees and a vegetable patch at the far end. The room looked well-worn, lived-in and homely. The walls were adorned randomly, it seemed, with photographs, paintings and sketches, and two sturdy bookcases filled the recesses either side of the chimney breast.

'Sit down, please,' said Tim. 'Make yourself comfortable. Jenny is out the back somewhere.' He shouted at the open door through which they had just entered. 'Jenny?'

Tara and Callum sat together on a wide sofa awash with cushions. Neither one was immediately conscious of how it looked to an outsider that they were seated together as a couple. Tim had returned to an armchair with a matching footstool upon which lay a copy of *The Daily Telegraph*. A large television in the far corner of the room was switched on with the sound muted. It appeared that Sri Lanka were playing England at Trent Bridge in a one-day match and required sixty-eight runs to win.

'Passing by, you said?'

'Yes,' Callum replied. 'We were down at Canterbury. Just on our way back to our hotel at Heathrow.'

'Right, right,' said Tim, his eyes seldom leaving the face of Tara, who tried her best to maintain a smile without looking demented. 'Glad to see you looking well, Callum. That you're getting on with things.'

'And how have you been?' Callum replied.

'Oh, I'm fine, but not too enamoured by our British summer. Plays havoc with the garden and the cricket.' He gestured at the TV screen.

A reliance on discussing the weather signalled that the conversation between father and son-in-law was already floundering. Tara sensed the growing awkwardness, but realised also that Callum had told her nothing about Tilly's parents. Did they get on with Callum? Did he like them? They seemed the most relevant questions. Callum didn't look terribly comfortable, but maybe that was down to her sitting close beside him, the significance of which he may have just realised.

'Have you been to the grave?'

'Yes. Left some flowers.'

'Good, good. Quite bright on that side of the church this time of year.'

Callum nodded agreement. His questions were gradually cutting all lines of communication, but Timothy Reason had someone to help relieve the tension.

'So, what do you do, Tara?'

Conscious of hesitating, for the second time today, she had no option but the truth.

'I'm a police officer.'

'In Liverpool? My, my, that must be an interesting job.'

'There's plenty of work for us to do.'

'Yes, of course. I'm sure there is.'

At that point an attractive woman, of similar height to Tara, in loose gardening clothes, appeared at the threshold. Her apparent confusion at being summoned by her husband evaporated on seeing she had visitors.

'Callum!'

He stood immediately, and she came towards him with her arms wide. They hugged then kissed on both cheeks.

'How are you, Jenny?'

'I'm fine,' Jenny replied already smiling at Tara, who noticed instantly the close resemblance between the woman and the photograph she remembered of Tilly. 'And who have you brought with you?'

The question sounded a little strange to Tara, as if it contained a hint of suspicion or even jealousy. After all, this was her son-in-law, a widower, here to visit his in-laws with another woman in tow.

'This is Tara, a good friend of mine.'

Tara felt elevated once again to the position of good friend.

'Hello, Tara, very nice to meet you. This man is a dark horse, you know? We hear nothing from him for months, and then he turns up at our door unannounced and with a new girl at his side, a lovely one at that.' There were slight tears in her eyes as she spoke. 'Tim, didn't you organise tea?'

'I was just about to.'

'Have you been to the grave?'

'Yes, Jenny. We've just come from there,' said Callum.

Once more the awkwardness descended upon the room.

'So, what have you been doing these last few months?' She asked Callum the question but, in the same manner as her husband had done, fixed her eyes on Tara.

'Nothing much.'

Jenny sat on the arm of another sofa, wringing her hands nervously.

'Sarah's still up in London,' she added, clearly struggling to find something worthwhile to say. 'That's Tilly's younger sister,' she said directly to Tara.

Timothy Reason looked at his wife and smiled sympathetically. 'Why don't you show Tara the garden,' he said, 'and while you're at it make some tea? Callum and I can watch the rest of the game?'

Tara was treated to a perfunctory tour of the gardens at the rear of the vicarage. Jenny named the plants and shrubs, while Tara affirmed their beauty. Tara observed a woman full of nerves. Maybe it was due to Callum having shown up unexpectedly, that seeing her son-in-law brought the tragedy to the front of her mind. To make things doubly worse, he had walked in with a new girlfriend.

'Jenny,' Tara began, while they stood among some pear trees, the sun emerging from dense cloud. 'I'm terribly sorry for your loss, and I realise how difficult this is for you.'

'What is?'

Jenny didn't seem more than fifty, not a line or wrinkle and not a grey hair among the dark brown.

'Me turning up here with Callum. It's not what you might think. I'm not his girlfriend.'

'I wouldn't mind if you were, dear.'

'Wouldn't you? I can't imagine the pain you and your husband have gone through with the loss of Tilly and Emily, but Callum struggles with it every day, too.'

'He wasn't exactly what we'd hoped for Tilly. But she seemed happy, and when little Emily came along I suppose we began to warm to Callum.' She pulled a crumpled tissue from the pocket of her trousers and blew her nose. 'If only he hadn't been so damned late for the train.'

'Jenny, I've been trying to help Callum put his life back together. Every day he dwells on what happened. It's not any life for him. It's not for anyone.'

'Are you his therapist?'

'I'm a police officer, a detective inspector.'

'Has he done something wrong?'

'No, I don't think so. He is convinced that Tilly and Emily were murdered. He's trying to find out who was responsible.'

The woman looked as though she'd been punched in the stomach. She drew a sharp breath but didn't dare exhale. Tara stepped closer, taking hold of Jenny's right arm to steady her.

'But why?' Jenny panted. 'Who would have done such a thing?'

'At the moment, we don't know. There have been other deaths, Jenny. They appear connected in so far as the victims were all graduates of Latimer College. Callum believes the answer lies in their student days, but he can't figure out what it is. Do you know of anything that troubled Tilly back then? Anything that may have led to someone wanting to kill her?'

Jenny Reason stood in tears before the woman she had met only a few minutes earlier.

'I can't think of any reason why someone would deliberately harm Tilly.'

Tara slid her arm around the woman's shoulders and walked her back towards the house. On the way, she told her as much as she knew about the deaths of Peter Ramsey, Zhou Jian and the mystery surrounding the sympathy card sent to Callum on the day Tilly and Emily were killed. By the time they reached the kitchen, where only a kettle had been boiled for tea, Jenny Reason had recovered some composure.

'Would you like to see Tilly's room?'

'I would love to,' said Tara.

A few moments later, they sat in a cosy room with a dormer window through which they could see over fields to the village primary school. They sat together on a soft divan bed. The décor was of easy shades of pink and blue, the furniture comprising a chest of drawers, wardrobe and small bookshelf, all of oak. The only books resting on the shelf were written by Tilly Reason. Jenny leaned forward, opened the second drawer in the chest and removed three photograph albums, placing them between her and Tara. From the bottom drawer, she lifted two scrapbooks with bright multi-coloured covers. Tara sat patiently, hoping the woman would quickly get to the relevant times and places in Tilly's life. In the meantime, she was treated to a complete biography in pictures: Tilly in the Brownies, the pony club, holidays in France and Italy, school plays and family gatherings, including Christmas and birthdays.

'We were overjoyed when she was accepted at Oxford, although she already knew that she wanted to write.'

Jenny opened another album, most of the photographs inside had never been fixed into place. There were several informal shots of Tilly in academic gowns taken outside the Sheldonian after her graduation. Tara also recognised the exterior of the chapel of Latimer College in a couple of pictures showing Tilly with friends celebrating, throwing their mortar boards in the air. Georgina Maitland was instantly recognisable, but Tara could not identify the three other girls.

'Do you have any pictures of Tilly with Callum when they were at Oxford?'

'Yes, I'm sure there are.' Jenny flicked through a pile as if she were playing cards. 'Although,' she added, 'Tilly and Callum didn't really get together until their final year.'

While Jenny continued her search, Tara took the liberty of starting her own. There were several envelopes full of old prints, taken with instant or thirty-five millimetre film. One set held around twenty pictures all of Tilly as a teenager. Then she came across a picture of Tilly, Georgina, a girl she assumed might be Charlotte and a tall young man. From what she could remember from Callum's ski trip photo, she guessed that it was Justin Kingsley. He stood between Tilly and Georgina, smiling broadly, his right arm around Tilly's shoulder.

The next envelope contained more pictures of Tilly's life at Oxford, featuring several buildings around the city and the interiors of several pubs that Tara recognised. One shot, composed of five girls, showed Tilly at the centre with Georgina, and three others crammed around a table in the White Horse in Broad Street. The first-years' rooms in Latimer also featured and again were familiar to Tara.

'That one was taken in Oxford, at Latimer College,' said Jenny, having ceased her own searching and taking notice of what Tara was doing.

'Yes, I know,' she replied. 'I went there, too, though not at the same time as your daughter.'

'Did you really? Isn't that remarkable?'

'Yes, I suppose it is.' Tara was jolted from her memories of Oxford by the picture she now held in her hand. It showed Tilly, in close-up and in the arms of Justin Kingsley. 'Forgive me for asking, but were Tilly and Justin together as a couple?'

'Oh yes. They were very close for a year or so. Justin used to come down here for weekends, and sometimes Tilly would go up to London to stay with his family. Tim and I really thought Justin was the one. A terrible thing, him disappearing like that.'

Tara didn't know what to make of the revelation, except that yet again Callum had not been forthcoming in telling her the details of the situation. Why hide it? Was Justin's relationship with Tilly the reason he now blamed Justin for her murder?

Several more photos were either of Tilly alone or of Justin alone by the river close to college, or by the Sheldonian, or the Bridge of Sighs, or at the boathouse. The last picture in the pack was the most confusing to a mind that had spent the last few days trying to uncover a motive for a student to stage his own disappearance and set about killing his friends. It was a photograph taken in one of the undergrad rooms in Latimer. Callum lay on the bed laughing; the slender body of Georgina Maitland beside him with her right leg draped across his groin. All perfectly innocent, she told herself. Besides, it was likely that Tilly had taken the picture. But Tara realised she needed to know more about these relationships. They held the key to this whole affair, and still her trust in Callum had yet to rise above zero.

'Thank you, Tara. It helps sometimes to do this – to face up to the memory of our daughter rather than trying to hide it away. Things got harder when Sarah left home for London and when her brother Jamie joined the army.'

Tara smiled, feeling inadequate in the midst of the woman's sorrow. For a moment, she wished she had been at Oxford when Tilly and Georgina had been there. They seemed to have much more fun than she did.

Loaded with fresh discoveries, she persuaded Jenny that they should return to the kitchen and finish making the tea. She was eager to be on her way. Seething, she had a whole new set of issues to fire at Callum. How could he not believe that the tangled relationships between this bunch of students were central to finding a killer?

CHAPTER 30

It is never easy to drive and hold a conversation. A full-scale row is downright dangerous.

'Who'd have thought it would only take a few hours for us to revisit the same conversation?'

'What do you mean?'

'I asked you to tell me everything, Callum, and then I find that you leave out stuff – important stuff.'

Her foot sank deeper on the accelerator as the blood rushed to her head. She felt her temples pulsating and her cheeks reddening.

'What stuff?' He sounded genuinely puzzled.

'You, Callum! You keep leaving yourself out of the story. If any of these deaths were murders—'

'Of course they were murders.'

'If they are associated with you and your friends at Oxford then it is a matter of relationships. That's where the motives lie. And still I have to find out the hard way.'

'Which relationships?'

'Justin and Tilly, for starters. You didn't tell me they had been a couple.'

'Didn't think—'

'Yes, I know, you didn't think it was relevant. What about you and Georgina?'

'Slow down a bit, will you?'

They hadn't yet returned to the motorway, but the speedometer quivered around seventy.

'This is your last chance, Callum. I'm not wasting any more time over this. The person I am trying to help is the biggest obstacle. You need to think about what really happened between all of your friends, and if you still want my help you have to tell me everything.'

'Of course I want your help.'

'Then shut up and start thinking!' She yelled the words at the windscreen then braked hard for the slip on to the M25.

They both welcomed the silence for a while. Callum wondered exactly what Jenny Reason had told Tara, while Tara wished she were somewhere else. She had to phone Kate and let her know that she was fine. Tara didn't want her getting into a panic because she'd heard nothing, and then go running to Tweedy for help.

They were almost back at their hotel when Callum decided to speak. If only he'd waited until she stopped driving. Her head throbbed; she was tired and hungry. She couldn't be bothered with this man's history; not right now. But she listened in silence.

'Justin and Tilly were together from the start. It stayed that way until our second year. I didn't know either of them very well. Everything began when Tilly, Charlotte and Georgina shared a flat in second year. They really hit it off.'

She stopped him when she stopped the car.

'Save it for later, Callum. I'm hungry. You can tell me over dinner.'

She bought two pints of lager at the bar, while they browsed the menu. She needed something to wet a dry throat and soothe a hoarse voice, a quick dinner and then to bed. She felt drained, her neck and shoulders were stiff and her eyes weary from driving and from glaring with incredulity at the man who was adding to her woes instead of easing them. She didn't think she could bear another conversation about murders, missing friends and revelations of things that went bump in Oxford ten years ago. As far as she was concerned, what happened in Oxford should have stayed in Oxford. Isn't that what happened in her case?

She opted for a bar meal rather than the formality of a restaurant. Described as a gourmet steakburger with French fries, in her language it was a burger and chips. She remained angry with her companion. It would take more than one lager to feel relaxed. She ordered another two pints from the waiter and sat back in her chair, her legs crossed and arms folded for full indignant effect.

'Right, let's hear it then.'

Looking nervous and struggling with the salad in his burger roll, he gave up and dumped the lot on his plate. He lifted his glass of beer and sat back.

'Georgina, Tilly and Charlotte shared a flat in second year,' he recapped. 'Justin and Tilly had split up. By then Justin had met the other girls, and he introduced them to his buddies at the rowing club, Anthony and Ollie. Peter wasn't a rower but he had been friends with Anthony and Ollie at school.'

'And where did you fit in?' she asked, in case he planned on leaving himself out of the story once again.

'Georgina.'

Tara recalled the picture she'd seen at the vicarage of the two of them lying on a bed.

'You were a couple?'

'Why look so surprised, Tara? Do you reckon she was out of my league or something?'

'I'm thinking more that you were out of your depth.'

'She was the first student I met at Latimer. We arrived at the same time on our first day. I carried her bags up to her room. It was a while before anyone else moved in. We got talking. She was fun and we sort of clicked. We became friends, although nothing really happened, not until the second year. If the three girls hadn't shared a flat, I don't think anything ever would have happened.'

'What do you mean?'

'I only heard this from Tilly after we got engaged, but apparently the girls deliberately set out to pass us men around.'

Tara couldn't help laughing at the idea.

'What? You mean they were going to take turns with each of you boys?'

'More or less. It was Georgina's idea, although the other two were just as bad.'

'Callum, that's ridiculous.'

'Maybe, but I ended up with Georgina. You heard her call me her Belfast Boy. We went out for a few months, but it was never going to be serious. That's how I met the guys, through Georgina. Ollie and Tilly had a thing for a while, as did Justin and Charlotte. Then we all changed around. Next it was Tilly and Anthony; that lasted about five minutes. Charlotte and me, about the same. Everyone could see that Charlotte really had eyes only for Anthony. Unfortunately, he was the only one not to notice. Georgina and Justin got together around the same time, and that was about it. Most of the fun stopped then. In our final year we all went to Austria on that ski trip.'

'What about Zhou Jian, where did he fit in?'

'Jian was my friend. We were classmates. He didn't really know the others until I invited him on the ski trip.'

'So he didn't get involved in all that… partner swapping?'

Callum shook his head and drank some beer.

'So, how come he was murdered?'

She noticed her phone screen flashing on the table. Callum delved into his food again. She picked up her mobile and saw the name: Alan Murray. She didn't really wish to hear from him. She didn't want to get into explanations of where she was and what she was doing. But maybe Tweedy had already learned of her contretemps with Sir Edward Kingsley, and Murray was calling to warn her. She stared at the pulsing screen in her hand, the sound of Lady Gaga wafting across the lounge bar.

'Are you not going to answer that?' said Callum, spearing chips with his fork.

His question prompted her to act. She hit the green answer symbol and spoke.

'Hi, Alan.'

'Ma'am. Thought I should give you a call.'

She was right; Tweedy was gunning for her.

'I know you're away with that Armour bloke, but I just wanted to check if you're all right?'

'I'm fine, Alan, thanks. Just having dinner.' Some relief that so far he hadn't mentioned Tweedy.

'Is Armour with you at the moment?'

'Yes, why?'

'How has he been with you?'

Murray was sounding strange. He'd lowered his voice, and she had some difficulty hearing.

'Everything's fine.' She looked towards Callum sitting opposite, his interest still fixed on his food.

'Can you talk?'

'No, not at the moment.'

'Just listen then. You need to be careful, Tara. I have a witness who claims he saw Armour going into the house with Audra Bagdonas on the evening before she died.'

CHAPTER 31

Tara felt her body stiffen, but did her best to look ahead impassively as people do when they're talking on mobiles.

'We're checking his place over at the minute, trying to get a match for prints,' said Murray.

'OK, good. Let me know what happens.' She glanced at her food growing cold on the plate, and yet she no longer felt hungry. The beer had lightened her head.

'The witness also claims to have seen you visiting Armour's house.'

'Do you have a name?'

'Mark Crawley.'

The lout in the Everton shirt and soon to be a father. As far as she was concerned, he also was a suspect in the case. More than likely, he was involved in the beating meted out to Callum.

'You think he's reliable?'

'No reason to think otherwise at this stage. If the prints match, then I reckon we have our man. You need to be careful. I can get the local police to take him off your hands?'

'No need for that.'

'Think about it, Tara. You're on your own with the prime suspect in a murder. Five minutes, and we can have him in custody.'

'Leave it for now. I'll let you know.' She realised that irritation had crept into her voice. Callum stared at her.

'Where are you?' Murray asked.

'Yes, that's right.'

'Tara, don't muck about, love. Keep me informed at least. When do you get back?'

'Sunday, and it's ma'am to you.'

'Right, sorry, ma'am.' She cut him off.

'Everything all right?' Callum asked.

'Fine. Other problems at work. At least, I still seem to have a job.'

'No thanks to me.'

She drew no comfort from his remark, trying her best to regard him in a positive light, while Murray's news hurt like a huge brick pressing on her chest.

'Don't know about you, but I'm whacked,' she said with a yawn. 'And I couldn't eat another bite.'

'You've hardly touched your burger.'

'The beer's filled me up. I'm off to bed. I'll see you in the morning.' She gathered her jacket and handbag and rose from her chair.

'Don't forget your phone,' he said, handing it to her.

'Oh, thanks. Goodnight.'

'Goodnight,' he replied, then called after her. 'Tara, we're still going to see Charlotte tomorrow, aren't we?'

'Yes. I'll see you in the morning.'

She could scarcely hold her hand steady to swipe the cardkey on her door. Once inside, she flicked the lock, dropped her things on the bed and bolted to the bathroom. Beer and what little food she'd eaten in the day found its way to the toilet bowl. Dropping to her knees, she pushed the flush button and felt the cool spray of water as it gushed from the cistern. Her eyes stung from tears, her nose from the acidic liquid erupting from her stomach.

A battle raged in her head. Murray was right; get the local force to pull him in. He was a killer. He'd fooled her completely. A clever man off his head, biting back at the world and at the people who had caused his misery. But it was ridiculously stupid. What had he done to her? He'd pissed her off, definitely. Keeping things from her. Never specific, discarding all he thought to be irrelevant. Had he harmed her? Had he threatened her? She'd witnessed his sorrow, so intense that he fell to his knees in soaking wet earth. He'd wept and reached out to her for comfort.

Slowly, she pushed herself to her feet and turned to the large mirror. Tears and mascara ravaged her face. She dabbed cold water on her face and patted it with a towel. Her retching of the last few minutes was soon overtaken by sobs. Angry, silly, and frightened sobs. She pulled her jumper over her head, loosened her jeans and peeled them down her legs, pulling off her boots when she reached them. A shower and she would feel better, but she craved sleep more than anything. She flopped on to the bed, unable to summon the urge to switch off the lights. Before sleep, came the worry of what to do next.

CHAPTER 32

The damned annoying ringtone woke Tara from a fitful doze. She couldn't remember what she'd done with her phone and by the time she fished it out of her handbag, the call diverted to voicemail. She rolled on to her back and prayed her head would soon clear. The display showed a missed call from Kate and two messages. Turning on her side, she curled herself to a foetal position and scrolled through her inbox. Both texts were from Kate: 'R U OK?' Times two. In no mood for conversation, she replied with a text to say that she was fine and would call her when she got home.

She crawled back under the sheet.

* * *

He made it to breakfast before her, and it was saying something when she reckoned he looked much better than she did.

'Morning,' he said with a smile that was not reciprocated. 'I thought you weren't meant to look like a cop?'

She felt like thumping him. No time or inclination to wash her hair, she'd pulled it back behind her head and secured it with a black elastic band. Black, it seemed, was the order of the day; she faced him in a black jumper and slim black trousers. The look would be complete when she donned her black jacket on the way out to the car.

'Needs must,' she replied coldly. 'And thanks for the compliment.' She realised how bad she must look.

'Are you feeling all right?'

'Fine. Eat your breakfast. We've another long day ahead.'

Callum had an address for Charlotte: Bridge Street, just off Botley Road in Osney. He seemed rather upbeat as she drove along the M40, and she allowed him to talk, if only to prevent her having to say anything. Murray had the facts that might well prove him to be a killer, but her instincts told her that whatever had occurred in Treadwater on the night Audra Bagdonas died did not point to Callum as a murderer. She was going to have to wrestle with those thoughts for the remainder of the day until they made it home to Liverpool. She hoped for a message from Murray to say they'd got it wrong; then she hoped not to hear anything at all. How would she handle the situation if she were to find out Callum was responsible? She needed something else to think about.

'Tell me more about Charlotte?' she asked him.

'She never really moved on after graduation. Loves Oxford, I suppose.'

'What does she do?'

'She works as a researcher in the Ashmolean. Lives on her own – last I heard anyway. We used to meet for lunch every couple of weeks when I was still in postdoc. Then there were the reunions.'

'Reunions? Is this another of your revelations I should already know about?'

'It was girls only: Tilly, Charlotte and Georgina.'

'How often did that happen?'

'About twice, maybe three times a year. Usually in Oxford at Charlotte's place. She was the main instigator. They came to our house a few times, and also stayed at Georgina's place in London. Once, I remember they went down to Anthony's house in Norfolk. I don't think I was ever told the half of what went on there.'

'I take it things stopped after Tilly…?'

'Long before then, actually. Georgina was always too busy, and the three of them could never quite agree on dates. There was no big row, or anything, more a breakdown in communication. Charlotte has tried to keep in touch with me since Tilly died, but I'm not good at replying to her letters. She's really looking forward to me coming, though. And I should have told you…'

'What?'

'She loves to cook. She'll insist on doing lunch.'

'Great,' said Tara. Something else to endure on this awkward day.

She found it hard to imagine a reunion for her in the same mould as Charlotte, Tilly and Georgina's. There were no close friends made from her time at Latimer. Her occupation with one guy, and his apparent obsession with her, did not leave time or space to develop close friendships. But in Liverpool she had Kate and Aisling, the three of them closer than sisters.

She thought she might feel something tug within as she approached Oxford, but today felt so much like a day of business her mind paid little heed to personal memories of the place. A dull sky sagging with low cloud didn't improve the mood, and by the time she turned into Bridge Street, stopping outside a compact-looking end-of-terrace, spits of rain streaked down the windscreen. Callum gazed at the red-brick house, its neat window boxes brimming with geraniums, petunias and lobelia. But he made no attempt to climb out of the car.

'You OK about this?' he asked.

'Yes, why shouldn't I be?'

'You don't seem yourself today.'

'So you know me well already?'

He smiled at her. She smiled back, intending it to be a sarcastic gesture. Still he wavered.

'I just want you to know, I really appreciate all you're doing for me. For the first time in three years I feel I'm doing something worthwhile. I'm getting justice for Tilly and Emily.'

She couldn't fashion a reply. Nice words, but if he was involved in the murder of Audra Bagdonas they meant nothing at all. She peered into his dark eyes, searching for the truth. He returned her gaze. Suddenly, she glanced the other way, worried that something inappropriate were about to happen. That, she could do without.

Eventually, he got out of the car and walked purposefully to the front door of the house. He pressed the bell, but got no immediate reply. Tara joined him by the door, looking up and down the narrow street but seeing no one. Callum pressed the bell again.

'Does she go out on Sunday mornings?' she asked.

'No idea, but she knows we're coming today.'

'Maybe she's at church?'

'Charlotte? I don't think so.' He tried again.

Tara stepped to the right of the front door and peered through the window. She saw a small living room, neatly furnished. It stretched all the way to the back of the house such that she could see through the rear window into an enclosed garden.

'What do we do?' he asked.

She didn't much care at this stage. She was thinking ahead to the drive home, to hearing whether or not Callum was implicated in the murder of Audra Bagdonas. She doubted they would learn much from Charlotte anyway. The rain became a heavy drizzle. They couldn't stand there all day. Callum persisted with the doorbell, while Tara returned to her car. She watched as gradually he got soaked, his long hair hanging in wet strings. He paced up and down between Charlotte's house and the next, a wide lane separating the two. Tara lowered the window on the passenger side of the car.

'Why don't you give her a call?' She reached her phone to him. 'Do you have her number?'

He shook his head.

'Take a look around the back. Maybe she's in her kitchen and can't hear the doorbell.'

She climbed out of the car again and followed him along a gravel-filled lane between the two rows of houses. They stopped by a wooden door in a high garden wall. Callum tried the latch, but found it locked. He looked again for inspiration from Tara.

'Help me up.'

She raised her hands towards the top of the wall and waited for him to grasp her waist and lift. She felt brief exhilaration by the height she gained as his solid hands locked on her hips and thrust her skywards. Once her arms were on top of the wall, she grabbed hold and managed to swing her legs over to sit on the ledge. Looking into the tidy garden, there were no obstacles in her way but neither was there anything to help her slip gently down.

Gazing at the house, the kitchen appeared deserted. She pushed off the ledge and landed, thankfully, on both feet in a soft patch of lawn. Quickly, she released the latch on the garden door and let Callum enter. She told herself they had already gone too far; there must be a perfectly rational explanation for Charlotte not being home. They should have had the patience to wait in the car. With no reply at the front door she should have insisted on driving away. Now she had climbed a garden wall, and that action alone filled her with apprehension of what they were about to do next.

Callum knocked on the back door, while she peered through the kitchen window. Everything looked clean and tidy, nothing out of place. Except one thing. A drawer in the kitchen unit lay open.

'Try the handle, Callum.'

He twisted the knob and, to his surprise, the door eased open.

'Charlotte? Hello. Anybody home?' he called. With no response, again he looked at Tara for guidance.

'We'd better take a look inside.'

He stepped into the kitchen, and Tara followed. She noticed that the open drawer contained cutlery. She walked through the doorway into a narrow hall with stairs to the right and a door to the left, tightly closed.

'Check upstairs,' she said. 'I'll look in here.'

The living room looked more spacious and brighter than she'd thought from peering through the window. A folded copy of the *Oxford Mail* lay on the two-seater sofa. A coffee table, between the sofa and fireplace, was cluttered with books, a box of tissues, sweet wrappers, two coffee mugs, an empty wine glass and a plate with three expertly decorated cupcakes. She heard a muffled shout followed by the rumble of feet on the stairs.

Tara stepped back into the hall. Callum shoved her against the wall as he rushed by.

'Callum?' She hurried after him, through the kitchen and found him bent double in the yard. 'What's wrong?'

Crying and retching, he could scarcely summon a reply.

'Charlotte,' he said, then threw up.

Leaving him in the yard coughing and gasping at the fresh air, she re-entered the house and climbed the stairs. Her heart thumped in her chest. Each footstep creaked on the landing, but her attention fell upon the walls and doors of the upper floor. Spattered blood and bloodied handprints had been swiped across the paintwork and wallpaper. Facing her, were two doors ajar and a third tightly closed. One room seemed bright beyond the open door, the other dimmed by drawn curtains. She chose the latter, nudged the door with her elbow, conscious that this was a crime scene and trying to avoid adding to the woes of those whose job it would be to investigate. Her eyes flitted to the centre of the room. The bed was empty. A plain duvet lay unruffled. Speeding up her actions, she rushed to the brighter room shoving the door wide open. It took all the strength she had not to replicate Callum's reactions. See the victim, and you won't stop searching for the killer.

A woman lay on the bed, her eyes open, her blood-soaked head set to the left as if keeping watch for those who might come and go from the room. It was impossible to judge the true colours of the duvet and the rug on the floor. All were drenched in blood that had spurted and seeped from the lacerations on the legs, arms and stomach of the dead woman. Her leggings had been ripped apart, the sleeves of her cardigan shredded, and her wrists and forearms sliced open. She'd put up a fight, Tara believed. Pillows were scattered about the room, a small television knocked over on the dresser, and a shattered wine glass lay on a bedside table.

In the murders of Peter Ramsey and Zhou Jian, as far as she knew, no weapons had been found at the scene. Not so this time. She forced herself to look at the wooden handle of the knife, its blade buried deep in the chest of Charlotte Babb.

Tara placed her hand on Charlotte's forehead. It was stone cold. She remembered the open drawer in the kitchen and assumed that the knife had come from there. It suggested that perhaps this killing had not been planned to the same extent as the others, not like Peter Ramsey or Zhou Jian. Was that the reason for such carnage? Had the killer struck out suddenly from rage? Had Charlotte angered her attacker to the point where they'd lost control?

Tara jumped at Callum's voice from downstairs and stepped onto the landing.

'We better get out of here, Tara. You can't get mixed up in this.' His voice sounded shaky. 'I can't take any more.'

'Too late, Callum. We have to call the police.'

'No. Let someone else find her. We haven't done anything.'

'It doesn't work like that.'

CHAPTER 33

DI James Saunders of the Thames Valley Police, a bulky man in his forties with dark spiked hair, wearing a navy-blue sports anorak, was grateful for Callum's positive identification of the victim.

'Why were you calling on Miss Babb?'

Callum glanced briefly at Tara who gave no indication of what to say.

'I was visiting old friends in London from university and Charlotte was to be my last call on the way home to Liverpool.'

'Do you know any reason why someone would want to harm Charlotte?'

Saunders raised an eyebrow when Callum's hesitation became a prolonged silence. Reluctantly, Tara decided the truth was the best option.

'Actually, we do, inspector.'

'Perhaps you should explain, DI Grogan.'

'Charlotte's death is the latest in what we believe to be a series of murders all connected in that the victims were former students from Latimer College.'

Saunders folded his arms as if in readiness to hear a good yarn, but first he had a difficult question for Tara.

'Latimer's a bit off your patch, don't you think?'

'Callum, go wait in the car.'

Callum, his head lowered, turned and slowly made his way across the street to the car.

'Very obedient friend you have,' said Saunders. 'Do I take it that you have something to say that's not for him to hear?'

Tara began her explanation of why she and Callum were together on a weekend trip to London. Saunders listened intently.

'And is Dr Armour a suspect in these murders?'

'There is a possibility that he is responsible for the murder of the young girl in Liverpool,' Tara explained.

Saunders massaged his forehead with his left hand, while Tara squirmed in her own discomfort. The connections between the different strands of this case grew more implausible each time she tried to explain them. She couldn't blame this detective for looking perplexed.

'I really don't know what to do with you two, Inspector. I don't have time for your mess.'

'I would appreciate it if we could be on our way. I've told you everything we know.'

Blowing air through his cheeks, Saunders cast his eyes about the street as forensic personnel carried out their duties around the house.

'I'll want a word with your boss before you go anywhere, Inspector. Seems an odd way to be carrying on, driving a murder suspect all over the country.'

She felt like a child standing before this hardened officer. For the first time she realised how ridiculous her method of dealing with Callum Armour looked to another detective, and she wondered how it would seem now to Superintendent Tweedy.

DI Saunders left her on the pavement and went off to make contact with Merseyside Police.

* * *

It was the late afternoon. Tara checked her watch hoping they might still make it to Liverpool before nightfall. Callum sat in her car, staring into space, while the house where Charlotte lay mutilated hummed with police and a SOCO team. Saunders had not returned with any news of his speaking with Superintendent Tweedy. Tara's unease grew, her mind simmering over what the two men might discuss. The last thing she wanted was to have Tweedy disturbed at home on a Sunday. It didn't help when she got a call from Murray.

'Is everything all right, ma'am? I heard from Tweedy that you'd come across a spot of bother?'

'To put it mildly,' she replied. 'We stumbled upon a murder, a friend of Armour's. Looks like his theories of multiple killings weren't entirely daft.'

'Any way he could have done it?'

A flippant question but she had to admit to having thought the same, if only briefly. Callum would have had to organise transport from the hotel at Heathrow in the middle of the night, either Friday or Saturday, drive to Oxford, kill his friend Charlotte and get back in time for breakfast. Possible, but not likely.

'I don't think that's helpful, Alan,' she replied. 'It's a big enough mess without adding another murder. Any word on the fingerprints?'

'We have matching prints taken from the murder scene and from Armour's house. We need to match those up with Armour himself when he returns.'

'OK.' She gave a long sigh of resignation. 'But I will bring him in. I've got him this far; I can drive him back to St Anne Street.'

'Fair enough, but if you need my help give me a call.'

She leaned against her car, waiting for Saunders to tell her they could be on their way. Thankfully, the rain had stopped although she was already soaked through. Standing in the street, however, was preferable to sharing her car with a man who completely baffled her. She wished DI Saunders would hurry up and let them go.

Her phone sounded once again in her hand. She was sick of that damned ringtone; she really must change it. She looked at the display, a number only, although it was vaguely familiar.

'Hello, Tara?'

'Yes. Who's calling?'

'It's Georgina here. Hoped to catch you sooner, but it's been a hectic weekend. Country retreats are supposed to be relaxing, or so I thought. My husband organises a shooting party and I'm supposed to play hostess. Anyway, after having met you on Friday, I wanted a quiet word.'

Tara recalled giving her number to Georgina when she'd promised to arrange a meeting for them with her husband. Tara wondered if she should tell her about Charlotte.

'How can I help you, Georgina?'

'Callum, of course! I could tell that you both care for each other.'

'You could?'

'Difficult thing to disguise. The way you look at each other, waiting for the other to speak and seeking approval.'

Very observant, Tara thought, but rather too much interpretation.

'We are not a couple, Georgina. I am helping him to uncover the truth about the death of his wife, his daughter and his friends. That's all.'

'Oh, I know you are a police officer – a detective inspector. Very impressive. It wasn't difficult: a quick check on the internet and the price of one phone call. You could have told me the truth, you know.'

'Is there something you wish to tell me, Georgina?'

'I merely wanted to pass on a few things about my Belfast Boy.'

'What sort of things?'

'You do know that he was totally devoted to Tilly?'

'Yes, I realise that.'

'When she died, Callum fell to pieces.'

Georgina really was stating what Tara had found to be obvious. She doubted if the woman had ever seen Callum's house in Treadwater and how he was living.

'I appreciate you telling me, Georgina, but I know how Callum lives.'

'He suffered a serious breakdown, Tara. Do you understand what I'm getting at?'

'I suppose you're trying to tell me that his theory of how his friends have died is not to be believed?'

There was a pause at Georgina's end.

'A lot more than that. Callum was, *is* a clever man but all rational thinking deserted him after Tilly and Emily died. He is not himself.'

'Are you suggesting that Callum is responsible for these murders?'

'Look, Tara, it may be one enormous but tragic coincidence. Callum is convinced that Tilly was murdered, and yet we both know her death was declared an accident. All I'm saying is that his frustration and despair over Tilly may have clouded his thinking. I'm just trying to warn you. Don't let him waste your time. I've witnessed the pair of you together. You could help him in so many other ways.'

'Thanks for the advice, Georgina. I will have to cut you short, I'm afraid. Callum and I called at your friend Charlotte's this morning. Sorry to have to break the news to you in this way, but we found her dead. She's been murdered.'

'No!' Tara heard a protracted cry followed by heavy sobbing.

'I don't know how this fits with what you have told me,' Tara continued. 'But I'm sure you can imagine that Callum is deeply shocked. I'll let you have a word.' She tapped on the car window, and Callum lowered it.

'Georgina wants a word,' she said brusquely, handing him the phone.

CHAPTER 34

As soon as DI Saunders let them go, Tara wasted no time in making for Liverpool. They had talked about visiting their old college to see if it might help with their investigation, but that was before they'd found Charlotte. All Tara wanted to do now was to get her car up the M6 as fast as she could and get back to St Anne Street station. It was a toss-up as to which felt worse: this journey home from Oxford, or the one she'd taken after her graduation, knowing then that her life was not going to work out as she'd hoped.

Callum was a wreck. Fortunately, he dozed for much of the journey and she was spared having to make conversation and having to stop herself from blurting out the truth of what was about to happen. She didn't believe he was a killer, but Georgina's phone call had unsettled her. She had a nagging ache in her tummy, like she was hungry but couldn't face food. She was nervous and didn't know why. If only she'd had the whole story from Callum at the outset. Instead, he'd played this stupid trade-off, and she'd got the poor end of the deal.

Tara thought that Callum would have mentioned his telephone conversation with Georgina, but afterwards he seemed to have shut down completely. If things didn't go well for him with regard to Audra Bagdonas, then the search for Kingsley and the attempt to solve the murders of the Latimer alumni would become a distant memory. If Callum had been lying to her all this time, she had no intention of giving his plight another thought.

She pulled into the services at Norton Canes and sent him to buy sandwiches. Reclining her seat, she lay back trying to think up the best explanations to appease Tweedy. None of them were pretty. From every angle she looked foolish. She realised, though, that what Tweedy respected most from his officers was honesty. Bizarre as it seemed, she would tell him the truth

By seven-thirty, they'd reached the outskirts of the city.

'You all right?' he asked her.

'Just tired. Didn't get much sleep these past few nights.'

She didn't take the M57 for Netherton. Instead, she drove towards the city centre, her destination being St Anne Street.

'Where are you going?'

'I need to stop at the office before I take you home.'

She didn't elaborate, and he made no further comment. Twenty minutes later, she pulled up into her usual parking space at St Anne Street station.

'You may as well come in. I could be a while.' She climbed out, hoping he would follow. If he decided to stay put then Murray would have to come and fetch him. But as she walked towards the entrance she heard the car door close and, glancing behind her, she saw Callum on her tail. Her body trembled; she hated arrests in any situation, but one involving someone she cared for... What the hell was she thinking? Cared for? Murray would have to do it. If he wasn't around, she would find someone else. Clearly, Callum had no inkling of what was coming his way. He followed her through the station reception, up a flight of stairs and into her office. Thankfully, she saw Murray seated at his desk. He came over immediately. Tara nodded for him to speak.

'Dr Armour, sir, I'd like to ask you a few questions, if you don't mind?'

Callum looked at Tara for guidance as he'd done several times over the weekend. Tara stared directly in his face. She did at least owe him some dignity.

'Bit late in the day,' Callum replied.

'Callum Armour, I'm arresting you on suspicion of the murder of Audra Bagdonas. You are not obliged to say anything—'

'Tara, what's going on? I haven't done anything. Tell this idiot to leave me alone.'

'Best if you do as DS Murray asks, Callum. No doubt we'll talk tomorrow.'

Murray continued to list Callum's rights, while Tara tried her best to zone it out by switching on her computer. Several things had occurred to her on the drive home.

'Thanks a lot, Tara,' Callum shouted. His voice sent a shiver through her spine, but she resisted the urge to reply, or to even glance in his direction.

'This way, Dr Armour,' said Murray indicating the door. 'Let's get you all signed in, and we can have a nice chat in the morning.'

'Tara, for goodness sake! Look at me. I've done nothing wrong, and you know it.' He shrugged off Murray and made for her desk. 'Tara! You were supposed to be helping me.'

Frightened by his sudden lunge towards her, all she could manage was to stare at his angry face. For a second, she lost herself in the darkness of his eyes.

'Please do as DS Murray asks, Callum.'

'Back off, Armour,' Murray shouted. He grabbed Callum's right arm and jerked it upwards behind his back. Callum gasped with pain.

'I didn't do it, Tara, and you know it.'

Murray bungled him through the door.

'Leave off. I'm going home—'

'Not tonight, sunshine.'

Their voices faded as they went down the stairs. When silence fell upon the office once more, Tara switched off her computer and went home.

* * *

195

Despite it being her own bed, she experienced another bad night's sleep. It seemed like only five minutes had elapsed before she was back at her desk. Nothing on the screen registered with her as she sat resting her chin in both hands. She felt rough: a dry mouth, chapped lips and an emptiness in her stomach that she'd done nothing to rectify. The coming day flashed before her eyes – none of it appealing. She would speak with Murray to thank him for his composed handling of an awkward situation. Then Tweedy. After that she might not have a job. She wondered how it would look to be sacked for incompetence. Detectives were supposed to solve problems, not add to the list. Scanning her computer screen, it seemed unlikely to yield any worthwhile answers. As Murray strode into the office, she made a mental note to phone Detective Muetzel in Switzerland.

'You look like death warmed up,' he said.

'You are just the sweetest-talking man I've ever met. Have you spoken with Armour this morning? Is he all right?'

'Yes, he's fine. Playing the victim. Then he moved on to the same game as before.'

'Which is?'

'Says he'll only speak to you.'

Murray pulled a chair from another desk and sat astride it with his arms leaning on the back.

'How's it looking?' she asked.

'For Armour? Or you?'

'Armour first.'

'This lad Mark Crawley insists that Armour went into the house with the girl. Once we cross-check his prints, it'll provide some corroboration.'

'Did Crawley say why Callum went into the house?'

'No. Apparently, Armour held the girl by the arm, and they went in by the back door. He didn't see him leave.'

'What a mess.'

'Tweedy will be looking for you this morning.'

'We meet every Monday?'

'You know what I mean, Tara. He called me at home yesterday. He was concerned for you.'

'I suppose he was furious at having to vouch for one of his officers who got mixed up in a murder way off her patch. I could be out of his squad by the end of the day.'

Murray had no words of comfort to offer.

'Might need your help later with this Armour bloke,' he said. He headed back through the door, and she was left to worry alone. She didn't think Murray would care in the slightest if she was thrown off Tweedy's team. After all, she'd always got the feeling that he resented her. She was younger than him, a detective inspector to his sergeant – her six years' service to his fifteen. Her departure would provide a career opportunity for Alan Murray.

* * *

Harold Tweedy, as he was prone to do on a Monday morning, stood behind his desk. Today, however, only one member of his team sat before him. Tara said exactly what she had planned to say. She gave Tweedy the absolute truth in chronological order, as best as she could recall. She was surprised by his interest. He asked about the circumstances surrounding Charlotte Babb's murder. His questions helped to relax her, somehow, and she no longer worried that he was about to ditch her from his team.

'An unfortunate set of circumstances, Tara. I can't see the matter going further now that Dr Armour is under our care, so to speak. Your prime objective is still to clear up the case of Audra Bagdonas.'

'Yes, sir.' She recognised her boss's language. A wonderfully polite way of noting that she'd messed up, that she had lost focus on her job, and that she should not run all over the country in a quest for justice for Callum Armour.

'If you call in the others we can get our week up and running.'

'Yes, sir.'

* * *

Late in the morning, Murray emerged from the interview room that played host to Callum, reporting that Armour persisted in his reluctance to answer questions. He'd also refused the offer of a legal aid solicitor. Tara was adamant that she would not concede to his request to speak only to her. No more favours. Murray would be with her, and they would only discuss the murder of Audra Bagdonas.

She started the video recorder and told Callum sternly that she wanted answers to her questions. He sat tight-lipped, as if he were ready to resist force-feeding, like a child refusing to eat his greens. Tara wasn't put off by his indignation.

'We have a witness who said you entered the house with Audra on the day before she was found dead. Have you any comment to make about that?'

'What witness?'

'Did you enter the house with Audra?'

She was quite content to tolerate his silence and wait for his answer. She kept the recorder running. He was no longer the man for whom, only two days ago, she had poured out her sympathy. Right now, she must regard him potentially as a man capable of killing a seventeen-year-old girl. She watched him and waited. He stared through her; his eyes looked washed out and stranded between fear and frustration. Tara met his stare with a coldness born of her disappointment in him.

'She needed help,' he said at last, his head bowed in defeat.

Tara bit her lip. She'd preferred the silence to his answer.

'I think we should bring in a solicitor, Callum, don't you?'

This time, she stopped the recorder.

CHAPTER 35

Ninety minutes later, the interview party had increased to four.

'Dr Armour has told me,' said Martin Grimshaw, a fifty-year-old solicitor with a red-blotched face, wheezy breath and white shirt straining at his belly, 'he is content to answer your questions fully, but would prefer to speak with Inspector Grogan alone.'

She heard Murray sigh in frustration.

'That's not happening,' said Tara.

Grimshaw looked at Callum, awaiting a response. Callum glared at Tara. She gave him no reason to feel that he had a friend on the other side of the table. He nodded once at Grimshaw.

'Very well,' said Grimshaw, proceeding to blow his nose in his handkerchief.

Tara restarted the video recorder.

'Tell me how you knew Audra Bagdonas?'

'She used to wait outside the house in the afternoon. One day when I was walking Midgey she stopped to ask the time and she stroked the dog. The next time she asked me for a light, but I don't smoke. Very bad for your health. Thousands of toxins in tobacco smoke.'

'Let's skip your fears over cigarettes, shall we? How many times did you enter the house with her?'

'I never went into the house with her.'

'We have a witness who claims to have seen you going into the house with Audra the day before she was found dead.'

'Your witness has got it wrong.'

Murray sat with folded arms.

'Did you meet Audra on the day before she died?' Tara continued, her eyes fixed on Callum's. Despite the brief time she had known him she believed she could tell when he was lying or at least holding something back. She realised also that he tended to answer only the literal question. He never elaborated upon his answers.

'Yes,' he said.

'Tell me where you met her, the time of day and what you did together.'

'She was standing at the back gate of number six.'

'What time?'

'About four in the afternoon.'

'Was she alone?'

'No.'

'Can you elaborate please, Callum?'

'Usually she was alone, but that day she was talking to a young lad.'

'Do you know this lad?'

'Mark Crawley.'

Tara glanced sideways at Murray. At least there was some coming together of two stories.

'What happened next?'

'I walked by on the other side of the road, and Audra called out to me. She waved me over, and Crawley backed away. He didn't look too happy to see me. When he was out of earshot, Audra told me that he'd been pestering her, asking her out, and inviting her round to his place. She asked if I would stay with her until her people arrived.'

'Her people?'

'That's what she called them.'

'Did you see or meet any of them?'

'Never met them, but I saw them each time Audra was there.' He raised his voice in frustration. 'I've told you this before, Tara.'

She wasn't having any tantrums. Callum Armour was not leaving the room until he'd told her everything. If she suspected he was holding something back he could stew in a cell for a month, for all she cared.

'Inspector Grogan to you. For the record this time, Callum.'

Grimshaw was about to speak, but Tara headed him off with a polite smile.

'Two men would usually arrive by car and go into the house with Audra. Then a few more women would appear. That would be it until late on. Sometimes they stayed overnight. I used to see bright lights in the rooms, especially upstairs. I told you I saw cameras and lights carried into the house. I reckon they were making adult films.'

'Why do you have a note of the house owner's name, Teodor Sokolowski, in your files at home?'

'I asked Audra what went on in the house. Nothing bad, she told me. Nothing wrong. I think she meant nothing illegal. I asked her who owned the house, and she gave me the name Sokolowski. She said he was a nice man, but she couldn't tell me any more or she would lose her job.'

'Did she tell you what her job was?'

'No.'

'Do you think she was frightened by what she was doing there?'

Callum shrugged then realised he should provide a verbal response.

'She never looked happy. Nervous, I would say. When the others arrived they went inside, but sometimes they were laughing and smiling.'

'Were you ever invited into the house by Audra or any of the others?'

'Never met the others. Even on the day she asked me to wait with her, she told me it was best if I went before the men arrived. I was never invited in.'

'So you watched what went on?' Murray asked, his eyebrows raised suggestively. 'Seems like you noticed quite a bit, Callum?'

Callum didn't respond.

'Why did you make a note of the house owner's name?' Tara continued.

'I grew concerned about Audra. She was very young, and she told me she hadn't been in Liverpool for long. Seemed a bit strange to me that she was Lithuanian, while some of the others were Polish. I didn't think they would mix socially. So I thought it was worth contacting Sokolowski to find out if he was aware of what was going on in his house. I couldn't find an address for him, but I contacted the Citizens Advice people, and they put me on to the local Polish Association. They provided me with a list of agents who were renting houses to Polish workers in Liverpool. I called with these agents, asking if they knew of Sokolowski. Didn't get anywhere, but in one of the offices I saw the two men who would meet Audra at the house. They appeared to be working in the agency. I didn't reckon it was a coincidence.'

'What did you do next?' Murray asked.

Callum smirked.

'I contacted your lot. Told them what was going on in the house and about the guys at the agency. I'm still waiting for a reply. I suppose, I'm regarded as the local nutter and not worth taking seriously.'

Tara ignored the remark.

'Where is this agency?' she asked.

'London Road, near the Odeon. I'm sure the two guys are long gone by now. They probably got offside after Audra was found in the house.'

'Do you think these men are responsible for Audra's murder?'

'That's for you to decide – not my job.'

If ever there had existed any warmth between Tara and Callum, with his reply to her question it had certainly dissipated. She called a break in the interview to let things rest for a while. Leaving the room, she instructed a uniformed officer to organise tea for Callum and his brief. When she met up with Murray in the corridor, she ran off a list of orders.

'Get down to that agency and check out those guys Callum was talking about. He'll have to identify them at some point. That's if they haven't scarpered. You need to round up as many of the girls as you can find who featured in those films, and especially the two who gave the ID for Audra. Then we need Callum to tell us which of them were at the house that night.'

'You believe him then?' said Murray, his shoulder pressed to the wall and a buff folder tucked under his right arm.

Tara didn't care much for his attitude. At times he forgot who he was speaking to.

'I'd certainly take his word over Mark Crawley's,' Tara replied.

Murray looked down at her with a satisfied smirk on his face – like a schoolboy playing chess who has just checkmated his teacher.

'Maybe you should look at this,' he said, handing her the folder. 'I've just picked it up from my tray. The results of the prints: Armour's are a match for those found in the house.'

She pulled out the sheets of paper and glanced at the text. Murray continued, gleefully.

'He was all over that house, Tara: back door, kitchen door, banister, bathroom and door frame of the room where Audra was found. If his DNA matches the semen found on the girl's body, he's finished. Sorry, I don't share your trust in him.'

CHAPTER 36

One by one, she placed five photographs of Audra Bagdonas on the table in front of Callum. All had been taken at the murder scene, in the back bedroom of the house.

'Did you kill her, Callum?'

Grimshaw, sniffing then breathing heavily through his mouth, attempted to whisper in Callum's ear. 'No comment.'

'No,' said Callum, ignoring his brief. 'I didn't kill her. How can you even think that?'

She remained standing, feeling she had more authority looking down on him.

'You have not been honest with me. I am trying to find the person who did this, Callum, and at every turn you have held something back. Now you're telling bare-faced lies.'

'I didn't kill her.'

'We have a witness who saw you going into the house—'

'He's lying. I didn't go in. I only went as far as the back door. The two men drove up, and I left her with them.'

'We have your fingerprints, Callum. Taken from inside the house, from the back door, the kitchen and upstairs. You were inside that house!'

He stared again at the photographs. Tara resumed her seat at the table. Murray came in and sat down beside her. That didn't surprise her. He would want to be here for the big finale – for the moment when she'd be made to look the fool. Bring Tweedy in too, she thought, just to seal her fate.

'Why did you kill her?' she continued.

His bowed head began swinging to and fro. Martin Grimshaw, his fingers entwined upon the table, had nothing to offer.

'I saw her dead, but I didn't kill her.'

'You need to explain that, Callum. Do you understand what I'm saying? You have to explain yourself, and this time it has to be the truth.'

'What I've told you is true. Mark Crawley was bugging her, trying to get off with her. I sent him on his way, and I stayed with Audra until the two men showed up. I left her at the back door of the house. I never went inside, not then.'

'What did you do after she went indoors?'

'I went home. I watched from my kitchen window until the other girls arrived.'

'How many girls?'

'Three. Two in their twenties and an older one, mid-thirties to early forties.'

'Had you seen them before?'

'Yes, but not all of them together on the same day. There were a few girls who came and went from the house on different days.'

'What happened after that?'

'During the evening, I kept an eye on the house. The maroon car was still parked outside when I was going to bed. I saw a bright light in one of the bedrooms. I don't sleep well. A couple of times I got up and went downstairs. I like to check the doors are locked. Can't be too careful. When I got back to my bedroom, I heard voices outside. I saw the two guys carrying stuff from the house and putting it into the boot of the car.'

'What kind of stuff?' Murray asked.

'Cameras, I suppose, lighting gear. A couple of bin bags. They drove off. Then I went back to bed. Next time I woke up it was about five. I usually take Midgey for his walk. On the way home, I passed by number six and I looked over the fence. I noticed the back door was open.

Ajar, not wide open. I took Midgey home and returned to number six. I didn't see anyone about, so I went through the gate and up to the back door. I shouted inside, but got no response. I went in. I kept calling for Audra, for anyone, but there wasn't a sound. I climbed the stairs and looked into all of the rooms. She was in the last room – the bedroom at the back. At first, I thought she was asleep; the light was poor because the curtains were closed, but then I saw the marks on her chest.'

He buried his head in his hands, sniffing his tears. Tara was content to wait, but Murray jumped in.

'What did you do next, Callum?'

Tara frowned at her colleague. She didn't believe they would ever make a team. Callum wiped his nose on his sleeve and sat upright.

'Take your time, Callum,' said Tara.

'I ran out.'

'Did you call for help? Phone the police?' Murray asked.

'I ran home. Threw up in the kitchen. All I could think about was Tilly and Emily.'

Murray looked perplexed. Only Tara could understand the remark, but she was in no mood to start explaining things. Besides, Murray already knew about Callum losing his wife and daughter. It wasn't her fault if the information had washed over him. She found it easy to picture Callum running away; she'd witnessed it for herself the day before at the home of Charlotte Babb.

'Is that how you left things?' she asked.

'I waited all morning. Nothing happened. The back door of the house lay open.'

'Why didn't you call the police?'

He fired them a look that managed to convey his disdain of the local police service and how they usually behaved towards him.

'I thought someone would come, but hours went by. I was about to go for help, when you lot suddenly turned up. I guessed a neighbour had beaten me to it.'

'You waited hours, Callum,' said Tara. 'The girl might still have been alive when you found her.'

He shook his head dismissively. 'No. I touched her arm. She was dead cold.'

Yet again Tara's frustration boiled as Callum persisted with his habit of gradually adding detail to his account, as if he was baking a cake where the recipe instructed him to add the flour slowly with stirring.

'Why have you waited until now to tell us? Don't you think Audra deserves justice? That her killer should be caught? You've been fighting to get justice for Tilly. Why not Audra? Why shouldn't I charge you now for withholding information? Or are you still lying to us?'

'I don't think Dr Armour deserves to be addressed in this manner,' Grimshaw put in. 'As far as I can tell he has co-operated fully with your enquiry. If you do not intend to press charges, I suggest you allow him to leave.'

'Dr Armour,' Tara began, with considerable heat in her voice, 'has told me nothing that we can prove is true. I'm afraid, he will be staying here for now.'

CHAPTER 37

They agreed to split for the time being. Murray went with a uniformed constable to fetch the girls from the house on Stanley Road. Attempts to find the two men who worked at the rental agency, and were responsible for running the adult film enterprise at the house in Treadwater, had so far proved fruitless. It seemed likely that they had left the country. Once identities were established for the pair, and their whereabouts traced, if necessary, they could be brought back to Liverpool. They sat below Callum on the list of suspects, but for reasons she could not explain, Tara didn't think them guilty of murder.

See the victim, and you won't stop searching for the killer. She could see the word burnt into the flesh of Audra Bagdonas. *Kurwa*: bitch, whore. Callum said he saw the two men leaving the house. He didn't mention seeing the other girls leave. Had they left earlier, before the men? She didn't believe so. She was on her way to visit the person who knew the truth, but who so far appeared determined to place Callum at the centre of the inquiry.

DC Wilson stopped the marked police car outside the house, three doors from the scene of the murder. The pair of them walked to the front door, and Wilson tapped heavily with the metal flap of the letter box. Through the lounge window, Tara saw a large television screen. Someone inside was playing a video game. Tara glanced at her notebook making sure she had the correct address for Mark Crawley, the youth she would always associate with a blue football shirt. The door eventually opened, and a heavily pregnant girl stared at them through pretty, but nervously darting eyes.

'Hello, Debbie. How are you?'

'All right,' the girl replied in a downbeat tone.

The bump was certainly increasing with each encounter. Debbie pressed her left hand against her back, clearly feeling uncomfortable. Barefoot, she wore a pale pink towelling bathrobe. Young Curtis, wearing only shorts and clutching at the living room door, stared intently at the callers.

'We were actually hoping to speak with Mark. Is he here? I didn't realise that you lived together, but this is the address we have for him.'

Debbie seemed unimpressed by all the civility aimed at her.

'Mark,' she called into the room. 'Bizzies want to see you.'

'Tell them to fuck off. I'm busy.'

Debbie glared at Tara as if to say, you have your answer, but Tara smiled back. She hoped to keep on the right side of this girl. From their first meeting, outside Callum's house, she had the feeling that Debbie was honest and trying her best to stay out of trouble. Tara still had difficulty believing that this young girl was happy to associate with the likes of Mark Crawley, never mind him fathering her child.

'Do you mind if we come in, Debbie?'

The girl glanced nervously towards the living room, her expression full of the dilemma facing her.

'This won't take long.'

Reluctantly, Debbie stepped away from the door allowing Tara and Wilson to enter. She remained in the hallway as Tara entered the living room. Curtis scuttled past their legs and reached for his mother. She took him by the hand but left him on the floor, unable to lift him into her arms.

'Hello, Mark,' said Tara in a civil tone. 'I'd like to ask you a few questions, if that's all right?'

Crawley, wearing blue jogging trousers and the Everton shirt, was sprawled in an armchair, his legs dangling over one side. He stared keenly at the television, a game controller held in both hands, his thumbs moving frantically across the buttons playing a combat game. It was easy for the youth to ignore his visitors, but Wilson had other ideas. He stepped between Crawley and the television.

'What?'

'Detective Inspector Grogan would like a word, mate,' Wilson said.

'Why did you claim to have seen Callum Armour going into the house with Audra Bagdonas?' Tara asked.

It was unlikely the boy would ever submit to eye contact with her.

'Cos that's what he did, all right?'

'What were you talking about with Audra before Callum turned up?'

'None of your business.'

'Did you threaten her? Were you trying to get off with her? Did she turn you down, Mark? Is that why you got angry? Is that why you decided to point the blame at Callum Armour? Because he helped her?' She fired the questions at him, hoping to rile him, eager for him to lose it.

Debbie stood by the door watching, biting at her fingernails, her uneasy gaze fixed on her boyfriend.

'How's your Polish, Mark? Know many words?'

'What are you on about? I don't know any Polish.'

'Did you talk to the other girls who came to the house? Ask them what they got up to inside there?'

The Everton shirt persisted with his silence, but Tara wasn't looking at him; she looked at Debbie, who with each question seemed to grow more uneasy, chewing on her nails then her bottom lip.

'Maybe you took part in some of their filmmaking? Bit of fun? Some cash in it, too?'

Debbie disappeared from the doorway.

'You know, Mark, if you did take part in one of those films we will find out. They're made to be sold. It is a business. Television, DVDs, internet. Won't be hard to track down.'

'Those films are only sold in Poland and Russia,' he said at last, and Tara knew she had him.

'Is that what they told you?'

'Didn't say they told me anything.' His attention returned to his video game. 'Are you gonna fucking move, or what?' he said to Wilson who stood like a nightclub bouncer, smirking and making it clear he was not intimidated.

'We haven't completed all the forensic tests on Audra,' Tara continued. 'There were traces of semen found on her body. If you took part in sexual activity with her, we'll soon know.'

He glared at Tara once again. For a moment, it seemed he was mulling things over. Then he resumed that look of cold aggression she'd witnessed on their first encounter. Finally, he cracked a disturbing smile.

'It was a porno film. Bound to be cum all over the place.' His grin was one of suggestion, but Tara no longer feared this insolent youth. She matched his smile with her own.

'What time did you go into the house, Mark?'

He laughed, nervously, but he laughed.

'Just tell her, Mark.' Debbie stood again at the doorway, rubbing the coldness from her arms.

'Ah, you stupid bitch!'

CHAPTER 38

'I think your friend Crawley may wish to change his story,' said Tara.

Murray looked at her doubtfully. She dropped into her desk chair, dumping her bag on the floor. She felt exhausted. It had been a long day, suppressing emotions and trying to wangle the truth from people determined not to give it. She was in no mood to debate matters with her colleague. He'd left the station a couple of hours earlier, convinced he was right about Callum Armour and that she was wrong. Now, if she wanted to, she could make him feel two feet tall. She was right. Not that she held Callum in any great spotlight of trust, but she had realised that Crawley was a hot suspect for murder when he suddenly came forward claiming to have witnessed Callum entering the house with Audra. He had been trying to deflect attention from himself, but he was too stupid to realise he had no need to do so. The investigation hadn't been heading his way, but once he opened his mouth then she was going to ask why.

Usually, around this time she would be getting ready for home; instead, she had four interview rooms occupied. Mark Crawley persisted with his tough exterior. To her, it was like boast plaster on a wall: one hefty tap and he would crumble to bits. The two girls, Laima Gabrys and Ruta Mankus waited to go over their story for her benefit, having already gushed to Murray when he picked them up. She'd left Callum to ruminate on his despicable behaviour. Her own face glowed with anger thinking of what he'd done to her, while all she had tried to do was help him. Murray was wrong about him, she knew that, but from recent harsh experience she also knew that Callum had more information tucked away in his scheming brain.

'Who's first?' Murray asked, ripping the plastic film from a pack of egg and cress sandwiches. He offered her some, but she didn't think her stomach could take it. While he ate, she fed him details of what happened when she questioned Crawley.

'His girlfriend Debbie knows the story. She's likely to give birth any day. I didn't want her waiting around here and getting into a state. Can't be good for the baby. But if Crawley clams up, we'll have to bring her in.'

By nine in the evening Tara and Murray, moving between the interview rooms, had learned much from the girls, little from Callum, and nothing at all from Crawley. Laima Gabrys and Ruta Mankus were stunned to learn they were even regarded as suspects in the case. Once that prospect sank in, they were only too happy to tell all they knew regarding Audra Bagdonas. Interviewed in separate rooms, their stories matched up perfectly. Both girls had been at the house with Audra that evening, but Audra was very much alive when they left and headed for home a few minutes after ten o'clock. Most significantly, they left the house before the two budding Fellinis, who had continued to shoot movies of Audra. Callum, it seemed, had missed their departure or had decided not to mention it. At that point Tara left the interview with the older woman Ruta Mankus and went to visit Callum. A constable opened the door, but Tara went no further than the threshold. Callum looked tired and rather vacant.

'What time did the two men leave the house that night?'

Callum pondered the question. He looked for a trace of empathy in her stare – in those usually warm eyes, but there was none. She'd come only for answers.

'Around midnight.'

'Did you see the girls leaving?'

He shook his head.

'No.'

'Do you think they were still in the house when the men left at twelve?'

He merely shrugged. She walked away without another word, and the constable swung the door closed behind her.

'Tara!'

She retraced her steps, nodded for the door to be reopened and once more stood on the threshold.

'There's something else I haven't told you.'

* * *

Tara went straightaway to the adjacent interview room where she found Murray questioning Laima Gabrys. His face was a picture to behold. Tara beckoned him outside, leaving the young girl frowning at the flurry of activity.

'It might be true that the girls left before the men,' said Tara. They walked a few yards along the narrow corridor. 'Armour said the men left around twelve, but he doesn't know if the girls were still inside.'

'Are you ready for this?' said Murray, gazing through a window into a darkening night pierced by streetlights and headlights of passing traffic on St Anne Street.

'What?'

'Gabrys just told me that Mark Crawley was in the house with them and was still there when they left.'

Tara burst into the room, where Laima Gabrys, looking nervous and pale, sat with her hands supporting her chin. Her eyes were reddened and filled with tears. Clearly, she believed herself to be in a lot of trouble.

'Laima, can you tell me what Mark Crawley was doing inside the house?'

She wiped the back of her hand across her nose and sniffed. Tara saw the woman's slender arms trembling and her chest heave in a deep sob. Tara, usually quick to offer sympathy to a distressed witness, decided in this instance that an outpouring of emotion was speeding things along. If Laima continued to believe she was under threat of arrest for murder, it would surely loosen her tongue.

'He wanted to be in movie,' she answered.

'Was this occasion the first time he'd been in the house?'

Laima shook her head vigorously, her hair wafting around her face.

'No. He came every day to ask the guys if he could help with the movie.'

'And did they let him help?'

'No – but he kept on asking. They let him come inside house three times, but not to do film.'

'OK. What did he do?'

'Make coffee – order pizza – he held lights.'

'He saw what went on in making the films?'

'Yes.'

Tara looked at Murray. He smiled, and she took it in the spirit in which he'd offered it: respect for a job almost done.

'Thank you, Laima. We will try not to keep you much longer.'

The girl nodded and pulled a crumpled tissue from her pocket.

Tara and Murray walked to the room at the end of the corridor. Murray stepped aside to let her go first. She smiled.

'Thanks, Alan.'

They sat down opposite a worried-looking Mark Crawley, although when he spoke his words carried only indignation.

'Can I go home now?'

'Not for a while, Mark,' Tara replied. Murray had already started the recorder. 'Were you really so keen to be involved in adult films?'

Crawley glanced from Tara to Murray. 'Thought you might show up, Tara.' He grinned proudly at his sick humour.

'Detective Inspector Grogan, if you don't mind. Our Lithuanian friends tell me you were the tea boy. Is that correct?'

'So what? I got paid for doing it. I was helping out.'

'But what you really wanted was to get some acting experience?' said Murray. 'You wanted into the action with the girls, isn't that right?'

Crawley shrugged, but made no reply.

'A yes or no will do fine, Mark,' said Murray.

Still, he refused to answer.

'What were the guys like? Friendly? They must have been OK to let you into the house?'

'They were great. They needed help.'

'Very kind of you to make the gesture. Which of the girls do you think was best at her job?'

Another shrug.

'OK, let me put it this way. Which one did you fancy having a go with?'

Crawley fell silent as his cockiness deserted him.

'Why did you claim to have seen Callum Armour going into the house with Audra?' Tara asked.

'Cos he's a fucking paedo.'

'Callum was trying to protect Audra, wasn't he? You were annoying her, and he scared you off?'

Crawley slouched in the chair, his arms folded and feet outstretched. It was enough of a show to prevent him talking. Tara didn't think he would hold out for much longer.

'I'm going to put my theory to you, Mark. I want you to stop me when I've got something wrong. OK?' His gaze fell to the floor. 'You intended going into the house that day. You were dying for a starring role in one of those films. Help out for a while and maybe those guys would give you a chance. You waited outside with Audra, but she didn't care much for your hanging around. When Callum Armour came along she had someone to help get rid of you. Off you go, no problem. But later on, Mark, maybe after dark, you came back, and the guys let you into the house. Laima and Ruta left about ten o'clock. Audra was still being filmed. With one of the men? Or did you get your chance? The two filmmakers left around midnight, leaving you alone with Audra.'

'No. I left before the men.'

'What about Audra? Why didn't she leave?'

'I thought the guys would give her a lift home.'

'So, you went back to the house later on to check who was still inside? Did she let you in, Mark? Or was the door unlocked? Don't forget to stop me if I get the story wrong. You were thinking how Audra does all sorts of things in those films. She does it with men, and she does it with other girls. She's up for it. It'll be the same thing with me, except there are no cameras running. You've seen the things she can do with her body, with her mouth and her hands. Maybe you picked up a few tips from watching the men.'

Crawley's face glowed red. Sweat beaded on his forehead. His gaze remained downward, but he stole glances at Tara as she continued with the description of Audra's final minutes.

'How am I doing, Mark? Sound familiar?'

'Nice story but no proof, cop.'

'You think?'

His eyes met Tara's then turned to Murray, as if he might find solace there.

'Let's talk about Callum Armour, shall we?' Tara continued.

He shrugged indifference, but Tara saw him wilt. She reckoned by now she'd planted enough doubt in his mind. He must be wondering who he could trust. Debbie perhaps? She was about to rub out his last hope.

'Why did you attack him with a stun gun?'

'Don't know what you're talking about.'

'Did you think he was going to tell us what he'd seen? Were you trying to scare him off? Kill him – shut him up for good?'

'He's a paedo. Shouldn't be allowed out.'

'He was the best friend you ever had, Mark. And you didn't even realise it.'

Crawley attempted a laugh; it died in his throat and became a cough.

'Whatever you did to Audra Bagdonas and whenever you did it, Callum saw you leaving the house.'

'Proves nothing. I didn't kill her. More likely to be him – friggin weirdo.'

'No, Mark. Too late with the denial, I'm afraid. He saw what happened later on, just before daylight. Once again, stop me if I get it wrong. You killed Audra and probably raped her, too, but we can prove that later. Then you went home to Debbie, who's eight months pregnant with your child. Hard to sleep after you've killed a young girl, isn't it? So, you lie awake thinking and you begin to wonder if, in your haste, things might look a bit obvious even to us

217

dumb bizzies when Audra's body is discovered. Maybe I should go back and clear up the mess I've made? Make it look like someone else is responsible. It's only three doors down. I'll slip back there and mix it up a little. Most nights, however, your friend Callum doesn't sleep well. His life is filled with more tragedy than you can possibly imagine. He sits by his window, gazing into the street. Once again, he sees the figure of Mark Crawley slipping in the back door of the house, where Audra is already lying dead. He could have called the police straightaway. Even when he'd heard that Audra was dead, a girl he knew well enough to stop and say hello, he could have told us that he saw you going in and out of the house during the night. He could have told us that he saw you taking away Audra's clothes, her bag and shoes. You did a pretty good job clearing the place. Busy night, wasn't it?'

Sweat and now tears poured down the youth's face. His hands moved nervously from under his arms to the table, to his pockets, to wiping his eyes. He was finding it hard to sit in any comfort.

'But you had a friend in Callum Armour, and you didn't even know it. He was never going to tell on you, Mark. Do you know why? Do you?' She shouted the questions, angry with him, angry with Callum but also with herself. She felt too gullible for police work. There were too many people spinning yarns. In future, she would take a step back and have a good hard look before accepting a story at face value. Now it was time to finish off this disturbed young man.

'You couldn't sleep that night, but neither could your girlfriend. She's expecting your child, and you're off with other girls but growing more frustrated as they reject you. Finally, you decide to take something that isn't yours. You rape and you murder, and then you return to your girlfriend's bed. Debbie can't sleep either. She's awake when you return to the house. She follows you right inside, into the very room where Audra lies dead. She is so frightened by what she sees, but you beg her to help you and to keep quiet. As the pair of you leave the house for the last time, Callum is still watching. Debbie knew it. But Callum was never going to tell. Audra is dead; telling won't bring her back. Debbie is heavily pregnant. Callum's not going to ruin her life and the lives of her children. You're only kids, he thinks. You were in the clear, Mark, until you opened your mouth. Until you tried to stitch up Callum. Only then did he decide we should hear the truth.'

She was already on her feet and looking down on the wasted youth, his head buried in his hands.

'How did I do, Mark?'

CHAPTER 39

Strong tea with sugar wasn't enough to shake out the dull feeling in her head. It went beyond tiredness, approaching nervous exhaustion. She hadn't really slept, merely dozed on the sofa as late night television ran from boisterous American sitcoms to gung-ho American police forensics.

'You look—'

'Don't say it; I know I look like shit.'

'I was going to say you look well considering the day you had yesterday,' said Murray, who certainly wasn't his dapper self.

She smiled thinly, striving to feel grateful for small mercies. Same clothes as the day before, hair unwashed and she'd taken no care with make-up; in fact, she had no recollection of doing anything in readiness for work. She'd woken up, drunk some orange juice and left the flat.

The pair of them sat in Tweedy's office ready to brief the superintendent on the outcome of their case. Murray attempted to treat his lack of rest by ingesting ridiculously strong coffee.

'Good morning,' said Tweedy quite jovially, entering the office and placing his leather-bound Bible at its usual spot on his desk. 'I gather this young man Crawley will make a full statement this morning?'

'That's correct, sir,' Murray replied.

'Very good work, both of you. Perhaps you could answer some questions for me? Crawley has a girlfriend who is pregnant?'

'Yes, sir,' said Tara, 'any day now. We intend to interview her, but we think it can wait until after she gives birth, assuming that Crawley makes his full confession.'

Tweedy nodded his approval.

'She helped bring closure to the case?'

'She helped confirm our thinking that Crawley was trying to fit Callum Armour for the murder. We believe also that Debbie was responsible, in the first instance, for contacting the police about the killing. If you remember, we received an anonymous call.'

'What about the people who were making the films?'

Only a man like Tweedy could make it sound like such an innocent pursuit, she thought.

'One of the two men is Teodor Sokolowski, the owner of the house. The Lithuanian girls told us that he owns several across Merseyside. Rents them to migrant workers, mostly girls; and he uses that as a platform for recruiting prostitutes and girls who are willing to participate in adult films.'

'Have you spoken with these men?'

'I'm afraid not,' said Murray. 'They high-tailed it back to Poland as soon as they heard about the murder. We're making contact with the Polish authorities to have them arrested. Although they're not implicated in the murder, they have some explaining to do regarding their activities.'

'And the two girls?'

'Terribly frightened by the experience,' said Tara. 'They were not surprised that Crawley was responsible for Audra's death, but they didn't speak out for fear of what Sokolowski might do. They couldn't draw attention to his operation.'

'Audra had marks on her chest, a word of some kind?'

'Crawley's handiwork, sir. *Kurwa* is a Polish word meaning whore. Ruta Mankus told me the men said it a lot to the girls during the filming. It became a play word. Apparently, Crawley asked what it meant, and he began using it. All of them thought it was funny.'

'So he burnt that word into the girl's flesh to shift the blame for the killing towards the Poles?'

'Exactly. I called with Debbie after Crawley folded. She told me that when she followed him into the house he was using a lit cigarette to brand the word on Audra's chest.'

'Terrible business,' said Tweedy, shaking his head and closing his eyes to shut out the disturbing vision.

Tara and Murray spent the rest of the day preparing formal statements from Mark Crawley in the presence of a solicitor. A night in a cell helped cultivate an attitude of remorse, and he didn't argue much over the content of his statement. The girls, Ruta Mankus and Laima Gabrys, had been allowed home the previous evening but instructed to return, after a night's rest, to make their statements. When it came to Callum's statement, at Tara's request, she and Murray worked together. They included the final piece of information Callum had revealed: that he'd witnessed Crawley coming and going from the house and also witnessed Debbie's involvement in the early hours of the morning.

It helped Tara confirm the sequence of events she'd put to Crawley, but it continued to rankle that Callum could have saved her days of trouble if only he'd been forthcoming when they'd first met. She realised, of course, he'd used his knowledge to bargain a favour and she had acquiesced. This morning, seated opposite his drawn face, she wanted nothing more than to be well rid of his scheme and his theories. When they finished with the statement, she told him he was free to go. He knew better than to raise the topic of his quest to find his wife's killer.

* * *

Aisling threw her arms around her in the middle of Liverpool One, dozens of shoppers and workers looking on as they tried to reach the escalator.

'We were *so* worried about you, love,' she said.

'I've been fine, honestly.'

Kate took her turn with the hugging then kissed Tara on both cheeks. Still holding her, she said, 'You are not good at keeping in touch these days, especially when you promised.'

'Sorry about that. Things got a bit hectic, but I was always safe. I can take care of myself, you know?'

Aisling didn't look convinced.

'When are you going to pack it in, Tara?' she said as they stepped onto the upward escalator.

It was a timely opportunity for a non-reply. She didn't need a lecture, not after the turmoil of the last few days. The three of them were out for pizza and then to the cinema. The subject of work, as far as she was concerned, had already been exhausted. She was determined to enjoy herself.

'What film are we going to see?' she asked.

'Has to be something funny,' said Kate. 'It's been a helluva day. I don't want to see anything violent or anything sad.'

'I'm with you, Kate,' said Tara.

Aisling was already knitting her eyebrows.

'Doesn't leave us much,' she said.

They consulted the listings at the cinema before heading to the restaurant. A romantic comedy was the obvious choice, Aisling outvoted.

CHAPTER 40

He made his own way home on the bus. Tara hadn't offered him a lift. She didn't even say goodbye. As far as she was concerned the previous three days hadn't happened. And where did that leave him? Back in exactly the same place he had been before they met.

'You been away, Callum?' said Billy Hughes, on his doorstep smoking a fag.

'London for a couple of days.'

'Missed all the fun round here, mate. That young gobshite Crawley was the one that killed the girl. And him gonna be a dad.' Billy shook his head. 'Crazy people round here.'

Callum smiled weakly and slipped his key into the lock. Billy stood watching, his belly poking out from under a faded T-shirt. He exaggerated his glance upwards at Callum's window screens.

'See those screens? You can probably take 'em down now that dickhead's inside for murder.'

Callum paid him the courtesy of looking up also, but tearing down the screens was hardly top of his list of things to do. He stepped inside, closing the door as his neighbour padded down the path to flick his fag butt into the road.

The house was quiet as it should be, but he found it unnerving. Moving from room to room, all he saw was Charlotte with a knife in her heart. He wracked his brain for a theory to account for the deaths of his friends. And why not him? If Kingsley were to blame, why hadn't he come for him? Why wasn't he lurking in a bedroom or keeping watch on the house from across the road?

Nothing made sense. Tara may have learned a lot more about the people who were dead; about Tilly, having met her parents; about Justin, having encountered his father, Georgina, Ollie and Anthony. But he had gained nothing. None the wiser. All he'd done was accompany a stroppy policewoman on a journey through England, through his life, and it ended with him losing another friend. Tara got what she wanted. She had eventually coaxed the story of Audra out of him. She had found her killer; he'd got nothing.

He needed food in the house, the bare essentials for living: milk, bread, butter and tea. Some beer, maybe. For now, he saw nothing beyond the accomplishment of that task. Decisions on his future were for later. Climbing the stairs, he went to the bathroom and opened the door of the hot press. Inside, concealed by a couple of well-worn towels sat a Victoria biscuit tin. He lifted it out and dropped to his knees, placing the tin on the floor. He had no idea how much cash was packed inside, but this was how he did his banking. There were half a dozen tightly rolled packs of notes: tens and twenties and several cheques, uncashed royalty payments from Tilly's books. From a loose bundle of fives, tens and twenties, he pulled out a twenty and replaced the lid. A Chinese takeaway might just hit the spot. He replaced the tin in the hot press and went downstairs. As he opened the front door, he noticed the mail on the floor that he hadn't bothered to look at earlier when he arrived home. He stepped outside, pulling the door closed behind him. Among the letters on the floor was one from the council, a gas bill, an invitation to sign up for a new credit card, notice of a clothes collection for a cancer charity, and the latest edition of the *Oxford Alumni* magazine.

* * *

Tara scarcely lifted her head all morning. It was one thing bringing a case to a close in the practical and verbal sense, it was quite another unenviable task to make sense of it all in writing. She thought that if she immersed herself in the business of detective policing and only in the area relevant to her unit and the Merseyside Police, it would suppress the irritation of how matters had been left with Callum Armour.

When she had told Kate and Aisling about her weekend their attitude surprised her. They saw something in her relationship with Callum that she hadn't seen or, being honest, had tried to ignore. She thought she was helping him. He played his bargaining game, but in the end, she got the truth about Audra and he was no closer to finding his wife's killer. Somehow, her friends had concluded that she had a thing for Callum. She had helped him, because deep down, she wanted him.

Murray invited her out for lunch. It was not a celebration, just a sort of wrapping up of one case before the next one came along. They drove out to Sefton village, to the same pub she'd taken Callum two weeks earlier. It was three o'clock when they got back to the station and Tara, having enjoyed the food and, surprisingly, Murray's company, felt quite relaxed. The feeling very soon evaporated. Waiting in reception for her was Callum Armour.

Murray had the good sense to leave them alone but as he climbed the stairs he cast an icy glare at the dishevelled creature. The dark stubble would soon be a beard once again, his two-week-old clothes, in need of washing, looking no better now than the decrepit jogging trousers and soiled T-shirts. His breath reeked once again of garlic and cheap lager. Callum waited until Murray departed. Tara waited also. She intended to be cool with him, to treat him in a professional manner. She could hide her true feelings from him with an un-smiling expression, but she couldn't hide them from herself. She felt a rise in her tummy, the sensation you get when a lift descends suddenly. She was pleased to see him.

'How can I help you, Callum?'

He had difficulty suppressing his excitement. Firstly, he planned to apologise and then ask after her well-being. Instead, he moved straight onto what he had really come to say. He passed her the latest *Oxford Alumni* magazine.

'Take a look at this,' he said.

Feigning indifference, she accepted the magazine and leafed through it in a cursory manner.

'Centre pages,' he said, urgently.

She opened the magazine up at the centre, but he didn't give her time to read anything.

'The Annual Alumni Reunion – third weekend in September – *in* Oxford.'

'So?'

'Look who's invited to Latimer as the guest speakers.'

She skimmed through the first column of the article.

'Anthony Egerton-Hyde and Georgina Maitland,' he said, gleefully.

She read the legend beneath the photograph of the couple.

'Successes of the last decade, Anthony Egerton-Hyde and Georgina Maitland. The husband and wife team will share some of the secrets of their amazing rise to prominence in British public life.'

She handed back the magazine but said nothing.

'Don't you realise what this means?' said Callum, brandishing the open pages. 'We need to go there, Tara. Kingsley won't miss out on the opportunity. If we show up and I convince Ollie to go along then all the survivors from our circle of friends will be there. It's our best chance to corner Justin and get to the truth.'

'It's not my business, Callum,' she replied, walking to the stairs.

'What? You want to find the killer, don't you? You're the detective.'

She returned to face him. The airy feeling in her tummy had flown, replaced by a fiery temper.

'Firstly, it's not my business. Secondly, it's no concern for Merseyside Police. They pay my wages. It's not on my patch. I'm not interested, and even if I was, I know from experience that I can't trust you.'

'But I can't do it on my own.'

'Can't trust you, Callum.'

'I'm sorry for the way I acted, but you would never have helped me. You would never have given the slightest thought to my problem if I had told you everything from the start. You'd have got your murderer, and I'd still be languishing in that damned house of mine.'

He looked sincerely into her eyes, the last point of appeal. It hung between them for a moment until her head began to shake from side to side.

'No, Callum. I gave you every chance to tell me all you knew. It wasn't simply about Audra's murder. You neglected to tell me about Peter Ramsey's relationship with Egerton-Hyde; you didn't mention Tilly and Justin having been a couple and, the best one of all, you thought it irrelevant that you'd shared a bed with Georgina. You have decided that these murders are all down to Kingsley and his disappearance, but there are secrets remaining, Callum, and they all point to this band of people. Anyone of them could be the killer, and that includes you.'

'I need your help, Tara. Please.'

Suddenly, she bent down to her shopping bag and pulled out a copy of the *Daily Mail*, shoving it into his chest.

'Page five.' Her eyes pierced him; her cheeks glowing.

He found the correct page, but Tara gladly recited the headline for him.

'Former aide to junior minister found stabbed at home. Something else you didn't tell me, Callum. Why? I thought you'd told me of all the relationships. Why didn't you tell me that Charlotte had worked for Egerton-Hyde?'

'I didn't—'

'Save it, Callum. But here's something else for you to think about. We met Egerton-Hyde last Friday evening. You told him we were intending to visit Charlotte, and we found her dead on Sunday. A connection? Go home and think of a reason why a government minister might want to murder his former aide. Think, Callum. Go home to that hovel of yours and bloody think.'

CHAPTER 41

Sometimes the silence of an empty room induces loneliness, at other times a feeling of tranquillity. Tara closed her door, dropped her bag on the floor and made for the fridge. A day-old carton of milk, a bottle of pressed apple juice and a glass's worth of a zinfandel rosé: nothing took her fancy. Defeated, she removed a glass from the cupboard above the sink and filled it with water from the tap. By the time she'd reached her sofa, she'd discarded both shoes. Legs outstretched, she faced the window and was blessed with evening sunshine over the Mersey, a giant cruise ship making for the docks. Alone once again with her thoughts.

She never thought she'd be back on the Treadwater Estate so soon. The phone call made to Assistant Chief Kurt Muetzel in Lucerne the next morning brought about a change of mind. The Swiss policeman had once again been most helpful, although he had made little progress in his investigation of the murder of Zhou Jian. The information he provided for Tara, however, suggested the identity of Zhou Jian's killer, though still not a motive. It piqued her curiosity and prompted her to pay another visit to Callum.

Life moves on. Time passes. Audra Bagdonas was now consigned to the history of this Netherton estate, the life of Mark Crawley changed irrevocably and that of the young mother Debbie.

Tara watched the girl approach, pushing a pram containing her newborn child. Curtis the toddler giggled in the arms of the scraggly kid who was his father.

'Hello, Debbie. You've had her then?' Tara noticed the pink trim of the pram and assumed a baby girl.

Debbie stopped and smiled warmly. She looked happy, the tension that had wracked her face when Tara last saw her had slipped away. She looked a proud mother.

'Do you want to see her?' She peeled back the nylon flap across the front of the pram. Inside, was a tiny bundle of pink wool, yellow-brown cheeks and a wisp of dark hair.

'She's lovely. Do you have a name yet?'

'Edie, it's me gran's name.'

'That's wonderful. I'm sure she's thrilled. Are you keeping well? Managing all right?'

'Got back with Jamie. He's helping me.'

Tara glanced at the youth. He still looked a mere child, his head was shaven, he wore a nose stud, his left arm obscured in tattoos, and a football shirt hung loosely on his skinny frame. He stared blankly, making no attempt at interaction. Tara hoped he was a better catch for Debbie than Mark Crawley.

'Take care of yourself, Debbie.'

She turned towards Callum's house, and to her surprise Jamie suddenly broke his silence.

'If you're looking for Stinker, I saw him down Marian Square heading for the park.'

'Thanks.'

The young family continued on their way, leaving Tara gazing at the changes to Callum's house. Those damned screens were gone; the windows looked clean and the front door, although still battered, was now devoid of graffiti. She smiled her approval and walked back to her car.

Parking in Marian Way behind a mini-market, she crossed the road and walked through the gates into the park. She found Callum sitting alone on a bench and staring idly across the green. It was a bright morning, but she felt the early September days growing cooler. Even as she drew nearer, he didn't seem to notice until she stood over him.

'Used to bring Midgey up here for his walk,' he said without looking at her.

'Nice place, lovely view,' she lied. It was as dull a park as she could ever recall seeing. She sat next to him on the bench and joined him in staring straight ahead.

'My father used to bring me here. He could remember the place before they built the houses and flats around it. Changed times.'

'I read one of Tilly's books.'

'Looking for clues to the murders? I've tried that; drove me nuts.' He suddenly turned towards her. 'You're thinking about the murders again?'

Her eyes widened, but his continued to stare, boring inside her and searching her. His question hung between them. She didn't feel inclined to answer. His staring didn't seem to require one. Without warning, he leaned over and his lips touched hers. At first she drew back, but then his arms encircled her narrow shoulders and he completed the kiss. Soon she gently pushed him away. It was sufficient to cool the moment.

'I see you've taken those awful screens down?'

He grinned, conceding that the moment had passed. His arms released their hold of her, and he slid away leaving a space between them.

'I've been thinking about the things you said. That I shouldn't have sunk to this level. There are loads of people out there who lose the people they love. I shouldn't be wasting my time here.'

She closed her eyes briefly. She had to or else her tears would flow. She couldn't help mixing his problems with her own, thinking of him losing Tilly, of her own experience at Oxford, her time spent with Callum and the kiss that had just occurred.

'What do you mean?' she asked.

'A fresh start.'

'That's great, Callum. I'm happy for you.'

'As soon as I find the man who killed Tilly and Emily, and I'm not going to do that festering away in Netherton. I'm going back to Oxford, to that alumni meeting. It's the most likely place for Justin to show up. And if he's there waiting to get the rest of us, I'll be ready for him.'

'In that case, I suppose I'd better come along, too.'

CHAPTER 42

Latimer College stands among those colleges bounded on the west by St Aldate's, on the north by High Street and to the south by Merton Field and Christ Church Meadow. Callum loved the place. Tara had also loved Oxford. Her dreams, however, always pointed well into the future, beyond student days, beyond the foundations of a career, to a time when she had a settled life with a husband she adored and children to love and inspire.

Walking along Merton Street with Callum beside her, she looked beyond the college that gave the street its name to a building similar in appearance, but only in the hue of its stonework, since Merton outdated Latimer by nearly seven hundred years.

'You all right?' Callum asked when she stopped suddenly. 'You don't look too happy going back to your old college.'

'Come on,' she said at last. 'Time to get this thing started.'

She took Callum's arm, and they walked towards the porter's lodge of Latimer College.

They were allocated rooms on separate staircases on opposite sides of the small quadrangle, its fountain in the centre a memorial statue to the Oxford martyrs of 1555. It was a small reproduction of the George Gilbert Scott memorial which stands between St Giles' and Magdalen Street.

She sat on the single bed, her back against the stone wall, shoes kicked to the floor and her suitcase open beside her. Upon her knee sat a folder containing some of the papers she'd taken from Callum's box-files. There was hardly a sound – the adjoining rooms so far were unoccupied – and little noise from outside, apart from the tap-tap of a gardener's hoe in the flower beds.

Before leaving Liverpool, in fact, even before she'd met Callum in the park, she had decided to keep the information she'd received from Assistant Chief Muetzel to herself. She had a name; that was all, and for now she assumed it was the name of Zhou Jian's killer. The reason for his death, however, remained a mystery. Apart from Latimer College, she could think of no logical connection between Zhou Jian's murder and the deaths of the other alumni. If she was right about the killer, then she must begin piecing together any possible scenarios that might reveal a motive.

Setting the folder to the side, she removed two books from her case: Tilly's novel, *The Clock-tower* and the manual given to her by its author Georgina Maitland. Leafing through this volume she hit on the section of *Live Your Life* devoted to healthy eating. Recalling Georgina's fabulous cupcakes, she wondered just how healthy they were intended to be. She got to thinking, too, on the health of the Maitland-Egerton-Hyde marriage. How had they got around Anthony's apparent homosexuality?

The only people who knew that she and Callum had intended to visit Charlotte were Ollie Rutherford, Georgina and Anthony Egerton-Hyde, and yet Callum persisted with his theory that Justin Kingsley was responsible for the murders. It would be quite a result indeed if he were to show up in Oxford on this weekend. Strangely, he was the only member of that circle of friends who hadn't actually graduated. He'd staged his disappearing act in his final year. He was not an alumnus of Latimer College.

* * *

Callum couldn't help looking forward to meeting up with old friends. At every turn, of course, he saw the sweet smiling face of Tilly. On the brief walk from the car park to the college he pictured her during those years after graduation when many of their friends had moved on, while he and Jian were busy with post-grad projects and Tilly wandered the city streets soaking up inspiration for her novels. She'd taken to some peculiar fashions in those days, Gothic in some sense, then New Age, a throwback to the Sixties with long flowery dresses, floppy hats and flowing locks of brown hair. He wondered now if, in some mystical way, she had been laying down her image for his future, for the time when he possessed only memories of her. Once she was published, after Emily was born and they moved to Shiplake, plainer fashion returned: she wore her hair in a bob, and when at home dressed in jeans and T-shirts.

He stood for a long time peering out of the small lattice window into the quad, watching people come and go. He recognised one or two of the dons, the head porter, Mr Winterburn, of course, and one of the old scouts, Mrs Simms. Several alumni arrived and found their rooms, and for a moment it felt like this was his first day here. How he longed to turn back the clock, to live it all again with no changes, bar the obvious, to have been on time for once, to have reached Tilly and Emily, for the three of them to have been far away when the killer came calling. He gazed at the Latimer Tower with its clock, the strangest part of the college buildings. It looked so quirky set against the traditional pale-yellow stone of Oxford; it didn't lend itself to any particular style of architecture that he could identify. Designed through a competition among students, it was a deliberate attempt to set Latimer apart from neighbouring colleges. In this they had been successful, and Tilly had used it as her inspiration for the time-travelling portal in her novels. A determined knock on his door interrupted his reminiscing. When he opened it, Tara stood in a brown half-length raincoat, woollen hat, jeans and high-heeled boots.

'Fancy a walk?'

Eager for the company, he grabbed his new anorak and joined her downstairs in the quad. She smiled warmly at him, and for the second time that day took him by the arm as they walked, the sound of her heels reverberating around the paved yard.

'Where are we going?' he asked, wondering if they were to behave as a couple on this weekend with her again trying to suppress the appearance of policewoman.

'Anywhere you like. I had to get out of that room for a while. Started to feel depressed.'

'Not reliving good old memories of the place?'

'That's exactly what I was doing, but my memories of Latimer are not like yours.'

'What do you mean?'

'They aren't all pleasant.'

They passed by Corpus Christi and Oriel on their way into High Street. She seemed content to walk in silence, but he couldn't help pondering her agenda. In the few weeks since their first meeting, he'd never known her to do something without having set an objective. He surmised that it was the way of a detective's mind, to have a reason for every action, for every question asked. He didn't realise that she was merely searching for comfort in the city where she'd endured so much grief, on the very day they parted company.

'Have a good look around,' she said at last. 'See if you can spot anyone you know. Someone who's been missing for a long time. That's why we're here.'

They strolled through the streets, browsing the shops, the city throbbing as always with tourists and still a couple of weeks from the student invasion. When they reached Broad Street she pinched his arm.

'Why don't you take me to one of your old haunts? I've heard all about the fun and games you had; why don't you show me where it all happened?'

He stopped and turned to face her. To all passers-by they appeared a natural couple, she dangling on his arm and smiling upwards at his roguish yet handsome face.

'I could ask the same of you,' he said. 'What did you get up to in Oxford that was so bad you never want to talk about it?'

She maintained hold of his arm, her eyes darting nervously as he waited for an answer. Neither one had mentioned the kiss in the park and now they seemed to be revisiting the situation. For a second she considered telling him her story, but a cool breeze suddenly flowed between them providing a sufficient distraction.

'Let's go for a drink,' she said. 'I'll choose the pub if you can't be bothered.'

She pulled on his arm, and he followed obediently. They headed off towards New College Lane, turned left down a narrow alley, and a couple of minutes later sat comfortably in the Turf Tavern, both of them sampling pints of special cask ales. Callum chose a pint of Broadside, while she self-deprecatingly ordered a pint of Bitter and Twisted. The bar was busy with a lunchtime rush, the aroma of sizzling beef and garlic constantly wafting towards them. They sat on low stools facing each other over a small table. Tara removed her hat and coat; Callum seemed comfortable to remain as he was.

It was tempting to slip into a holiday mood, to pretend they were away together, getting to know each other, working towards the moment when they hurry back to her room, pull off their clothes and jump into bed. Each time the mood lightened, she reminded herself of Callum's circumstances, of what they must achieve on this visit, of the dangers one or both of them might face in finding a murderer and bringing him to justice. It had the same effect as the cold rush of air that passed between them earlier. Warm, cosy feelings needed dousing with a bucket of cold water. Visions of murder had the same effect.

'Do you know if Ollie Rutherford is likely to show?' she asked as he set down another pint for each of them.

'Wasn't able to contact him. I left a message on his answerphone. Does it matter? As long as Kingsley shows up and we catch him we'll have our killer.'

'If Kingsley is the killer he will only appear if he has business to attend to.'

'You mean, if he intends to kill again?'

'I mean, if he needs to kill again. These murders, Callum, are all born out of necessity. There can be no other logical reason. Why kill Tilly seven years after most of you left Oxford, and then wait nearly three more before killing Peter Ramsey? Then we have two in quick succession. The killer is beginning to panic, to lash out.'

'Exactly why I think Kingsley will turn up in Oxford. He aims to finish us off.'

'And what if it's not Kingsley?'

'I know, you've said that before. You really think an MP, a government minister, is going to kill somebody to hide the fact that he once had a gay affair? There's no longer a scandal in being gay.'

'Tell me again, who knew that we were going to visit Charlotte? Certainly not Kingsley.'

CHAPTER 43

Around eight o'clock, the alumni of several Oxford colleges began to arrive at The Head of the River for an informal evening of drinks and buffet food. Tara and Callum were eager to discover who, if any, of their old friends and classmates would show up. Both were to be disappointed. Yes, each was recognised by one or two of the academic staff from their days at Latimer, but Tara did not see anyone who was a student during her years there. Callum only seemed interested in whether Georgina would show up.

'She's not likely to appear until it's time for her talk, and that's tomorrow night at the college,' said Tara. 'Georgina and Anthony are far too busy, I'm sure, to spare two nights from their diary for the likes of this.' She used her hand and wine glass to indicate the gathering.

Most of the sixty people appeared old enough to be her parents, or at least graduates from thirty years ago. One or two others, she guessed, were recent alumni, or perhaps postgrads, working through the summer and not likely to miss a free bash. What were they to do if none of that ill-fated bunch put in an appearance?

'I don't know about you, but I've had enough of this.' He held his glass up for her to see. 'Don't like wine very much these days. Fancy a pint?'

'I'm with you,' she said.

After a pint at lunch and two glasses of poor wine, her head felt woozy. Callum disappeared to fetch the beers, while she sat alone beneath the awning on the terrace by the river. She felt the cool of the evening descend, and with it the hopelessness of their situation. Then someone spoke from behind her.

'Hello, Tara.'

'Hi, there,' Tara replied, startled and trying desperately to recall the girl's name. 'Stephanie?'

'That's right,' said the pale girl with chopped brown hair.

She stood by the table in a short black skirt, black cropped leggings and sandals with block heels. Her black and white hooped T-shirt, gathered in at the waist with a broad belt, was overly large on her bony shoulders. Tara invited her to sit.

'I didn't realise you were a Latimer alumna.'

'Oh, I'm not. I went to Surrey. Ollie dragged me along.' She looked inside the building towards the bar. 'He's just met up with Callum.'

'Did Ollie get Callum's message then?'

'Mmm – freaked him out a bit. He didn't want to come, but I told him he must. Do you really think this Kingsley chap will show up?'

Surprised that Stephanie was even aware of the reason for the visit, never mind recalling her name and that of Kingsley, Tara tried her best to explain the situation, as she understood it.

'I'm glad you're here, Tara. It all seems very creepy to me. I'm frightened by the whole thing, but you sounded quite at ease when we last met.'

Tara didn't think Stephanie had taken much notice of the conversation she and Callum had with Ollie in London. She'd seemed too engrossed in her mobile phone.

'I wouldn't say I was at ease. Callum believes the answers to why his family and friends were murdered are to be found here, this weekend. I came along to help him.'

Stephanie rubbed her bare arms. It was growing colder, and the bar staff were lighting the patio heaters as the place began to fill with former students.

'Do we have to do anything?' Stephanie asked. 'Or do we lie in our beds and wait for the killer to strike again?'

It was a fair question, and one for which Tara could not provide a practical answer. Callum returned with the promised beer, closely followed by Ollie Rutherford, casually dressed in an olive-green sweatshirt and blue jeans.

'Hello, Tara. Nice to see you again. I gather we're on a for a real-life murder mystery weekend?'

Considering what Stephanie had just told her, she knew it was false bravado from Rutherford. He and Callum sat down at the table, and a rather inappropriate toast was proposed.

'Here's to nailing the sucker,' said Rutherford in a freakish American accent.

Tara didn't think she could bear a whole night of his quips but, fortunately, conversations soon paired off; Ollie talking to Callum, while Tara chatted with Stephanie. It became clear after a few minutes that everyone was now aware of Tara's background as a police detective. This knowledge implied that the group expected her to take the lead if anything were to happen. She hadn't a clue how to react if they were to encounter Justin Kingsley, although it seemed that she was the only one to doubt that he would make an appearance.

'What does this Justin Kingsley look like?' Stephanie asked.

'Nobody's seen him in ten years,' said Rutherford.

Tara opened her bag and pulled out Callum's well-studied photograph of the skiing party.

'That's him.' She pointed out the young man seated, his arm resting on the back of a chair.

'He's lovely,' said Stephanie. 'Doesn't look like a murderer.'

'And what does a murderer look like to you?' Rutherford asked.

Tara cut them both off.

'That's the trouble, isn't it? There's no set face for a murderer. They won't necessarily stand out from a crowd.'

'Or even a small group like ours,' said Callum.

'I see you've been teaching him well, Tara,' said Rutherford, who continued to look bemused by the situation.

'The reason I asked,' said Stephanie, 'was that I thought someone was watching us just now.' The other three glanced around the terrace and inside towards the bar.

'Here we go,' said Rutherford nervously, taking a hefty gulp of his wine.

'I don't think it was him,' said Stephanie. 'He didn't look like the guy in this photo.'

'Might have changed his appearance since that was taken,' said Callum.

'Looked nothing like him, but he definitely seemed interested in us. Can't believe you lot didn't notice. He was standing on the steps.' She pointed to where three steps separated an upper terrace from the lower in which they sat. 'Watched us for about ten minutes. Soon as I made eye contact, and gave him a look' – she made a not unattractive pout then winked playfully – 'he upped and left.'

* * *

They parted company around eleven. Tara and Callum walked along St Aldate's towards Latimer, but Stephanie and Rutherford called for a taxi to take them to their room at The Randolph. Ollie Rutherford, despite his nonchalance, Tara thought, was clearly spooked by the idea of hunting a murderer and wouldn't consider walking back to his hotel. At his suggestion, however, they agreed to meet for lunch the following day. In fact, Rutherford was intent on not being alone in Oxford for the entire weekend.

Tara wondered if his unease was merely down to a spineless disposition, or did he perhaps have something more to worry about if they were to bump into Justin Kingsley.

She took Callum's arm again on the walk back to college. Neither one said much – too many mixed emotions for Tara, thinking about the case, about how to move things forward, wondering what she really meant to Callum and whether she had become his plaything? To be discarded when this sorry mess was behind them?

It wouldn't be the first time it happened to her in this city. What could she tell Kate and Aisling about this developing relationship? Why on earth did she even regard it as such? She hoped that when they reached her staircase, she could release his arm. Let him go.

They passed through the porter's lodge and bid the night porter, whom neither of them recognised from their student days, a pleasant good evening. A portion of moon appeared in a clearing sky, adding an aspect of shadow to the dim quadrangle, its fountain silent, the spire of the monument thrusting upwards phallic-like from the dark mass of its stone base. The yellow light from the clock face in the tower glowed feebly against the vastness of space above, the hands reading eleven twenty-five. They should have parted there, by the fountain. They should have bid each other goodnight and walked to opposite corners, to separate staircases. But she didn't release his arm.

* * *

He didn't step away from her, as he knew he should. For somehow he believed he would only get one chance. He'd pulled down the screens from his windows, cleaned himself up, made plans for his future, and had begun to embrace life once more. But Tara, he realised, would only give him one more chance. They walked to her staircase in silence.

Reaching the entrance, she dropped her hand behind her taking hold of his, leading him up the narrow stairwell. Kiss him goodnight. Send him on his way. She couldn't do it. He pressed her against the door of the room, bending slightly at the knee for his mouth to meet with hers. One kiss, long, probing, hopeful and bold. Somehow she freed herself from his grip, sufficient only to unlock the door and tug him inside with her.

Later, she lay beside his sleeping body, her pleasure fading. In the darkness of the room, she feared terribly for tomorrow.

CHAPTER 44

Outside, the morning was bright sunshine. Early autumn leaves had blown from the sycamore and horse-chestnut trees in the gardens through the open gates into the quad, swirling around the fountain and rising and falling with each gust of wind. Tara's mood did not complement the promise of the new day. Instead, gazing through the window, she felt cosseted in a blanket of regret and fear. Worst of all, a deep-seated loneliness ushered a hollow sensation through her tummy, an urge to eat indulgently but with the experience to realise it would not satisfy.

Washed and dressed in a blue stretch T-shirt, jeans and boots, she paced the carpeted floor of the student room, retrieving the papers she'd scattered in that urgent moment of desire. She'd found her bra draped over the edge of the waste bin, her pants on the floor close by, and Callum long gone. It was still dark when he released his hold on her body, trapped between him and the stone wall. A few moments of him searching for his clothes, then the click of the door handle, the squeak of hinges, and he was out. Free. She had never experienced such passion. Certainly not with Simon. But it was like any fleeting moment. She had the memory, but the warmth, the gentle touch and the love had gone. She couldn't bear to think that it might not happen again. That she may never again share his bed or feel him inside her. She realised that wanting him may not be enough.

She made no arrangements to meet up with Callum for breakfast. After all, he'd taken his leave of her in the early hours without a word. A late sleeper, she imagined, if her previous experience of Callum was anything to go by. Instead, she went alone to the Latimer dining hall and tried her best to feed the empty sensation in her stomach.

Despite the bright sunshine, it was cool outside. Fresh air, however, was what she needed most. With no particular objective in mind she walked at a brisk pace, her heels clicking on the pavement, into Merton Street but sub-consciously selecting the most convenient route to Balliol College. Stephanie's mention of a stranger watching them in the pub the night before had her thinking.

CHAPTER 45

Disappointed by her morning, walking, thinking and searching, and frustrated with all three activities, she resorted to shopping. That too proved a disappointment for she bought nothing more than a pair of fine denier tights from Debenhams. Not long after one o'clock she entered The Randolph Hotel by the main door into the wood-panelled hall and, turning to her right, proceeded directly to the restaurant. A pleasant and foreign maître d' was intent on escorting her to a table for one, and as she explained that she was meeting friends, she spied them at a round table by a window overlooking Beaumont Street. Ollie Rutherford, Stephanie and, to her chagrin, Callum were already present. She couldn't manage eye contact with the man who a few hours earlier had shared her bed, and when she stole a glance he seemed more taken with the menu. Quite deliberately, she angled her dining chair to face Stephanie who looked to have experienced as rough, or perhaps as passionate, a night as she had.

'One rule before we start,' Rutherford announced, looking directly at Tara. 'Please, no more talk about killings and missing friends. Let's have a good time, enjoy the food and get to know each other better.'

'I agree,' said Stephanie, raising her wine glass. 'Besides, I need a stiff drink.'

'Hair of the dog?' said Callum, raising his glass also.

'Absolutely.' Stephanie took a healthy gulp of white wine.

Tara felt cajoled into joining the toast, but as far as she was concerned this was a working lunch. She might have to disguise the fact, but she was there only to get information.

'So, Callum,' Rutherford began. 'What's this fresh start you've been hinting at?'

Rather than see it in his face, Tara sensed Callum's discomfort: shifting in his chair, glancing at her, his eyes darting before attempting an answer to the question. Rutherford wasn't prepared to wait.

'You coming back to Oxford?'

'No. Nothing's settled yet, but Georgina has offered me a job.'

Tara instantly recalled the conversation in Georgina's office, when a fairly vague but open invitation had been laid before him. It seemed to Tara that the offer had been made several times over the last three years. She wondered if anything more specific had been discussed since the day they met in Georgina's office or perhaps when Georgina had telephoned on the day they found Charlotte.

'You've spoken with Georgina?' she asked him.

He nodded sheepishly.

'When?'

'About a week ago.'

Now she had good reason to feel used. The masochist within her was having a field day. For the second time in her life she'd allowed, heck, she'd encouraged a man to share her bed when he already knew, when he already had plans laid for a future that did not include her. For added humiliation, on both occasions, Oxford had provided the backdrop to her heartbreak.

'Did you tell her we were coming to Oxford? To the alumni meeting?'

'I mentioned it, yes.'

'Why, Callum?'

Tara closed her eyes in anguish. She couldn't decide on the worst part of the news, his leaving Liverpool to go and work for Georgina, or him telling Georgina they were coming to the alumni gathering in Oxford.

'What's the problem?' he asked.

'Come on, chaps,' Rutherford jumped in. 'I thought we weren't going there?'

Tara's head dropped to her chest. She sensed Stephanie's eyes upon her. While Callum and Ollie plodded on into bland conversation, she felt a growing urge to run. But she was made of stronger flesh. She'd been walked over once before. Never again. She was here to help Callum find a murderer. She was determined to find the truth. That's what she had resolved to do when she signed the enrolment forms for the Merseyside Police. To hell with upsetting poor Ollie. She ploughed in.

'Can either of you men, distinguished alumni of Latimer College, suspects in a murder investigation' – she saw Rutherford blanch at the suggestion – 'tell me why Charlotte stopped working for Anthony Egerton-Hyde?'

Rutherford, in a fluster, helped himself to more wine from the bottle. Callum filled the silence.

'I don't think she worked that closely with him. She was more a party member, a constituency worker.'

Tara looked at Rutherford for input.

'Matter of trust, I believe,' he said finally. 'She helped Anthony get elected. Once he'd taken his seat in Westminster, he didn't think she could be trusted having access to the information available to an MP.'

'How do you know this?' Tara asked.

'He told me. What the silly sod never seemed to realise was that Charlotte worshipped him. She would never have done anything to hurt him. Not intentionally.'

'I wonder if Georgina has ever told him that Charlotte was in love with him,' said Tara.

'Might well have done, and he chose to ignore it,' said Rutherford.

'Hardly matters, now that she's dead,' said Callum.

'Not relevant either, if Kingsley is your man, Tara.'

She ignored Rutherford's comment. For a man who, two minutes earlier, wasn't keen to discuss the subject he was now defending Anthony Egerton-Hyde.

'Kingsley's the one with the axe to grind, isn't that right, Callum?' Rutherford continued.

'I think so,' Callum replied.

Rutherford stared with a glib expression at Tara, while she for a brief second clung to his metaphor. An axe to grind, was that coincidental or Freudian in origin? Did Rutherford realise or was he well aware of the weapon used to cut Peter Ramsey to pieces?

'And what says our resident beauty from the Merseyside Police?' he said.

She took it in the manner in which he'd intended it: sarcastic, patronising and arrogant.

'I'd be very surprised if Justin Kingsley turns up in Oxford this weekend,' she said. 'Firstly, he's been missing for ten years and no one has seen him. Secondly, he has no reason to attend the alumni meeting because he never graduated. Thirdly, he's unlikely to show just to quench Callum's thirst for justice, especially since he is not the murderer. If he is alive, I doubt that he is even aware of these murders. Now, if you'll excuse me, I need some fresh air.' She dropped her napkin on the table and rose to leave.

'Come on, Tara,' said Callum with some incredulity in his voice. 'You said yourself that Justin has probably been in contact with his father all this time. He's no longer listed as a missing person. If he's alive he must be the killer.'

'Aren't you going to eat something?' Stephanie asked.

'No thanks. Not that hungry, and I'm tiring of the company. Do you fancy a walk, Stephanie?'

'Wouldn't mind actually.' She rose from her chair. 'You boys, stay and enjoy the wine. We'll see you later.'

The girls had reached the door of the restaurant when Tara turned swiftly and marched back to the table. Leaning both her hands on Rutherford's shoulders, she faced Callum and said, 'Here's something for you to mull over while you have lunch. I still haven't figured out why Zhou Jian was murdered, but guess who was attending the same conference in Lucerne when he was killed?'

Rutherford was already reaching for the wine again; Callum stared at Tara in amazement. Now he would know how it felt to be drip-fed information. Assuming neither man would contribute an answer, she filled in the blanks.

'Our junior minister for health.'

CHAPTER 46

After they'd wandered about town for half an hour, Stephanie suggested a walk by the river.

'Ollie talks so much about his rowing days at school and at Oxford. Sometimes,' Stephanie said with a sigh, 'I wish he would take it up again. I told him he's getting lazy. He goes to the gym a couple of times a week, but that's about it. I've asked him to come running with me. But no. He thinks running is for people who don't have a life.'

'You do a lot of running?' Tara asked.

'I still compete. Middle-distance stuff. I'm cutting back now; Ollie isn't keen on me travelling all over the place.'

Tara realised how the ultra-slim, bony physique and pale complexion were typical indicators of such an athlete. For now, though, she was more interested in what Stephanie had to say about her partner.

'How long have you two been together?' she asked.

Tara had steered them into Christ Church Meadow, taking a path leading down to the Isis. Her feet were getting sore from wearing the high-heeled boots, having spent the morning traipsing the streets, but she managed to slow the pace as she chatted with Stephanie.

'We've been living together for a year. Before that we were on and off for about two.'

'You seem to get along all right.'

'Sweetheart at times, selfish bastard at others. That's Ollie.'

Stephanie sounded neither happy nor sad with her description of her boyfriend. She walked with her head down, concentrating on her feet in blue espadrilles, kicking out at pebbles strewn on the path. Tara got the impression that Stephanie was keen enough to talk openly of her relationship, sensing also that she was looking for some advice.

'Is there any reason why Ollie is particularly nervous about being here this weekend? You said that he didn't want to come.'

'Big coward, isn't he?' Stephanie laughed.

'Understandable if you believe your life may be under threat, but do you know if Ollie has any reason to be more frightened than the rest of us?'

'You mean does he have enemies among this bunch of people?'

'Justin Kingsley, for instance. Has Ollie ever mentioned anything that happened between them?'

Stephanie shook her head as they came to a halt by the water's edge. Two scullers, having passed Cox Stone and made the turn, were now headed downstream towards the boathouse. She watched them gather speed.

'He has only ever spoken about the night Kingsley disappeared,' Stephanie replied. 'And that's only since we met you in London.'

'They didn't have a fight? Ollie doesn't believe that Kingsley would hold any grudge against him?'

Stephanie shook her head.

'Don't think so.'

'What about Ollie and Anthony?'

'They're pretty close friends, although they fight all the time.'

'What do they fight about?'

They remained on the spot, Tara hoping for a break to help ease the discomfort in her feet.

'Money and things... Look, Tara!' Stephanie nudged her and whispered, 'That's the guy who was staring at us in the pub last night.'

To their right, thirty feet and closing, was a couple walking hand in hand. The man wasn't tall, about five-eight or nine. He had a fine complexion, delicate, as if his face might be his living – a model or an actor, perhaps. Casually dressed in brown slacks and a brown chunky-knit cardigan, his face broadened to a wide smile revealing whitened teeth. His companion was taller by at least two inches, although her black ankle-boots had heels much higher than Tara's. The girl had long brown hair, blowing around a narrow face with a rather prominent upper lip and pushed-up nose. Attractive, but Tara would not have said she was pretty. She wore tight-fitting black jeans and a half-length brown tweed coat. So many emotions flooded Tara's head before the man spoke. She'd spent all morning searching; walking through Balliol, wondering if the man

249

Stephanie had observed watching them the night before was her Simon. She cringed at even thinking of him now as her Simon.

'Hello, Tara,' he said in a sprightly way, as if he'd purely by accident, by a freak of time, nature and fate, bumped into her.

When he added, 'Fancy seeing you here,' she could have lashed out at the supercilious face. Deep breaths, she thought.

'Hello, Simon. How are you?' She attempted to add a smile, aimed more at his girlfriend, but she was sure it looked more like a snarl.

'Great,' he replied. 'You remember Louisa? From our year?'

'Hi,' the girl said with a smile and a slight wave of her free hand.

'Sorry, Louisa, I don't think I remember you,' she lied, proud of herself for doing so. Louisa had indeed been in their year, but not in their social circle. Evidently, she now fitted the picture for Simon, her background seemingly more agreeable than North of England middle class. 'Very surprised to see you in Oxford, Simon. I thought student days were consigned to the past for you?'

Unfortunately, her sarcasm seemed lost on her former lover, the man she thought she'd be spending her life with, the man who had stamped on her dreams and gouged out her heart.

'Louisa dragged me along. She's really into all this reunion caper. It was either come along with her, or stay at home to look after the sprogs.'

'You have children?' Tara felt her heart sink to her feet. One shock laid upon another. Simon a father, a painful twisting knife in her gut.

'Two girls, four and two,' said Louisa, proudly. 'My husband loves them dearly, but he's not terribly domesticated, not when it comes to potty training.'

Tara scoured her mind for something meaningful to say. How should she react to learning that Simon was married and a father?

'I'm sorry, this is Stephanie,' she managed. Simon and Louisa shook hands with Tara's companion.

Suddenly, her attention shot past the couple. Twenty yards behind them, under the shade of a sycamore, a man dressed in dark trousers and leather bomber jacket stood with his shaven head bowed. She could hear Simon prattling on, networking with Stephanie about living in London, while she strained to see the man's face. She really needed to see him close up.

'Excuse me a moment,' she said, stepping around Louisa, while keeping her eyes on the man beneath the tree. She didn't think he was aware of her approach, but she'd only taken a couple of steps when he swung round. Now she felt certain. The strong jaw, serious eyes, her mind switched rapidly to the first time she'd ever seen him. The photograph in Callum's box-file, now in her handbag. The man came towards her. She couldn't help staring at him. But he didn't know her. He must have been faintly aware that she had been watching him, because he looked startled as his gaze met with hers. He strolled on by, taking the path through the meadow towards Christ Church. When she turned around, Simon, Louisa and Stephanie were looking on in silence.

'Sorry, I have to go.'

'Tara?' Stephanie called after her.

'Maybe we can meet up later, Tara,' Simon said.

'Nice talking to you,' said Tara, sarcastically, already on the trail of the man she never believed would show up in Oxford. She'd been so terribly wrong, instead building a case in her mind against Egerton-Hyde.

'What's wrong, Tara?' Stephanie said, jogging to catch up. Tara glanced over her shoulder; Simon and his wife watched them go. She'd abandoned him. Great to think it was poignant, but she hadn't time. She stopped dead.

'Tara?' Stephanie, fast becoming a bystander looked confused as Tara suddenly rushed back towards Simon.

'Tara? Is there something wrong?' Simon asked.

She veered to her right, under the trees, a grey squirrel hopping out of her way. Papers, news cuttings, lists and photographs rolled through her head like movie credits on a cinema screen. The question of what the man had been doing under the tree lay before her, and yet she believed somehow that she already knew the answer. Stephanie walked by her side as they moved under the sycamore to the place where she'd first noticed him.

'Tara? Can I help you with something?' Simon called out.

'Fuck off, Simon. That's all I need from you. Just fuck off!' Never even bothered to view his reaction, her mind already lost in something else, something more important. She stood before a small rectangular plaque made from brass but pitted black from weathering and welded to a single metal stake pushed into the earth beneath the tree. Her former lover and his wife moved away, whispering between each other, but Tara was no longer aware of their ever having been there. She had moved on, too. She read the inscription on the plaque.

'The Baby Isis?' said Stephanie. 'In memory of Baby Isis whose remains were discovered here. What's this mean, Tara?'

'Not sure yet.' She hurried away. 'Come on, we have to follow him.'

'Who?'

'Justin Kingsley.'

CHAPTER 47

The man she believed to be Kingsley was now more than a hundred yards along the path heading, she guessed, for the gateway from the Meadow into St Aldate's or to Merton Street and beyond, or to Merton Field towards Latimer College. Terrible misjudgement to have worn heels, but this morning she never thought she'd be haring around Oxford on the trail of a murderer. Stephanie peppered her with questions as they hurried along. Some she answered, others she couldn't and one or two, wouldn't. Fortunately, the man didn't alter his walking speed seemingly unaware of his pursuers. Tara realised that if he made it to St Aldate's and to the streets crowded with Saturday afternoon shoppers and tourists, she would lose him. All the while the one question swung to and fro before her eyes. What connected Justin Kingsley to the Baby Isis?

The man was nearing the end of the path through the Meadow. Tara watched carefully for the direction he chose.

'You were saying that Ollie fights with Egerton-Hyde?'

'They've had a couple of blow-outs,' Stephanie replied.

'About what?'

'Money, investments. It's all gone quiet though since Anthony got the ministry post.'

'Are they business partners?'

The man turned left. They were only forty yards behind, but they needed to reach the exit gate before he entered St Aldate's. Once there he could go left, right, straight across the road, or even hop on a bus. She broke into a run. Stephanie had no problem picking up the pace.

'Ollie handled some financial deals for him; one didn't quite go to plan; that's all I know. Why are you asking me these questions, Tara? If the man we're following is Justin Kingsley, surely that proves he's the killer? He's come to murder again.'

'That's why we need to follow him.'

The man had reached the open gate leading to St Aldate's but once he passed through, he stopped and gazed up and down the road. Tara and Stephanie slowed to walking pace, and twenty yards off came to a halt. She had to do something inconspicuous, while at the same time get another look at the man's face.

'Do you have your phone?'

Stephanie pulled her mobile from the pocket of her anorak.

'Call Ollie. Get him to tell Callum that I may have found Kingsley.' The man set off again, heading up St Aldate's towards the city centre. The girls followed, maintaining a distance of forty yards behind him. Still, he seemed unaware of his stalkers. His pace quickened, however, and it seemed to Tara that he now had a specific destination which was at odds with his dithering earlier by the gates to Christ Church Meadow. Tara needed Callum and Ollie to give a positive identification. All she had to go on was the ten-year-old photo that she'd just removed from her bag and periodically examined as they hurried along the street, passing by Christ Church College.

She wondered where he was going. She wondered, also, what to do when she had him at a fixed location. Call the local police? To tell them what exactly? I've discovered a man who's been missing for ten years wandering the streets of Oxford? He's responsible for the deaths of five people? But sorry, I can't place him at any of the crime scenes, and I can't provide a motive for any of the killings. She'd be the one locked up. She worried how Callum would react if they managed to corner Kingsley at a house or flat. Listening to one side of the telephone conversation between Stephanie and Ollie, it didn't sound pleasing.

'Ollie's coming to meet us,' said Stephanie. 'I'll keep him posted as to where we're going.'

'Where's Callum?' said Tara, a sudden note of panic in her voice.

'He's gone off to visit some old colleagues from the lab,' Ollie said.

'Shit. Why does that man think he's here on a jolly?'

'I take it you two had a row? Things seemed a bit frosty over lunch.'

Tara couldn't speak. She had a sudden urge to turn around and walk away. But her fear and her determination to find the truth behind this bunch of people, dead and alive, drove her forward. Thankfully, this man was proving easy to follow. Crossing High Street, he entered Cornmarket, a pedestrianised zone. His pace slowed again as he paused to browse at shop windows, and each time the girls had to stop, look the other way and pretend to be chatting.

'Call Ollie again,' said Tara. 'Tell him to go find Callum. I need him here with me.'

They set off once more, but in a few seconds the man entered a burger bar, and they could do nothing but wait outside. Five minutes later Ollie was standing beside them.

'So where is Lord Lucan then?' he said, chortling. His bluster and lack of discretion continued to grate with Tara.

'Let's move away from here,' she said, ushering him to the opposite side of the street to stand in the doorway of a clothes store. 'Keep watching that burger bar. I'll tell you when the man I think is Kingsley comes out. You tell me if it's really him. Try not to let him see you.'

Tara stepped away from Ollie and Stephanie, thinking it wise that if Kingsley did notice Ollie she would not be associated with him, and could continue to follow Kingsley when he walked off. She didn't get the chance. Before Ollie managed a good look at the man, he was out of the shop, turning right in the direction of Broad Street and moving at a much greater pace than before. It seemed likely to Tara that the man had spied Ollie through the window of the burger bar, and he'd decided that Ollie was not a person he wished to meet right now.

'Did you get a look at him?' she asked.

Ollie shook his head.

'You two go and find Callum. I'll keep following this guy.'

'But, Tara,' Ollie protested. 'If it is Kingsley–'

'Give me your number, Stephanie, and I'll call you if anything happens. Phone me when you find Callum, and we'll arrange to meet.'

As soon as she'd punched Stephanie's number into her phone she hurried off, trying desperately to pick out the man among dozens of people moving along the street.

What should she do if she managed to corner him? Wait for Callum to show up? They could beat each other senseless? Questions did little to aid her chase. If she still had her eye on the right man, he hadn't slowed his pace and was putting greater distance between them. When he reached the corner of the Cornmarket he paused by Waterstones bookstore, and looked over the window display. Suddenly, he glanced in her direction. There was nothing she could do. She had to keep going. Any sudden jink to her left or right, dropping her head, or coming to a sudden halt would look conspicuous. She fixed her gaze dead ahead and maintained her pace. At least it gave her the opportunity to look at his face, while she hoped he had taken little notice of her.

She was almost upon him before he moved off again. Once his back was turned, she had time to pause and allow some distance to develop again between them. From the bookstore, he crossed into Magdalen Street, on the same side of the street as the Church of Saint Mary Magdalen. Concentrating on crossing the road, she momentarily took her eye off her quarry. When she next peered down the street he'd gone. She stopped and looked around her. He'd vanished. She hurried along by the railing of the old graveyard, scanning the pavement on the opposite side of the street, crowded with shoppers and several queues of people waiting for buses. He may have crossed the road and gone into one of the shops, she thought. Searching each of the stores was futile. Too many people. She'd lost him. Further along the street she noticed the open door into the church. He couldn't have gone much further beyond this point. She'd only taken her eyes off him for a second. It had to be. Worth a try anyway, she thought.

The overhanging trees cut the light, giving the impression of dusk as she made her way to the church porch. There would be others inside, she told herself. She could get a good look at the man as he wandered around. Stepping into the wide porch, she entered the ancient church through very modern plate glass doors. The interior was gloomy, with a pervading smell of burning incense. Standing at the back, she gazed toward the sanctuary but saw no one. Cut off from the bustling street outside, there was total silence. Glass panelling behind her separated a small office and sacristy, lit by a single dim spotlight, from the main church. It also was deserted. Stepping into the south aisle, she noticed a door opened slightly revealing a hallway leading to the south door. She'd lost Kingsley. He had not entered the church, or else he'd given her the slip by leaving through this door. After a last look around the church, she hurried into the hallway.

She gave a yelp as a hand took firm hold of her hair, pulling her into a darkened corner. She managed a brief scream before another hand covered her mouth and nose. She felt a body behind her, squeezing her tight. She fought for breath. Her eyes bulged, her face tightened as the hand twisted and pulled her hair backwards. Panic gripped her. She struck out with her foot, trying to stamp her heel into his shoe. Why weren't there other people around? Why couldn't someone help her? She moaned, but the hand remained locked around her mouth. He released her hair and slung his arm around her waist, pulling her close to his body. She tried pulling away, but without breath she had no fight. Her head spun. She felt close to passing out. Then he spoke in a harsh whisper.

'One scream and I'll break your neck. Understand?' His arm squeezed tighter into her stomach. She wanted to heave. 'Understand?' he repeated as he twisted her head and body to face him. His eyes drilled into hers. The hand on her face slipped downwards allowing her to breathe through her nose. He was too strong, too big. Forcing his right leg between hers he thrust his knee upwards pressing it to her crotch. She cried out, but his hand gripped ever harder to her mouth, and her head thumped against the stone wall of the church. Why didn't someone come? She attempted another escape, trying to force her hands between their bodies to get leverage, to shove him off. She felt a stinging pain in her side, just below her ribs.

'Next time I won't stop with the knife, and you can bleed to death. Now, tell me why you've been following me? Scream and I'll cut you again. Understand?'

This time she attempted a nod, and slowly he relinquished his grip on her mouth. She gasped a deep breath and felt the knife jagging into her flesh.

'In there,' he ordered, his arm locking around her tiny waist, her T-shirt raised and the knife still pricking at her side. He bundled her through the door into the south aisle of the church. It was quiet and empty, and she felt shattered by disappointment and bereft of hope. He bungled her to the right-hand side and into a rear pew. Jabbing the knife into her side, he slid her across the cushioned seat until she hit the wall. He pressed himself tightly against her; the knife, she was sure, had again pierced her skin. He repeated his question, as if she could possibly forget.

'Why were you following me?'

'I don't know what you're talking about.' His right arm moved around her shoulders mingling with the strands of her hair. He grasped and pulled back sharply. She cried out.

'No more games. Who are you? What do you want with me?'

This time she got a closer view of his face. Clean-shaven, smooth taut skin. His eyes she judged a blue grey, wary but not evil in the way she had known others to be. His breath smelled of onions and vinegar after his meal in the burger bar. Most striking was his tanned complexion. Unless he slept every night under a sun bed, this man had spent serious time in the sun.

'I'm a police officer,' she replied at last. She watched his eyes dart as his brain dealt with the implications. 'Detective Inspector Tara Grogan. I think it's time you let go of my hair and put that damned knife away.'

He did neither.

'What do you want with me?'

'I saw you by the river; you were looking at a plaque about the Baby Isis, why?'

'And that's a reason to follow me across town? Try again.' His grip tightened on her hair. She drew a sharp breath and felt the cold blade on her skin.

'I know who you are, Justin,' she said. The knife cut her. She cried out.

'You've got the wrong man, cop.'

Judging by his reflex action with the knife as she spoke, she knew that the man squeezing the breath from her was definitely Kingsley.

'Please, Justin. Listen to me. I'm trying to help you. Put the knife away, and we can talk.'

He laughed nervously then pressed his forehead into hers, pushing her back against the wall. He pulled ever harder at her hair, and she cried in fear that she'd got things terribly wrong in her mind. That Justin Kingsley was indeed the killer, Callum was right, and he was here to finish off this group of Latimer alumni. But first, he intended to kill her.

'No, you listen to me. I don't know what you're talking about. Whatever you're doing you've got the wrong man. Leave me alone, or next time you won't get to speak before the knife goes in.' Releasing her, he shoved her hard against the wall. He was out the door before she'd crawled into the aisle. She tried going after him, to make him understand, but as she struggled to her feet she saw her blood dripping to the floor.

CHAPTER 48

Finding her shoulder bag lying in the porch where she'd been grabbed by Kingsley, she retrieved a small pack of tissues and struggled back inside to sit in a pew. Using her compact mirror, she inspected the cuts. A lot of blood but, she hoped, no real damage. There were at least three gashes in her side, and a rip in her T-shirt where he'd forced the knife point to break her skin. Had he been deliberately careful with his cutting? she wondered.

While she pressed a tissue against the cuts in her side, the silence in the church was broken as the door opened. She had no time to run. A man of around seventy, bald, squat, with glasses and a sagging face, ambled through the doors. A woman of similar age with silver hair and remarkably similar build followed behind. They did little more than glance at the young woman seated in the back pew, her hair sticking out at every angle, her face pale with shock, and tears drying slowly in the corners of her eyes. The woman managed a brief smile, and Tara tried her best to return it. A bit bloody late, she thought.

Fresh air helped, although her body still trembled, and she wondered if the people in the bus queue opposite noticed the little girl lost rocking on her feet. She steadied her hand and managed to call Stephanie's number.

Thank God they were close by. She propped herself against the railings of the churchyard and waited for them to appear, watching all the while in case Justin Kingsley had decided to keep tabs on her.

Stephanie and Ollie took her immediately to A & E at the Radcliffe Infirmary. Fortunately, the wait was brief and soon she'd been seen by a staff nurse and momentarily by a junior doctor who assessed the damage. Not as bad as it looked, was the medical opinion. She'd had to explain how she came by such an injury, and in doing so had to point out that she was a police officer involved in a case which was ongoing. No time for rest or written reports to her superiors. Eight stitches and a tetanus jab later, she was released to her waiting companions. Ollie went off again in search of Callum, while Stephanie escorted Tara to their room at The Randolph.

* * *

Callum appeared with Ollie thirty minutes later. His face was pale, his eyes frightened.

'Are you all right?' he said, rushing to her and going down on his knees.

'I'm fine, just a little shaky. You were right, Callum. He did show up.'

Ollie had a glass of brandy for her, although Tara knew she couldn't manage it. She sat gingerly upon the bed as Stephanie boiled water in a kettle and made some strong coffee. Callum hadn't taken his eyes off her since he came in, listening in silence while she spoke of her encounter with Kingsley.

'You're certain it was him?' Ollie asked her, helping himself to the glass of brandy.

'Might not have been one hundred per cent until I called him by his name. That definitely touched a nerve.'

'So, we have our man then?' said Ollie.

Callum appeared to wait for Tara's view on the matter.

'We don't have anyone, Ollie,' she said. 'Kingsley didn't hang around for a reunion with you lot. We have no further evidence that he's the murderer.'

'He stuck a knife into you, Tara,' said Stephanie, alarmed. 'Isn't that sufficient evidence?'

'If he killed the others, why not kill me?'

'Did you tell him you're a police officer?' Callum asked.

'Yes, I did. But if he's a determined killer my being a police officer wouldn't have stopped him.'

Ollie shook his head in despair, throwing the remainder of the brandy down his throat.

'I don't understand coppers. If you can't see a killer from close up, what hope is there for the rest of us?'

Only now was Tara able to sip at her coffee, it having been much too hot when Stephanie poured it. Something inside her, despite her shaking, enjoyed seeing Ollie Rutherford a bundle of nerves. He looked a strong man, but lacked something substantial in the courage department. Regardless of his mental state, she had a couple of questions to ask him.

'Tell me about you and Egerton-Hyde, Ollie.'

'Here we go. You still reckon Anthony is the killer?'

She wasn't about to argue the toss over her suspicions. She simply wanted information about Egerton-Hyde. The rest of them seemed convinced that Kingsley was the murderer, but as far as she was concerned nothing had changed. No one had identified a motive for any of the murders.

'How much business does he put your way?'

Rutherford glared icily at Tara, his face paling into the most serious expression she'd so far witnessed in the man. For a moment, she wasn't certain that he would answer.

'I handle a fair number of private investments for him. Strictly business. Nothing that interferes with his political activities.'

'If he were to take a fall would you go down with him?'

'This is ridiculous. The man's a close friend of mine. We were at school together. He's not a murderer.'

'Is he in your debt, Ollie, or are you in his?'

'We've worked together for years. I helped him raise money outside of his political career. It went to saving his ancestral home. Most families with properties like his have to open their doors to the public to keep going. I earned Anthony enough money to save him having to consider such action. You're out of your mind, Tara, if you think Anthony would be trying to kill me or anyone else.'

'I hear you have had quite a few rows with him. What about?'

He fired his girlfriend an unhealthy stare.

'Well informed, aren't you?' He gave a deep sigh. 'Yes, we have rows, usually about money.'

'Not always money?'

'No.' He fixed his gaze on Stephanie and looked as though he might be on the verge of tears. 'I once had an affair with Georgina.'

'When?' Stephanie demanded. She'd been sitting on the double bed next to Tara, but she jumped to her feet and stood before him. 'When, Ollie?' she repeated.

'Years ago, before us,' he said with some resignation in his voice. 'He and Georgina argue about it, and she throws in his gay fling with Peter. They beat each other up with it all the time. I think he would use it against me, but he needs me to earn money for him. Nowadays, he seems resigned to needing me.'

'What about Georgina?' Tara asked.

'She hates my guts, because Anthony is so reliant on me. He could get himself another investor, but I think he keeps me around just to spite Georgina.'

Tara looked at Callum for input. None was forthcoming. She'd believed that she and Callum were in this together. Now, however, she realised she was very much on her own.

CHAPTER 49

They shared a taxi back to Latimer. Neither one spoke. Tara's side below her ribs continued to sting from the wounds, and she wanted to get back to her room to rest before the evening reception for the alumni. Emotionally, she was in agony from the ordeal at the hands of Kingsley, but also from the treatment she'd received from Callum. It crossed her mind to run, to clear off and leave these people to their own sorry mess, but part of her still wanted to help the man she'd come to love. What infuriated her most was that every suggestion she'd made to counter the argument that Kingsley was the murderer, Callum had put down and dismissed completely. She had been wrong about Kingsley showing up, but she didn't think she was wrong about Anthony Egerton-Hyde.

She enjoyed a couple of hours' sleep in her room and felt refreshed by a careful shower. She downed a couple of paracetamol and a cup of hot, sweet tea before getting dressed for the evening.

The Old Members' Building sat directly behind the buildings that formed the quadrangle. Built in the nineteenth century of Bath stone, the three-storey block stood on the far side of a tidy lawn. The Meeting Room, fully panelled in oak, had an arched wooden-beamed ceiling and a polished floor. It was laid out at one end, close to a huge stone fireplace, with red-cushioned straight-back chairs. Slightly off-centre, an oak lectern awaited the invited speakers for the evening reunion of college alumni. To the right of the main door, stood two long tables neatly stocked with canapés, wines, tea and coffee.

Tara was one of the last to arrive, deliberately so. Whatever way she regarded this evening's event she couldn't feel comfortable in attending. Rather than parade herself, which is exactly how she felt in her expensive, staggeringly high shoes and a dress much too extrovert for her tastes, she longed to be home in her flat at Wapping Dock, a light-hearted film on the telly, a bowl of crisps in her lap and a glass of apple juice in her hand. She hadn't devoted any attention to what Callum was thinking on how she looked. His jaw-dropping reflex, when she came into the room, made her feel better.

'Any of our distinguished guests arrived yet?' she asked him.

'Ollie and Stephanie are helping themselves to the food and drink.'

They looked across the room to where Ollie was trying his best to hold a flute of sparkling wine in each hand while attempting to eat a spiced prawn wafer.

'No sign of our guest speakers?' she asked.

He shook his head.

Perhaps it was best if they didn't show at all. She wondered what Kingsley was planning. There was no doubt in her mind now that his appearance in Oxford was designed to coincide with this evening's gathering. If, as she believed, he was not the killer, then what role was he here to play?

* * *

Twenty minutes later, the assembly of Latimer alumni took their seats at the top end of the room. The chairs were arranged four rows deep in an arc around the fireplace. Tara sat next to Callum at one end of the third row, and to the far right of the lectern. Ollie and Stephanie sat one row in front, close to the centre aisle.

A panelled door to the right of the fireplace opened, and to warm applause, Georgina strode into the meeting room. She acknowledged the welcome with a beaming smile, although Tara thought the distortion of facial muscles made her look ten years older. In reality, she was little more than four years older than Tara. The reddish-brown hair she'd noticed at their first meeting had grown such that, had it not been curled inwards at the bottom, it would have rested upon her shoulders. It looked perfectly smooth, and it shone beneath the bright candle bulbs of the room's chandelier. She wore an exquisite metallic, silver-blue dress, a slim fit that hung just below her knees. The silver strap-shoes seemed excessively high for a woman so tall, but she walked with confidence to take her place behind the lectern. Her smile remained on show until the applause subsided, and then she dropped her head to examine the few pages of notes she'd brought with her.

Before she began, the door behind her opened once again, and Anthony Egerton-Hyde, in a plain dark suit and bright multi-coloured tie, made a less elaborate entrance and took a seat on the front row of chairs. Following him was a girl Tara remembered as Georgina's PA, the plump Scottish redhead Katrina. She tiptoed unnecessarily and took a seat beside Egerton-Hyde.

'Thank you for joining us, dear,' Georgina said to her husband. Laughter swept around the room.

For the next forty-five minutes, the gathering of alumni were treated to a well-rehearsed, Tara thought, anecdotal telling of life after Oxford for one Georgina Maitland. She spared the technical details of her world, and was well used, it seemed, at omitting succulent details of her private life, the type of information to flame the jowls of any tabloid journalist. She offered a few light-hearted reflections upon her time at Latimer, dropping in a few names of the fellows, some of whom were seated in the audience. Georgina was adept at public speaking and exuded a charm that, as Tara had already discovered through Callum and through her own experience, drew people to like her immensely. She was a driven woman in every aspect of her life. She enjoyed her success and her fame, but Tara wondered if, in her armour of Prada, there might exist one small chink. How far would she go to preserve the life she'd created and nurtured for herself?

Following a round of applause, she concluded her chat by inviting questions from the floor. One question, posed by a quietly spoken lady whom, Tara supposed, was of pensionable age, regarded a recipe she had very much enjoyed using for a recent Saturday lunch, had Georgina referring to her latest book. Following that Tara decided it was time for her to speak.

'Georgina,' she called. Georgina's eyes widened in recognition, but the smile that came with it was forced and strained.

'Tara, how nice to see you again. And my close friend, Callum.'

'I wanted to ask you about something you've written in your latest book, *Live Your Life*. You mention that a mother, even one with a busy career, should set aside time to be with her young children. You wrote that newborn babies deserve to have their mother around in the early years.'

'That's correct, Tara,' Georgina cut in, then proceeded to quote from her writing. 'Taking time out from a career is a must. If you can't provide this level of care then you should reconsider becoming a parent at all.'

'I agree entirely but, considering your words, I was wondering if you intend to have children at any stage?'

'Perhaps you may wish to answer the question, husband?'

Everyone laughed as Egerton-Hyde played at being in a quandary.

'I'm happy to make decisions in government,' he said, 'but I leave all the really important stuff to my good lady wife.'

There was more laughter, while Georgina scanned the room for the next question. Tara hadn't finished.

'Georgina, do you think early motherhood would have hindered or helped a career such as yours?'

Any pretence of smiling left her face as Georgina stared coldly at Tara. To many present in the room the question had little significance. Georgina's failure to reply, strangely, provided answers to a whole set of questions for Tara. Now, she believed she understood what lay behind the mystery of the Latimer alumni and why so many lives had been destroyed.

CHAPTER 50

'Who knows, Tara?' said Georgina, with an undercurrent of disdain. 'I suppose motherhood is a life experience I don't feel qualified to discuss beyond what I have stated in the book. If I had been a mother when my career was just beginning, I imagine it would have added to my experience and not detracted from it.'

Georgina appeared relieved to have reached the end of her time in front of the audience. During the applause she moved away from the lectern, her gaze lingering on Callum and Tara.

Anthony Egerton-Hyde stepped forward and kissed his wife on the cheek. But Georgina's sparkle had deserted her. She looked dazed, preoccupied, and instead of taking her seat while her husband spoke, she made for the door.

'What was all that about?' Callum whispered to Tara. 'I've never seen Georgina act like that before. She didn't appreciate your questions.'

'Good, I'm glad.'

'You don't like her much, do you?'

'Not a lot.'

* * *

Callum felt uneasy about Tara's attitude. They had to make it through this evening. He waited nervously for the moment he was sure would arrive. Justin Kingsley had come to Oxford for a reason. Callum was convinced that Kingsley was intent upon a confrontation with the surviving members of the group of friends from student days. He was grateful that Tara had instructed him to ensure that everyone would be there. Now he wondered if Georgina would return to the meeting following the awkwardness of the last few minutes. He couldn't fathom Tara's motives in asking Georgina obtuse questions about motherhood, when she knew that the Maitland-Egerton-Hydes had not yet produced children. As he kindled his attention for Anthony's address, he moved his hand to the left and placed it upon Tara's.

* * *

She let it rest on hers for a few seconds, but was concerned over Georgina's whereabouts. Tonight was not the time for moving forward in a loving relationship. She watched the door, eager for Georgina to reappear. Katrina, her PA, didn't seem sufficiently concerned to go and check on her employer. Tara, on the other hand, with several conflicting theories swirling in her head about who had murdered who, could no longer settle. She lifted Callum's hand from hers and gave it back. He glanced at her with disappointment in his eyes. She had no time to offer him explanations.

'I'm going to check on Georgina,' she whispered. 'Don't let Egerton-Hyde out of your sight.' She lifted her handbag and was out of her seat before he could reply.

Trying to avoid drawing attention away from Egerton-Hyde at the lectern, she padded as quietly as she could to the back of the room, exiting by the main door. Once outside, she turned to her right and made her way along a flagged path to the corner of the Old Members' Building. There was a small car park, sufficient for twenty cars and usually reserved for Fellows, the librarian and assistants to the college principal. On this weekend, on a first-come, first-served basis, members of the visiting Latimer alumni had been granted access for their vehicles. Staying close to the wall, remaining within the shadow of the building, she peered around the corner and saw her Ford Focus parked by the boundary wall of the college. It sat flagrantly between a silver Mercedes and a dark-coloured Jaguar. Parked or, more accurately, abandoned in the middle of the yard was a black Range Rover, its windows heavily tinted making it impossible to tell if anyone was sitting in the vehicle.

Suddenly, appearing by the bonnet of the Range Rover with her back to Tara, was Georgina. She stopped, placed her hand on the wing of the car, one foot supporting her weight and the other touching the ground only by the toe of her shoe. So much for advocating a healthy style of living: a thin cloud of smoke ascended from the cigarette perched between the forefinger and middle finger of her right hand. No doubt she had felt the need for some relief after the uneasy finale to her presentation.

Tara didn't expect to receive a warm reception, but she couldn't care less. She was in the midst of a murder investigation. No time for bruised egos. Besides, if her updated thinking on the matter was correct, she was looking at a beautiful, intelligent, successful and utterly charming murderer.

Stepping from the shadow, she turned the corner and had taken a couple of steps toward the Range Rover when the figure of a man emerged from behind the Jaguar, parked next to her Focus. Fortunately for her, the man stood sideways on to where she had paused in open space, stranded. When he moved toward the Range Rover he had his back to Tara, and she scurried to the safety of the darkened corner from where she'd emerged seconds earlier. She watched, as the man's body seemed to merge with Georgina's. He spun her around, his hand cupped over her mouth and nose, taking her weight by pulling her tight against him. Exactly the same operation Tara had endured earlier in the day. This time Kingsley was not reacting badly to someone who had been following him; he'd come for Georgina.

Unsure of what to do, whether to challenge him, call for help or remain in the shadows and witness a murder, she saw Georgina clamber into the Range Rover, followed at close quarters by Kingsley and his knife. She had to do something. She darted from the shadows to the centre of the courtyard.

'Georgina!'

Georgina saw her, but too late. Kingsley paused for a second, looking Tara's way. The car door slammed with a deep clunk. The engine burst into life, revving loudly as it moved off. She was nearly upon it. She reached for the door handle, but the car swerved for the exit. Her hands touched the door but instantly bounced off as the car straightened and roared to the open gateway. Tara hurried to her Focus, fumbling in her handbag for the keys.

By connecting all the outlandish notions she'd considered over the past few days, she wasn't guessing where the Range Rover was going. She knew exactly the place. What was to happen there had still to be decided.

When she'd exited the college into the laneway leading to Merton Street there was no sign of the car, but it didn't deter her. She hoped she'd got it right and drove for the river. Turning off St Aldate's immediately before the pub by Folly Bridge, she rolled down an alley which opened into a small residential car park. She saw that Georgina and Kingsley had done the same, the Range Rover abandoned in the centre of the square. Tara parked close to a wall at the rear of the pub. Before getting out, she pulled her phone from her bag and quickly composed a text message. She hoped that Stephanie, already bored silly with the alumni meeting, was browsing on her mobile as she had been the first time they met. Tara explained where she was going and told Stephanie to alert Callum and the police.

Easing the car door closed, she hurried into the darkness under the trees close by the river. She realised it was only fifty yards to the place where she'd spied Kingsley earlier in the day. This also was the spot where she'd told her former lover to fuck off. Right now, she needed more of that same courage.

She automatically kept to the path at first, but quickly realised how foolish it was to announce her arrival by the clicking of her heels upon tarmac. Stepping onto grass beneath the trees, her heels sank into the softer ground with every step. Her bare shoulders tingled from the chill in the night air. The cut in her side stung, the pain shortening her breath. Instinct was her only navigation in pitch darkness, while the hum of cars crossing the bridge and music from the pub slashed through the silence. With each pant of breath, she thought she would give herself away. The cool air lodged in her throat, the sensation one gets from drinking cold water after sucking a mint. She heard shouting. Kingsley's voice at first, then Georgina's.

'It has to stop, Georgina. No more.'

'But it can't. It's too late. They all know. You told me they all know. I can't let them live when they have the power, the knowledge, to destroy me.'

Tara heard deep, painful sobs.

'That's a pathetic excuse for what you've done,' said Kingsley.

She saw his silhouette against the light cast from a lamp-post on the path beside the river. The blade in his hand sparkled briefly, the one he'd raked across her flesh in the church. Tara slipped behind the trunk of a sycamore, but peering round it, she still had sight of Kingsley. In daylight, and wearing a purple cocktail dress, she wouldn't stand a chance. In darkness she hoped to remain undetected until the police and the others arrived. When she peered at the tree under which Kingsley stood, she at last spied the figure of Georgina. On her hands and knees, she crawled around in the dirt like a child in a sandpit.

'Why have you brought me here, Justin? Are you going to kill me? Is that how you're going to finish it?'

She looked up at Kingsley, like a destitute slave awaiting her punishment. The bubbling, effervescent Georgina *in absentia*. She was a mighty tree felled.

'I wanted to remind you of where it all began,' said Kingsley. 'But it ends here, too, Georgina. Tonight.'

CHAPTER 51

'Look at it, Georgina. Read what it says.'

Georgina was crying. She crawled around on all fours like a pig on a truffle hunt. Then Tara watched as Georgina laid her hands upon the brass plaque, fixed to a spike lodged in the soft ground under the tree.

'Baby Isis,' said Kingsley, his voice growing louder and splintering with emotion. 'He was never given a proper name.'

'I know,' Georgina sobbed. She kept a hold of the plaque and, pulling hard, withdrew it from the earth, clasping the cold metal plate to her chest.

A volley of car doors closing and voices calling out interrupted the exchange between them. Kingsley glanced to the source of the noise, and in doing so he spotted Tara lurking by the tree.

'What do you want, cop?' he shouted. 'This is none of your business. Go away.'

He turned to face her. His right hand wielded the knife. She was well aware of what he could do. But his focus upon Tara was his downfall. He'd turned his back on Georgina. On her knees, three feet from her ex-lover, she had a firm grip of the plaque, and she pointed the metal spike towards Kingsley. Tara gasped. Kingsley spun round, but too late. Georgina drove the spike upwards through his side. It pierced his clothing, his skin and sank easily into soft flesh. He cried out, groaned and dropped to his knees. His knife landed at the hands of Georgina.

Tara ran to stop her.

'No, Georgina! Leave him be. You've done enough.'

She looked at Tara and smiled.

'Tara?' Callum shouted. She couldn't yet see him, but she could tell there were others with him. Suddenly he emerged from the darkness, stopping exactly at the spot by the tree where she had been hiding. His voice distracted her. Georgina held Justin's knife. In a fluid movement she rose to her feet and stepped behind Tara. Her left arm enveloped Tara's narrow shoulders, and her right hand pushed the knife at her throat. Kingsley lay on his side bleeding heavily, struggling to raise himself onto one arm.

'Not so fast, my Belfast Boy,' said Georgina, sniffing tears, but sounding more her old self. 'One careless move and your little friend's blood will spoil her lovely dress.'

'Let her go, Georgina. She's done you no harm.'

'Georgina!' Anthony Egerton-Hyde stopped abruptly on the path. Ollie, Stephanie and Katrina stood beside him.

'Hello, my dear husband,' Georgina said. 'And Ollie Rutherford. Now we're all here.'

Anthony ventured towards his wife. 'Georgina, what's going on? Let the girl go free.'

'Don't come any closer, or I swear she'll die. She means nothing to me.'

Tara felt the cold steel at her throat, the same blade that drew her blood earlier in the day. She didn't think it possible to feel a greater fear than when Kingsley had pressed himself against her in the church. Now she knew how it felt to be in the grip of a murderer. Georgina was taller and much stronger than Tara. Everyone around her stood powerless. Georgina had assumed her dominant role among this group of people. She was in control. She would dictate what would happen. Tara glanced from Callum to Egerton-Hyde. Neither one seemed brave enough to rescue a woman in distress.

'Please, Georgina, let her go,' said Egerton-Hyde. 'We can talk about this. I love you. I'm your husband for goodness sake. You can tell me what it's all about.'

'None of them knew, Georgina,' said Kingsley, his words peppered by shallow breaths and weak laughter. 'The people you've killed didn't know, except for Tilly, and she was never going to tell. She was your best friend, Georgina. She helped you, and you killed her.'

'He tricked me, Anthony.' The breaking tear-soaked voice returned. She sounded like a six-year-old stamping her feet in the playground because the other children wouldn't play to her rules. 'He told me that everyone knew.'

'Who tricked you, darling?'

'Justin.' She stepped backwards pulling Tara with her to indicate the bleeding man cowering on the ground.

'Kingsley?'

'Yes, bloody Kingsley,' she yelled.

'Why don't you tell them what happened, Georgina?' Tara said.

'You shut up. I don't take orders from you.'

Georgina pulled her arm tighter around Tara's neck. Tara cried out as the knife cut at her bare shoulder. She saw confusion and frustration pull at Callum's face. Trying to figure it all out. He should have been looking at Kingsley threatening with the knife. Not Georgina. He'd come face to face with the person who'd killed his wife and daughter, but it wasn't Justin Kingsley.

'Justin told me they all knew, Anthony. They were going to ruin me if I didn't pay him.'

'Tilly helped you,' said Kingsley. 'You would have died out here, but for her.'

Callum backed away, disappearing in the gloom of the trees. Tara's heart sank. Somehow she hoped he would be the one to save her. Instead, he'd run off to deal with the news in his head that the woman he admired, the woman who promised him a fresh start was the person who had taken away what he loved most.

'I couldn't take the risk,' said Georgina.

She addressed the words pleadingly to the onlookers rather than the wounded Kingsley.

'When he blackmailed me, I couldn't take the risk that Tilly wouldn't talk. Justin told me they knew, and they would go to the police if I didn't pay him.'

'I needed money, Georgina,' Kingsley said. 'That was all. You ruined my life that night, here on this very spot. But it didn't stop you; you became rich and a big success. You didn't stop to look back. The least you could do was pay for destroying my future. No one had to die, especially not Tilly.'

Her nervous laugh sprayed over the stricken Kingsley.

'You think?' she said. 'Tilly was the easiest. Yes, she knew my secret; she helped me, but she also had Callum.' She looked around her, but Callum was gone. 'Callum! Do you hear me? She took you from me, Callum. You were always my Belfast Boy.'

'Why didn't you stop this after Tilly?' Tara asked Georgina. 'Three more people died, Justin? Because of your blackmailing three more innocent people died.' She tried to shout the words, hoping that Callum, wherever he'd got to, might still be in earshot.

'Didn't realise…' Kingsley said, his voice trailing off.

There were sounds of car doors closing, a blue flashing light reflected off a building next to Folly Bridge. Georgina edged further from the onlookers and closer to the stricken Kingsley. His voice resumed, breaking Georgina's attention upon the arrival of the police.

'At first I thought Tilly died in an accident,' he said. 'Never believed Georgina was capable of murder. I needed more money from her, and she paid every time. But when I heard that Peter was dead and then Zhou Jian, I realised it was Georgina. She was out of control. I tried to stop her. I tried to warn Charlotte, but she wouldn't listen.'

'They were going to ruin us, Anthony,' said Georgina.

'None of them knew, Georgina. I never told them.' Kingsley winced as he drew breath.

'But Peter still had the power to ruin us. He and Anthony—'

'That's enough, Georgina,' Egerton-Hyde called out, panic shrouding his usually calm voice.

'Why Zhou Jian?' said Tara.

Georgina swung around to face Kingsley. As her heels sank in the ground, Tara's body twisted but she managed to adjust her stance. Georgina's grip on her had not weakened.

'You told me he heard us talking in Austria, Justin. You told me he heard everything.'

Tara recalled something Callum had mentioned. Zhou Jian once asked him if Justin had a child. It seemed the Chinese scientist had stumbled upon a conversation between Justin and Georgina. The mention of a baby. He'd known little else. He'd overheard a snippet of a quarrel, and it led to his death.

'Did you kill Charlotte?' Egerton-Hyde asked his wife. He spoke forsakenly in the voice of a man who sees his life and career lying in tatters before him.

'She had to die, Anthony. Don't pretend you weren't relieved. She could have ruined you, too, remember.'

Two police constables, one male the other female, came into view from the darkness of the path. It didn't take long for the girl to realise they needed back-up, and she spoke into her radio. Their arrival sparked greater panic in Georgina.

'Stay back. I'll kill her.' She wrestled Tara, tightening her grasp around her throat, with the knife now jabbing at her side.

'They've come to help you, Georgina,' said Tara, grimacing as the woman's fingernails squeezed into the bare flesh of her shoulder.

'Too late for help,' she cried, her trembling body fusing with Tara's.

'Talk to us, Georgina,' said the female constable. 'We can sort this out. No one needs to get hurt. Let the girl go.'

Her well-meaning words had the opposite effect. The blade cut at Tara's dress. She screamed out.

'Please, Georgina,' she said, her vision blurring from tears. 'Tell us about the baby.'

Georgina seemed to reassess her situation, glancing from one anxious face to the next. Stephanie had a firm hold of Ollie's arm. Beside them Katrina stood in tears, hands clutched to her cheeks. Egerton-Hyde looked forlorn, arms hanging to his sides, eyes fixed on the figure of his wife desperately locked in a place from where she would never emerge unscathed. The police officers mumbled words to each other, but seemed resigned to the stand-off, awaiting those more expert in handling this kind of incident.

'I didn't know I was pregnant,' Georgina wept. 'You have to believe me; I had no idea. Just a terrible pain. We were out here, walking in the darkness. It all happened so quickly.'

The bystanders looked on, their faces suddenly swept by fear. Callum crept silently from the trees behind Georgina and Tara.

'I didn't know what to do,' Georgina continued. 'A baby? I couldn't be a mother. Not then. I had plans.'

'You killed our baby, Georgina.' Kingsley tried to raise himself onto one arm. 'You gave birth to our son, and then you squeezed the life from him.'

Pain coursed through him, and he cried out. Georgina's scream met with his. A terrifying harmony released to the night. Callum edged closer.

'It was the wrong time. Don't you see? Now I could be a mother, but not then. I wasn't ready. I had so many things to do.'

Callum took another step. He could almost reach out and touch her.

'I could have raised him, Georgina,' Kingsley wept. 'I wouldn't have left you. We had a child together—'

Georgina screamed again, a horrible mocking laughter filled the night as yet more flashing lights bleached the darkness, and sirens came in answer to the madness.

'Your child? It wasn't yours, Justin.' Georgina laughed hysterically. 'Isn't that the great irony? All this time you believed I'd had your baby.'

Kingsley's face, wracked with pain, fought with something so much more than he could bear. His life destroyed all those years ago, and now the realisation that it need not have happened this way.

'Where are you, Belfast Boy?' Georgina howled in the air. Tara sensed time was running out for her. 'Callum? Do you hear me?'

'I hear you, Georgina.'

Startled, she turned her head to face him, and her voice softened, dropping to a whisper. 'Callum, my darling. I'm so sorry. I didn't know what to do. Our baby. I couldn't keep it. You understand, don't you?'

'Listen to yourself, Georgina. How could you do that to your own child? You killed your best friend, my wife and daughter. Did we mean nothing to you?'

'I loved you, Callum. I loved Tilly and Emily, but I was so scared. It would have been fine if Justin hadn't come back. He tricked me.'

Kingsley gave a loud groan. Georgina flinched, squeezing Tara closer. Her hand was shaking, trying to keep the knife pressed at Tara's waist.

'Let Tara go, Georgina.'

'I can't.'

'Please, Georgina. I love her. Please don't take her away from me. I couldn't bear it.'

'Callum,' Tara cried.

'I'm so sorry for getting you into this, Tara.'

Kingsley raised a trembling hand and caught the hem of Georgina's dress. She looked down and tried to pull away. Kingsley held firmly, crying in pain. Tara felt the grip loosen around her neck. Suddenly free, she pulled away, falling to the ground. Georgina slashed with the knife at Kingsley's outstretched arm, the blade slicing into his wrist as he struggled to keep hold of her dress. Callum seized his moment. He rushed at her. His arms swung out for the tackle. The knife came up; Kingsley lost his grip on the dress and flopped to the ground. Callum caught Georgina. Took her at the waist. He pushed on through as the knife pierced his stomach. His legs pounded on the pathway. Georgina tumbled backwards, crying out, fighting desperately to stay on her feet. Callum pushed on. The path ended by the water's edge. They splashed into the dark river.

'Callum,' Tara cried out. She regained her feet and ran to the river. 'Callum!'

The police sprang to action, but when they reached the riverbank, there was nothing to see. Seconds passed.

Something, fifteen yards downstream broke the surface. The head and shoulders of Georgina. A gasp for air to feed her scream. She fought, splashing wildly to stay on the surface, but something more than the flowing waters of the Isis finally claimed her.

Tara dropped to her knees and wept.

'Callum! Please! Don't leave me, Callum.'

There was nothing to see in the blackness of the night. He was gone from her life. Broken-hearted in Oxford for a second time.

EPILOGUE

Ripples of nerves fluttered across her tummy. Her hand trembled as she sat on the edge of the bath holding the plastic stick in front of her, her eyes fixed on its digital display. One minute from now she would know the answer. Her best friends sat in her kitchen drinking coffee, munching biscuits. They would be the first to know. And why not? They were her best friends. They'd been together since first form at school. Everything, fun, laughter and occasional tears, shared between them. Her rising joy was tempered with trepidation at what the next few months might bring. Her life changed forever. It was only the briefest of moments, but she closed her eyes and drew a long slow breath before letting go. Then she saw the display and smiled contentedly before tears rolled down her cheeks. Hurrying from the bathroom, she raced along the hall into the kitchen.

'Well?' said Aisling.

'I'm pregnant!' Kate sang, hoisting the little stick in the air as if it were a trophy.

Tara, Aisling and Kate rushed together for a group hug.

'Congratulations, Kate,' said Tara. 'You'd better call Adam and let him know he's going to be a dad.'

'Sure his part is over,' said Aisling.

'Don't you even think it,' Kate snapped, reaching for her phone on the worktop. She left the room to share her news with her partner, and Aisling went to use the bathroom.

Tara sat alone in the kitchen, feeling pleased for Kate, but so easily these days her mind didn't have far to stray in order to see Callum. He was there in everything. Her waking, driving, working, and when at times he slipped from her consciousness, she would meet him in her dreams and awaken to feel the reminders in the pit of her stomach.

She'd told the story a dozen times or more. Each new occasion as painful as the last. She'd told it to the police in Oxford, to DI Iain Barclay in Canterbury, to Superintendent Tweedy and to Assistant Chief Muetzel in Lucerne. She spent those first few painful weeks on the road explaining how each murder fitted into the story. How Georgina Maitland had strived to conceal a terrible secret – that late at night, beneath a tree, she had killed her son within seconds of his birth. That Justin Kingsley, as he was about to fetch help, saw Georgina cover her son's mouth and nose with her hand, denying him all but those first few breaths. He'd looked on in horror as Georgina callously scraped away the earth beneath the tree and laid the child in a grave six inches deep. Beside him she placed the afterbirth, covered the hole with soil and scattered crisp leaves over the grave. Afterwards, they'd told Tilly that the baby was stillborn. Georgina swore her to secrecy as Tilly nursed her back to health.

Justin Kingsley, recovering in hospital from his wounds, related the events of that night to Tara, a night that tragically altered the lives of so many people. Trying to avoid bringing scandal to his family, Justin could no longer share his life with someone capable of murdering their newborn child. At his first opportunity he'd walked away from everything. It was only the need for money, at first, and later his greed that brought him to blackmail Georgina. He had a girlfriend and two children to support in Greece. It wasn't right that Georgina should live a life of riches and glamour without having to pay, at least to him, some penalty for what she'd done. The trouble was he'd done too good a job in convincing her that all of the alumni friends knew her secret and were prepared to report her to the police if she didn't give in to Justin's demands.

Tara's long-held suspicion that Anthony Egerton-Hyde had murdered Zhou Jian proved unfounded, when Muetzel confirmed that Georgina Maitland, though not a delegate at the food safety conference, had accompanied her husband on that particular trip, presumably after discovering that Zhou Jian was to give a presentation. By then, Justin had realised, Georgina was out of control and was intent on removing anyone who might be aware of her ghastly secret.

Without a murderer in custody, to bring charges against and to put away for life, it wasn't the most satisfactory conclusion to a murder investigation for any of the police forces involved.

It was when she travelled to Lucerne to meet with Assistant Chief Muetzel that she began to feel unwell. She passed it off as a tummy bug, hurried through her meetings as best she could and jumped on a plane for home. It was never the conclusion that she had envisaged. She took time to visit Tim and Jenny Reason to help bring some closure to the death of their daughter, grandchild and now their son-in-law. They buried Callum next to Tilly and Emily.

Kate and Aisling re-entered the kitchen together. Tears and smiles all round.

'How did Adam take the news?' Tara asked.

'I think he was in tears,' Kate replied before breaking down again.

'Hey, come on, Kate,' said Aisling, her arm around her friend. 'This is supposed to be a happy time.'

'I am happy. That's why I'm crying.'

Aisling looked at Tara and rolled her eyes. Tara braved a smile despite feeling inside a deep loneliness and a longing for different circumstances. She would cope. She had coped so far. She had her parents, and she had Kate and Aisling.

'And what am *I* supposed to do now?' said Aisling.

'You need to find a man,' Kate replied. 'And then–'

'I know what to do after that, thank you very much.'

The quip brought laughter to Tara's face. She loved her friends dearly. And Callum would never leave her. She would always have him around, wherever she was, wherever she looked. She moved a hand to her swollen stomach and stroked it gently. Her baby kicked again.

If you enjoyed this book, please let others know by leaving a quick review on Amazon. Also, if you spot anything untoward in the paperback, get in touch. We strive for the best quality and appreciate reader feedback.

editor@thebookfolks.com

ALSO IN THIS SERIES

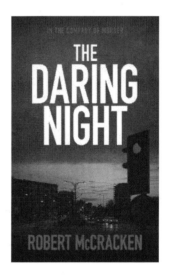

THE DARING NIGHT (Book 2)

Liverpool is on high alert after a spate of poisonings, but DI Tara Grogan is side-lined from the investigation. Yet when she probes into the suicide of a company executive, she becomes sure she has a vital lead in the case. Going it alone, however, has very real risks.

Available on Kindle and in paperback.

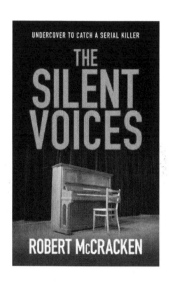

THE SILENT VOICES (Book 3)

When bodies turn up on a Liverpool council estate, DI
Tara Grogan goes undercover to get inside information.
But she risks everything when the cover story she adopts
backfires. Can she work out the identity of the killer before
she is exposed and becomes a target?

Available on Kindle and in paperback.

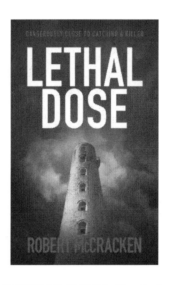

LETHAL DOSE (Book 4)

Investigating the death of a journalist, DI Tara Grogan
stumbles upon his connection to a number of missing
women. Is it possible the victim was actually a serial killer?
Tara closes in on the truth but can she evade a fatal jab?

Available on Kindle and in paperback.

OTHER TITLES OF INTEREST

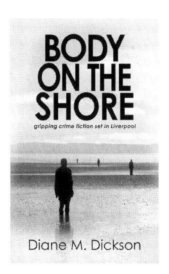

When police retrieve a body from the flat sands of a popular beach, DI Jordan Carr is presented with his first murder case. The victim is a woman, but they know little more about her. Tracing the events that led to her death will take the detective on an uncomfortable journey into the dark side of Liverpool.

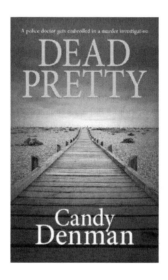

A police doctor gets embroiled in a murder investigation

DEAD
PRETTY

Candy
Denman

When a woman is found dead in Hastings, Sussex, the
medical examiner feels a murder has taken place. Yet she
feels the police are not doing enough because the victim is
a prostitute. Dr Callie Hughes will conduct her own
investigation, no matter the danger.

Printed in Great Britain
by Amazon